CATCHING
the COWBOY

USA TODAY BESTSELLING AUTHOR
KENNEDY FOX

Copyright © 2020 Kennedy Fox
www.kennedyfoxbooks.com

Catching the Cowboy
Circle B Ranch Series

Cover design by Outlined with Love Designs
Cover photography by Wander Aguiar Photography
Copy Editor: Jenny Sims | Editing 4 Indies

All rights reserved. No parts of the book may be used or reproduced in any matter without written permission from the author, except for inclusion of brief quotations in a review. This book is a work of fiction. Names, characters, establishments, organizations, and incidents are either products of the author's imagination or are used fictitiously to give a sense of authenticity. Any resemblance to actual persons, living or dead, events, or locales is entirely coincidental.

I love it when you just don't care
I love it when you dance like there's nobody there
So when it gets hard, don't be afraid
We don't care what them people say

"Life of the Party"
-Shawn Mendes

PROLOGUE

DIESEL

TEN YEARS AGO

I STARE AT HER.

I stare at her *a lot*, actually. An embarrassing amount of time.

But Rowan doesn't notice. She hardly acknowledges me, except for when she brushes me off and rolls her eyes at my lame attempts to flirt. I *shouldn't* be flirting with her, considering she's my best friend's little sister. Riley's three years older than her, which makes him even more protective. She's only a year younger than me, though.

Tonight's her eighth grade winter formal, and since I'm a freshman in high school, I can't go to protect her from those little pricks. They mindlessly stare at her tits and long, tanned legs and aren't subtle about it. I spent the better part of middle school giving them threatening glares. And even though I told myself it was for Riley's sake—as his friend—that was mostly a lie. I did it because none of them deserved her, and I wanted her for myself. Still do.

Given that she pays no mind to me, I've resorted to making

fun of her instead. It's not the type of attention I want, but for a moment, it means I have hers, even if she's telling me off or smacking me. It's childish—like a boy chasing a girl to pull on her pigtails on the playground—but it's the only way Rowan will actually look at me or speak to me.

Pathetic as hell, I know.

One of these days, Rowan Bishop will notice me as more than a nuisance or her brother's best friend. Guaranteed.

"Boys!" their mother screams out the second-story window. River's like a mom to me, considering how long I've known the Bishops and how much time I spend on the ranch. "Hurry up! She's ready to go, and I need to take pictures!"

Riley and I jump out of his dad Alex's truck and rush toward the house. Even though we're still dirty from the day's work, we try to brush off as we head up the steps to the porch. I help on their family ranch on the weekends and during the summer. It's my own personal escape, and I can't wait until school's over so I can be here every day. It's much different here than in town where I live, and I never want to leave.

The front door whips open, and we enter. I wait with bated breath for Rowan's grand entrance down the staircase. My clothes and hair are a mess, and I'm embarrassed by how much of a disaster I must look, but when Rowan rounds the corner in a bright pink gown, my throat goes dry. Even if I were dressed in my Sunday best, I'd still be out of her league.

She smiles wide, her adorable dimples peeking through, as she holds the railing and walks down. Alex and River wait by the bottom step with pride filling their faces. Pulling out her phone, River begins taking pictures, then demands a daddy-daughter photo. Alex is wearing his typical cowboy hat, Wranglers, and work T-shirt and smiles next to Rowan who looks like royalty.

"Get in the picture, Riley," River orders, waving him over

after she gets a few good ones of just the two of them. She snaps several more, and then I step in.

"You need a family photo with all of you," I tell her, reaching for her cell. "Get in the picture, Mrs. Bishop."

She hands it over. "Oh, you're a gem, Adam!" Aside from my mother and grandmother, River's the only other person who uses my real name. I've repeatedly told her to call me Diesel—a nickname I've had for as long as I can remember—but she insists I'll always be Adam to her.

"No problem, Mrs. B."

River stands on one side of Rowan, and Riley and Alex are on the other. I step back, then click a few shots. Aside from their different hair color, Rowan looks identical to her mother. Riley's always resembled his dad, even when he was younger.

"One more," I say, then motion for them to move closer and tell them to smile wider.

Rowan doesn't look at the camera. Rather, she flicks her eyes to mine, and when the corner of her lips tilts up, I imagine that smile is for me. A grin fills my face, and my imagination goes wild with thoughts on how I'd make this night memorable for her if I were her date. It'd be nothing short of perfection as we danced to her favorite songs, drank punch, then ended the evening with a quiet stroll under the stars.

"Alright, I'm gonna be late!" Rowan lifts the front of her ball gown, revealing cowboy boots, then walks out of the group. I smirk at her shoes, knowing she'd never wear heels unless she was forced. Hell, I'm surprised she's even wearing such a poofy dress. She's worn sundresses to church before, but never something this fancy. She's a natural tomboy, born and raised on a ranch, and has always preferred getting dirty over pompoms. Riding horses is second nature to her, and she often gives me a run for my money when it comes to hard work and getting chores done. It makes me like her even more.

"You sure you don't want a picture of you shoveling shit in

the barn? You in your natural habitat?" I tease, knowing it'll annoy the hell out of her.

"Now, now, Adam. Be nice and watch your language." River steps forward, grabbing her phone from my grip, and gently pats my cheek.

"Yeah, *Adam.*" Rowan huffs and crosses her arms over her chest, which was a really bad thing to do. The movement pushes up her tits, and I immediately avert my gaze, trying not to stare. "Maybe you should go back into *your* natural habitat, in the mud, with the *pigs.*"

Riley howls, cracking up so hard, I'm worried he'll piss himself. This is an ongoing thing in the Bishop house. Me teasing Rowan, her throwing it right back, and Riley laughing at my expense.

"You ready to go, princess?" Alex asks, digging his keys out of his pocket.

"You sure you don't want me to take her?" Riley interjects. "I'm her big brother after all and way cooler than you."

"Excuse me?" Alex nudges Riley in the arm, wearing a playful grin. "I managed to land your mother, didn't I? I smooth-talked her into moving to Texas, after all. She had it *bad.*"

"According to my math," Rowan chimes in, "and my sources, Mom was knocked up with Riley and came back to tell you, which means y'all had sex before marriage."

My cheeks heat at Rowan's bold words, but honestly, I expect nothing less from her.

"Rowan Rose Bishop!" River scolds. "Who told you that?"

"Grandma," she reveals. "Like it's a secret? Riley was born *before* your wedding date."

"So Riley's a bastard. What else is new?" I tease.

"Language, Adam." River gives me a firm look before turning to Riley. I can't help but laugh, considering the conversation. "We're taking Rowan to the dance, but I need you to pick her up at midnight. I'm trusting you to be there *on time*."

It's Saturday night, and knowing Riley as well as I do, he's not gonna like this.

"Ma, what? Why do I have to pick up the little rug rat?"

"Because you're *so cool*. Also, your father and I are going to bed early so we can *all* get up for church in the morning," she says pointedly. "I expect you to be there tomorrow, too."

Riley groans with an eye roll, which causes me to snort.

"Yes, ma'am," he begrudgingly mutters.

"Good boy." She sweetly pats his head like he's a five-year-old.

The three of them leave, and I'm anxious the moment Rowan's out of sight.

"Thank God, they're gone. Let's go drink in the barn!" Riley shouts, pushing me toward his room. "I'm gonna shower first, though."

"Did you suffer a blow to the head?" I ask as he follows me down the hallway. "You have to pick Rowan up in four hours."

"So?" He shrugs without a care in the world.

"So you shouldn't be drinkin', smartass."

"I'll be fiiiiiine. Quit worryin', pretty boy." He slaps my shoulder. "You can be my DD."

He knows damn well I'm only fourteen and don't have my license, but that hasn't stopped me from driving his drunk ass around before. I drive around the ranch sometimes, and I've had to take him home from partying in town a couple of times but never with Rowan in the truck.

Over three hours pass, and I'm stuck dealing with a shit-faced Riley in the barn we hang out in on the weekends. He invited a few friends who brought an ice chest full of their parents' booze. I tried to slow Riley down, but he downed six beers and four shots of bourbon like there were no consequences. Now he's three sheets to the wind.

"Dude, you're supposed to pick up Rowan in forty-five minutes. You need to start chugging water," I tell him. My last beer was over an hour ago, and I only had two total.

"Stop being a pussy," Riley slurs.

I check my watch. By the time I manage to get him into the back seat and drive into town, it'll be close to midnight. I don't want to keep Rowan waiting around by herself or worse, with those little dicks from her class.

"Say goodbye. We're going." I stand and tower over him. Riley might be muscular from working on the ranch, but I have a good four inches and fifty pounds on him. Grabbing his arm, I lift him to his wobbly feet. "You're gonna be puking your fuckin' guts out."

"Whatever you say, *Dad*," he mocks, and the other guys laugh. If he wasn't my best friend and a decent human—sober—I'd leave his ass out here for his parents to find in the morning.

With fifteen minutes to spare, I pull into the parking lot. Since Riley's passed out in the back seat, I leave the truck running and hop out. Parents are already starting to arrive to pick up their kids, so instead of waiting out here, I go inside to check on Rowan.

I spot her under the disco ball dancing with a bunch of girls. She's smiling, but it seems forced. Her cousin Mackenzie is with her, drawing tons of attention, as usual. Ten minutes later, the DJ announces the final slow song of the night. He then tells the guys to find their sweetheart, and one approaches their circle but grabs Kenzie's hand. She grins wide, and the two of them walk away. I watch Rowan's fake smile drop as do her eyes before wrapping her arms around her waist and leaving the dance floor.

What the fuck?

As much as I don't want guys near her, I don't understand why the hell none of them at least asked her to dance.

I warned most of them off last year, so it must've actually worked.

After thirty seconds of watching her stand alone with that sad expression, I can't stand it. Suddenly, I'm halfway across the gym, moving toward her.

"Row…" I grab her attention, and she looks shocked as hell.

"What are you—?"

I tilt my head toward the dance floor. "C'mon. Let's dance." Holding out my hand, I nod for her to take it.

When she finally does, I don't even try to contain my smile. I lead her out into the middle under the sparkling disco ball, then pull her into my chest and wrap my arms around her.

"What're you doing here?" she asks, holding my shoulders because she's too short to place her arms around my neck. But holding her this way is perfect.

"Your idiot brother is as drunk as a skunk, so I drove us here. Came inside to check on you and didn't want you to miss out on dancing to the last song."

She licks her lips and swallows. "The boys here don't like me. They say I'm too much. Too loud. Too—"

"They're fuckin' morons," I interject.

Rowan looks down and shrugs. "Oh well."

I tilt up her chin and gaze into her gorgeous brown eyes. "Trust me, none of them are good enough for you."

"You *have* to say that." She sighs, her shoulders rising and falling. "You're my brother's best friend."

I scoff. "No, I don't. I'm not *your* brother."

She shrugs casually. "Close enough. You pick on me worse than him. Always around. I'm surprised you haven't tried to pants me in public yet."

Our laughter eases the tension. "That's Riley's specialty," I tease, remembering the time he did it to Rowan a few years ago at one of their family's picnics. She was livid and ended up sucker punching him between the legs.

"Middle school boys are dumb," she states.

A smile spreads across my face. "High school ones are too. Don't forget that."

When she's a freshman next fall, I'm going to have to try not to be so overbearing. I'll be a sophomore, and we'll be on opposite sides of the building, but I'll still keep my eye on her. It'll be better than her attending another school altogether. Hopefully, I'll see her around after class, considering I play football and baseball, and she'll probably try out for the softball team.

Everyone in this town is well aware of my family ties with the Bishops. I make sure Rowan and her cousins aren't messed with, especially when Riley isn't around.

"I love this song," she says softly.

I know she does. She plays it on repeat in her room. I've noticed she likes listening to slower songs while she studies and does homework.

"Who's the singer?" I ask as if I'm clueless.

"Shawn Mendes," she tells me and I nod, pretending it's brand-new information. If Rowan knew how much I watched and obsessed over her, she'd think I was batshit crazy. Hell, when it comes to her, there's no doubt I am.

Riley would kick my ass if he ever found out.

As the music begins to fade, I frown at the anticipation of losing her touch. She blinks up at me, and a small smile plays on her lips that are only inches from mine. Forgetting where we are, *who* we are, I slide my hand up her arm and cup her cheek. I study her expression, waiting to see if she pushes me away, and when she doesn't, I lean in closer.

She inhales sharply as my lips softly brush hers. I taste the fruit punch she must've drunk earlier, but we're harshly interrupted before I can deepen the kiss. We pull apart when a loud commotion echoes through the gym.

"Fuck," I mutter under my breath as I see Riley staggering toward the middle where we're standing. "C'mon, we gotta go."

I reach for her hand, but then think better of it and drop my arm. Riley's wasted, bumping into tables and students as he nearly falls on his ass.

"What the hell?" I steady him, grabbing his arms. "Why didn't you stay in the truck?"

"I couldn't find you," he stutters loudly. "You left me."

Everyone stares, and when I look at Rowan, her cheeks are beet red. She's embarrassed as hell, and it's all my fault. If I had just waited outside for her, Riley would've never stumbled in here looking like a fool.

"You were passed out," I tell him between gritted teeth. "I came in to grab Rowan."

He blinks, looking around me as if he just realized his sister was next to me. "Oh." He wobbles from side to side, and his eyes are in slits as he stares at us.

Ignoring his suspicious look, I straighten my shoulders and try to get us out of here fast. "Let's go."

I turn Riley around and walk him to the exit, hoping no one gives her shit for this later. While he picks on his sister regularly and has zero qualms about embarassing her in front of family, he'd never intentionally humiliate her in front of her classmates.

"Shotgun!" Riley shouts once we're outside. How the hell he's still standing is beyond me. He's plastered, and if he doesn't sit the fuck down, he's going to vomit all over his truck.

I manage to get him into the passenger seat, and Rowan follows me to the driver's side. She gets in the back, and I sit behind the wheel. Once we're all buckled, I glance up in the rearview mirror and see her stunning brown eyes. We barely kissed, but I felt it all over. I wonder if she did too, but now isn't the time to bring it up.

We're halfway to the ranch when Riley perks up and looks over at me.

"I know I'm a little drunk…" he begins, slouching. "But did I see you kissing my sister in the gym?"

My eyes round, and I swallow down the panic streaming through my veins. He's too drunk to really kick my ass at the moment, but that doesn't mean I won't pay for it tomorrow.

"Dude, what?" I contort my face. "You must be more hammered than I thought if you're seeing me lock lips with your kid sister."

He leans back against the seat. "I know what I saw," he grumbles.

"You're wrong," I tell him flatly. "You must've seen another couple."

Riley turns just enough to look at his sister. "Rowan?"

"What?" she asks as if she's annoyed.

"Were you kissing my best friend?"

Without any hesitation, she replies, "Gross, no. He offered to dance with me, and that's it."

Riley scoffs, not believing her. "Then why was his mouth so close to yours?"

"Do you really think I'd waste my first kiss on him?" she spits out.

Jesus fuck.

That was her first kiss?

"He's your annoying best friend who follows me around like a sad puppy," she adds. "The *last* person on earth I'd ever want to kiss. If his mouth ever touched mine, I'd knee him in the jewels."

Ouch.

Her words hurt like a thousand needle pricks. If her plan was to convince him it wasn't real, she's golden. If it was to hurt me in the process, then mission fucking accomplished.

"*Dayum*." Riley whistles, slapping his knee.

I glance up into the mirror, seeing her narrowed eyes and tense jaw. *What the hell*? I denied it to save my friendship, but she went a step further, dragging me through the mud in the process. Did she expect me to tell him? Is she pissed I didn't?

Silence draws on until we pull up to their house. Riley passed out against the window, and drool is sliding down his chin.

"Can you cover for your brother?" I ask Rowan when I open the back door and hold out my hand to help her out. She dismisses me and jumps down. "Tell your parents he's sleeping over at my house tonight?"

She shrugs, then nods. "Alright, fine."

I shut the door and follow her to the porch. "Rowan, wait."

She spins around, her face emotionless.

"You know I only denied it so he wouldn't beat my face in, right?" My eyes plead with her to believe me.

"It doesn't matter, *Adam*. I don't care."

I flinch at her harsh words. She leaned into me, I know she did, so why is she acting as if I'm the biggest inconvenience of her life?

Furrowing my brows, I step closer. "Was that really your first kiss?"

She bursts out laughing, crossing her arms. "Yeah right."

"What the hell is your problem?" I finally ask.

Before she can respond, the front door swings open. "I thought I heard voices out here." Alex looks at the two of us, squinting. "Where's Riley?"

"We're gonna hang out at my house if that's alright?" I step away from Rowan. "I'll make sure he's at church tomorrow, though, sir."

Alex nods, then looks at Rowan, smiling. "Did you have fun at the dance?"

Rowan glances at me before climbing the steps and nods. "It was fine, Dad. I'm tired, though."

"Okay, kiddo. Let's get you to bed then."

"Good night," I call out, waving to both of them. Alex waves, then shuts the door.

I drive Riley to my house in town and hope I don't get pulled over in the process. My parents are asleep, so I quietly help him to the couch in my room. The asshole can sleep there without a pillow and blanket for putting me through this shit tonight. Hopefully, he'll forget what he saw between his sister and me.

It seems as though Rowan already has, so perhaps I should too.

Though there's really no way I can.

What she doesn't know is that was my first kiss too, and I've been waiting for her.

I don't understand why she's so pissed, but I'll do whatever it takes to figure it out.

CHAPTER ONE

DIESEL

PRESENT DAY

"Damn," I mutter as I roll out of bed, realizing I'm late as fuck for work. I probably shouldn't have stayed up until two drinking, and I sure as hell shouldn't have made out with that woman at the bar. I don't remember her name, just her long legs and revealing neckline. As quickly as I can, I rush to the bathroom to piss, then brush my teeth, and that's when I see the dark purple hickeys on my neck. Not one or two, but three are in plain sight. I should've called her Hoover, considering they're the size of a vacuum hose.

"Shit," I say after spitting out the toothpaste because I know I can't cover them up. Wearing a turtleneck sweater in June might be more of a red flag than just owning up to my stupid mistake. I shrug, then rinse my mouth, and hurry to get dressed. This is why I stopped staying out late and drinking so much, but sometimes, those old habits reappear. Before leaving my modest cabin located on the Bishop Ranch, I text my boss, Alex, and let him know I'm running late.

Alex: I knew that an hour ago. Hurry your ass up.

Diesel: Yes, sir. I'll be right there.

With a smile, I crank my truck and rush down the long dirt road toward the shop where we do our morning roundups. Riley's dad holds staff meetings every morning so we're on the same page. What's needed around the ranch often changes for reasons like the weather or emergency repairs, so doing this each day is necessary. About six months ago, I was promoted to help manage a group of ranch hands, and together, we tend to the cattle. It's a group effort, considering how large the property is, and while it's a lot of hard work, I nearly sold my soul for this opportunity. There are days when all I do is sit in a saddle in the hot, blazing sun, sweating my ass off, but I wouldn't have it any other way. The Circle B Ranch is my home, and I don't plan to ever leave. I could be shoveling shit and be as happy as a hog here because this place is my own personal heaven on earth. I've grown up here, and the Bishops are my chosen family.

Trust me, I've done my fair share of bitch work over the years because nothing is handed to anyone. Everything here is earned, which I respect and appreciate.

I pull up to the metal building and see no other vehicles except for Alex's old beat-up truck he drives around the ranch. The bumper is dented from dumbasses backing into random things, and there are scratches all over the paint. Honestly, I don't blame him for using it because I've done my fair share of damaging it, too.

Before I get out, I grab my cowboy hat and place it on my head, then take in a long, deep breath. When I walk inside, he's drinking a cup of coffee and gives me a smug look. He's like my second dad, but I'm actually afraid of Alex's repercussions. The man could kick my ass all the way to the border of Texas and back. I'd never want to intentionally cross him.

His steel blue eyes glance up at the clock on the wall, then pierce through me. "One hour and twenty-three minutes *late*."

"Sorry," I say. Walking over, I grab a cup and pour some steaming hot coffee into it. "I…"

"Don't lie to me," he snaps.

"I wasn't going to. I drank too much and—"

"What's on your damn neck?" Riley asks. I didn't even realize he'd walked in. I glare at him as he wears the cheesiest expression ever. He comes closer and tugs on my shirt to fully reveal the marks. All I can do is smirk.

"That's how you get a disease," he explains. "Lettin' strange women suck all over ya." Riley chuckles, but Alex shakes his head, unamused.

"Well, not all of us went to Vegas and came back with a wife," I throw at him. Three years ago, as a twenty-first birthday present, Riley took me on a surprise trip to Las Vegas. When I think about it now, I smile because it was a weekend to remember. Riley found Zoey, and I ended up hooking up with one of her friends. The only difference is I didn't put a ring on it, and I don't even remember her name. However, a lot has changed since then because while I go to the Circle B Saloon often and have a few drinks, I'm not into the one-night stands like I was years ago. That's why Ms. Hoover Vacuum didn't come home with me last night, which is probably for the best. I might not have survived her sucking powers.

The Circle B Saloon is also owned by the Bishops. Riley's uncles John and Evan invested in the property and fully remodeled an old building downtown. It now consists of a large beer and liquor selection, a pool table, and a quaint seating area. Before the Saloon opened, there were zero places for people to hang out at after dark, so it became an instant moneymaker. It's done really well, and everyone in the family helps run it, especially Rowan, who's taking over now that she's graduated. Their cousins Ethan and Kenzie bartend a few nights a week when they're home during college breaks.

"It looks like she bruised you from the inside out," Riley taunts with a grin. "You might wanna get that checked out."

"I'll live." I glower, ready to give him a snide comment about wishing it was his sister who marked me. But since their dad is within earshot, I hold my tongue. I'm already in the hot seat with him for being late so I don't push my luck. These Bishops aren't always mild mannered—the men or the women—if I'm being honest.

"Anyway," Alex drawls, "it's supposed to start raining this afternoon, so I'm not sure how much you'll be able to get done, but you can try. I had Grayson start since you were nowhere to be found."

Grayson was hired this past year to help with the cattle. He's my right-hand man and super dependable, so it doesn't surprise me that he stepped up today. He saves my ass when needed, which is great, considering Riley and I work in different areas now and can't cover for each other anymore.

"Sorry about that, sir," I apologize again, taking a sip of coffee because I need to wake up. "Won't happen again."

Riley chuckles. "Yeah right."

"Shut the hell up." I punch his shoulder, then look at his dad. "It won't."

"Since it's getting hot out there, ya need to ride around and check the wells and make sure the water troughs are full. I know the pond out in the far pasture is drying up, and we can't have those cows getting dehydrated. It's so dry the rain ain't gonna do nothin' but evaporate as soon as it lands. Not much shade after all. Can't afford to lose any of them due to the heat," Alex explains.

"I'll get right on it," I tell him, finishing every hot drop of coffee, then head out.

Riley follows behind me, laughing his ass off.

"Way to make me look bad in front of your old man." I scowl, narrowing my eyes.

"He already knows how you are, Big D." He waggles his brows. "Don't forget, we gotta drive to Houston tomorrow and help my sister with all her stupid shit."

I grin at him with a smug expression. "You know I won't."

He shakes his head. "Oh God. Don't you be gettin' that look in your eyes like that. You know she hates you."

"I think that means she's got the hots for me. Maybe you can put in a good word and have her start calling me Big D, too?" Just seeing him squirm is worth every second.

"Shut your damn mouth, you dumbass." He groans. "Tomorrow morning, we leave before the sun rises. Four o'clock sharp. It's a long ass drive, and I wanna get there and back as fast as possible."

I know it's because he wants to be with Zoey, and I can't blame him, considering she's eight months pregnant. He's supposed to be on pre-baby duty right now, but he can't seem to stay away from the ranch life, even if it means meeting at the shop for ten minutes. He's addicted to this, just like the rest of us. Tomorrow, we'll be on a tight schedule, and I'm sure he'll be in a mood. If Zoey goes into labor while we're gone, I'm not sure he'll ever forgive Rowan or his dad since we were voluntold to help.

I throw him a grin. "Whatever you say, *Daddy*."

He pretends to gag as I hop in my truck and crank it. I roll the window down and holler at him. "See you in the morning after I dream about your sister sittin' on my face."

As expected, he flips me off and walks away, but it's all in good fun. Though when it comes to Rowan, I'm never joking. If she'd let me, I'd hang the damn moon for her. We haven't spent much time together because she's been at the University of Houston for the past four years and only comes home during her breaks, but it doesn't matter. My feelings for her haven't changed.

Something about Rowan makes my blood pump a little faster and my adrenaline rush. Rowan Bishop's a goddamn firecracker, sassy as can be, and Southern to the core with her values. One day, I'm going to make her mine, and I've been telling Riley that since we were kids, even if he's been warning me away from her for that long too. He thinks I'm too unreliable and unable to settle down, but he's wrong. She may be dead set on loathing me, but I'm still convinced she'll eventually get on board. *Hopefully.*

I drive out to the old barn where Grayson is busy saddling the horses. He looks at me over his shoulder and shakes his head before tightening the strap. Hopping out of the truck, I walk over to him.

"Where the fuck have you been?" he asks.

"That is no way to talk to your boss," I snap, then grin. "Overslept."

"You dumbass. I already sent the boys out to the far pasture to round up the cows and move them. Saddled Meadow for you so we could ride over to the wells and make sure they're good. I think the pump on the east side needs to be rewired. It was making a noise a week ago."

"A noise?" I prompt. "And you decided to say something *now*?" Releasing a deep breath, I shake my head and walk over to Meadow and climb on. He's a red quarter horse who loves to run and ride through the mud. We've had some great days together even though he's young, spunky, and doesn't always listen.

Once my feet are in the stirrups and Grayson is on his horse, we take off down one of the yellow trails that shortcuts over to the little water shack we need to check. Looking up at the sky, I see the dark clouds in the distance and know we don't have much time.

"Should we take the four-wheelers instead?" Grayson asks, looking out over the horizon.

"Nah, I think we'll be okay if we get going and don't lollygag any longer. We're already halfway there."

"Alright. You're the boss." He snickers and follows me as we continue forward.

The temperature is dropping, and the wind is picking up, but I focus on the task at hand so we can get it done before getting dumped on.

"You gonna talk about those bruises on your neck?" Grayson finally asks, trotting up beside me.

"God, not you too," I huff. "Riley's ragged on me enough this morning for it. In front of Alex, too."

"Well, it's impossible to ignore it when they're like beacons in the night." He chuckles.

"I drank too much, but luckily, I wasn't drunk. One more beer and I might've gone home with her, but I've had enough one-night stands to last me a lifetime," I admit.

"And it's not because Rowan's coming home tomorrow?" He arches a brow.

All I can do is smirk. "Maybe I'm not as transparent as I thought."

"Better get something to cover up those marks, or she'll notice."

I nod, agreeing. I honestly didn't think about it. Rowan will use every opportunity to bust my balls, and these stupid hickeys will be enough to get her wrath for a month.

We continue riding until we arrive at the water well. We dismount and tie the horses to a fence post before walking over. Grayson was right; it's making a noise, but I'm not sure what it is exactly.

"Go check the water trough and turn on the water so I can hear this pump kick on and off," I order, and he jogs across the pasture. I take the casing off the pump and continue to listen closer. After everything is filled, Grayson joins me in the small shed.

"I'm pretty sure it's the bearings. They need to be replaced before this thing burns up. We'll need to look in the supply room and see if we have a few extra." I pull out my cell phone and take pictures of the model number and type of pump it is. "And we're gonna have to hurry. This storm's movin' in quickly."

Grayson unties the horses as thunder rumbles in the distance. After hopping on, we decide to gallop for a while and run into my ranch hands, who are moving the cattle to where we just were. We don't have time to stop and chat but exchange words in passing.

"I'll catch y'all at the B&B for lunch," I yell, and several of them give me a thumbs-up. The Circle B Bed & Breakfast has been around for decades on the Bishop's ranch. It's an old farmhouse Riley's grandparents converted into a secluded Southern getaway. It's known for many things: the rooms are named after colors, they serve the best damn food in this part of Texas, and horseback riding lessons are offered. Riley and Rowan's cousin Maize is the chef now. She uses all of Grandma Bishop's homemade recipes, and a kitchen staff prepares every meal fresh. John has been in charge of it for years and gets his panties in a knot anytime us ranch workers come in and overstay our welcome. But just thinkin' about Maize's buttermilk biscuits makes my mouth water. The B&B's booked year-round with repeat guests who love visiting the ranch and animals.

I can't blame anyone for wanting to return because I've been obsessed with this place since I met Riley. During my high school summers, I started at the bottom of the barrel doing grunt work and all the shit assignments. I hoped after years of busting my ass, I'd get promoted, and once Herbert announced his retirement, Alex offered me the job.

The only thing that would've made things better is getting promoted earlier so I could rub it in Fisher's face. He's Riley's cousin who lives in California and worked on the ranch during the summers and busted my balls on a daily basis. He conveniently started dating my ex Gretchen and constantly pissed me off and pushed my buttons. While we had a small rivalry for years, we ended our feud and became friends. After Fisher got married, he took a full-time job in Sacramento and stopped working here. If only he could see me now.

"What're you smiling about?" Grayson asks when we climb off the horses.

"Nothing." I quickly change the subject. "I'm gonna run to the shop and see if I can find the parts we need. We'll take the side-by-side so we can get out there quicker if you wanna put the horses up before the storm hits."

"Sounds good," he says, leading them into the barn.

Running to my truck, I haul ass to the storage building where the spare parts are kept. After digging around, I find an extra pump that's the same model and quickly disassemble the housing and remove the bearings. I stuff them in my pockets and head back. By the time I meet Grayson, he's finished and waiting for me. We hop in the side-by-side and take off.

Less than ten minutes later, the bottom falls out of the sky, and when we finally make it to the pump house, we're both soaked. Grayson isn't amused as he parks and follows me inside. I pull some tools from my pocket, turn off the pump, and change the bearings as fast as I can because lightning's striking too close for comfort. Thunder booms, making us both jump.

"Hurry the hell up," Grayson urges, looking out the door as the rain pours down around the little shack we're standing in. It takes every bit of strength I have to loosen the bolts, and the constant rumbles have my nerves on edge. For us to be out here like this is dangerous, and I can tell Grayson is just as unhinged as I am. The storm seems to have stalled right above us, and we're already soaked from head to toe, but in this part of Texas, we pray for rain, especially during the brutal summer months. There have been too many years when we've suffered droughts, so we never take it for granted. After tightening everything and replacing the casing, I start the pump and thankfully, the loud squealing noise is gone when it comes on.

"Thank fuck," I mutter, wiping my greasy hands on my jeans. "Let's get the fuck outta here."

We run to the side-by-side and hope we don't get struck by lightning as we rush to the barn. Though it's nearly impossible to see the trail, when the building comes into view, I let out a sigh of relief and feel better once we're inside. Grayson turns off the engine and shakes his head at me.

"If you wouldn't have been late this morning, then we would've finished earlier."

"And if you would've told me that shit was rattling like that last week, we wouldn't have had to do it in the rain."

Grayson rolls his eyes. "Yeah, yeah. Whatever," he mutters, knowing I'm right.

Lightning cracks in the distance, and we leave. Once we're inside my truck, I pull out my phone and text Bradley, one of the guys who works for me, to check in with him. Considering it's pouring, I don't expect a text back anytime soon, but I hope he and the other ranch hands are being safe. While I'd never admit that Grayson is right, I am actually annoyed I overslept because it really did fuck up our schedule.

Instead of immediately pulling away and heading to the B&B, I tell Grayson I want to wait a few minutes to see if the guys come back. He doesn't care because he's getting paid either way, so he pulls out his cell and scrolls through his phone. After thirty minutes, they ride up on horses and once they're in the barn, I get a call from Bradley.

"Hey boss, first herd of cows are moved. What do ya want us to do now?"

"Thanks. Unsaddle the horses and I'll call Alex. Don't want you out there with all that lightning. Meet you at the B&B once y'all are done."

"Yes, sir. See you there," he tells me, and I end the call.

"See, now that's what you call respect. He called me sir." I crank the truck and glance at Grayson.

He rolls his eyes. "I'm not really into stroking your ego. It's big enough."

On the way there, Grayson does nothing but chat about Maize's cooking, and it makes me even more hungry. We park on the side of the large house and walk up the steps of the porch. As soon as we enter, John shakes his head when he sees us dripping wet. We should've changed clothes, but my stomach is rumbling, and I didn't want to wait.

I suck in a deep breath, and the hearty smell fills my nose. I can't grab a plate fast enough. Grayson and I sit and immediately dig in. I look around, and laugh because there are more ranch hands than guests in the dining area. If Maize comes out and sees us eating up all her food, she's gonna lose her shit. Honestly, though, she should be used to it by now. It's been a longtime tradition among the workers, which was started by John, Jackson, and Alex themselves, not to mention it's Grandma Bishop approved.

The next morning, I'm up before I get a text from Riley because I'm so damn nervous to be around Rowan. It's time for us to drive to Houston to help her move all of the shit she's accumulated while at college back home. The last time she was in town was spring break two months ago, and even then, we both worked, so I didn't actually see her that much. I'd be lying if I said I wasn't excited for her to be here permanently.

I meet him at the B&B, then we hook up the lowboy and get going. It's a six-hour drive to the campus, and Riley calls Zoey almost every hour to check on her. It's disgustingly cute.

After all the boxes are loaded, we immediately drive back. Rowan's following us, and Riley notices the smug grin on my face. If looks could kill, I'd be six feet under.

We don't stop to eat a proper lunch, just some shitty fast food to go because Riley wants to get home before dark.

"You know this ain't gonna tame the beast," I tell him, unwrapping and nearly devouring the burger within three bites. I can barely hear him scolding me for making a mess as I sip my Coke.

Though we're not supposed to speed while hauling a trailer, Riley doesn't follow the rules. He goes as fast as he wants and takes curves like a bat outta hell. Rowan's boxes are sliding around, and I know if any of them fall off, she'll kick someone's ass. And for once, it won't be mine.

We finally make it back to Eldorado, and Riley nearly flies down the long dirt road that leads to his parents' house. He parks, hops out, and already has a box in his hands by the time Rowan catches up with us and gets out of her car.

"Seriously? I'm telling Zoey how you were driving." She throws Riley a glare with a hand on her curvy hip. Soon, the two of them are going back and forth as we carry the boxes. Rowan's trying her hardest to ignore me, but each time I pass her, our eyes meet.

After thirty minutes, we're still unloading. Her shit is heavy, as if she packed the boxes with bricks, so I peek inside one and see a few romance books and souvenirs from her college life. I walk into her bedroom she had when we were kids, and it brings me back in time. The walls are still purple, and some posters of her favorite boy bands are still hung. It's like a time capsule of Rowan's teenage years.

"I plan to have a life, thank you very much," I hear her say.

"Yeah, hanging out with me," I interrupt, hauling in an oversized box and dropping it.

"Hey! That could've been fragile!" She stands and gives me a scowl. She's so cute when she's mad.

"Relax, princess. I looked inside, and it wasn't." I flash her a shit-eating grin.

She pushes her finger into my chest, but I don't move an inch. "Don't look through my things, you weirdo!"

I chuckle as Riley interrupts our moment. "She literally just moved back. Can't you two be adults and stop antagonizing one another?" he asks, then laughs.

"Between Diesel and me, there's only one adult here," she says, narrowing her eyes at me.

I press a palm to my chest. "Now that just hurts. You wound me."

She rolls her eyes and pushes past me, all worked up.

"Alright, children. Let's get this shit done so I can get back to my pregnant wife." Riley scolds, following her. By the smile on his face, I can tell he's thinking about Zoey. I take a few minutes to look around her room and remember coming in here when we were kids. Before she gets weirded out that I'm lingering, I leave and pass them as they continue bickering.

I look at the boxes and see one has clothes written on it in black Sharpie. If she was worried about me looking through her romance books and pictures, this will really get her fired up. Happily, I grab it, walk inside, then set it down.

"I went through this one too." I smirk at Riley, knowing he's going to be annoyed at our banter, but I don't care. "You have a thing for red thongs, huh?" I tease Rowan.

"You ever gonna grow up?" she snaps at me.

Shaking my head, I shoot her a wink and grin. "Never, baby."

Rowan heads outside, and we're on her tail. As she bends over, I stare at her plump ass, imagining her completely naked and in my bed. Riley's glaring at me, and I can tell he's getting pissed, but I just can't help it. For years, he's warned me how off-limits his sister is, but it hasn't stopped me from finding ways to antagonize him. They walk past me and continue their conversation, but I'm too busy laughing to care.

It takes nearly an hour for us to put all of Rowan's stuff in her room. She gives her brother a hug and me a firm handshake accompanied by a glare.

I lean down and point at my cheek. "I'll take a kiss and a thank you."

"Will you turn back into a toad if I do?" She playfully slaps my arm, and a jolt of electricity streams through where she touched me.

"No, sweetheart. I'm already your prince." I pucker my lips, which only causes her to groan and walk away. I deserve a medal for trying.

As we climb into the truck, I'm beaming with joy. Once we're inside, I turn to Riley. "I think she likes me."

He snorts. "I think you're still drunk from last night."

"Nope, totally sober," I say, giving him my mini version of a sobriety test by touching my nose with the tip of my finger.

"Don't forget I'll kick your ass if you fuck with my sister. She's off-limits," he warns, being completely serious. Rowan deserves the world, and I wish I could be the one to give it to her.

I snicker. "What you don't know won't hurt ya, Daddy."

"Dude! It's sick when you call me that."

When I start the engine, my mood shifts, and Riley notices

my frown. I'm trying not to sound like a jealous stalker, but I'm not happy. "I might've seen who she was texting earlier."

Riley looks at me.

"You're not gonna like it." Hell, I don't either.

"Who was it?"

"Trace. That guy she hung around a couple of years ago." Just knowing Rowan is chatting with him again makes my stomach turn. He's old as dirt, at least ten years older than her, and I hated when she hung out with him.

"That fucking thirty-year-old?" Riley's livid, and as I recall the memory of when she brought him to the Fourth of July party, it has me seething all over again. At least Riley hates the guy as much as I do.

"I think he was twenty-seven at the time, so almost, I guess."

Riley lets out a growl and grips the steering wheel even tighter as he drives me to my truck that's parked at the B&B. "What the fuck is he doing texting her?"

I suck in a deep breath, growing more agitated with every passing minute, but Riley needed to know. She won't listen to me if I say anything, but she might listen to Riley if he tells her he doesn't approve of him. "The message said 'Can't wait!' so it sounds like they're planning to meet up," I explain, agitated as hell over it.

"Over my dead body," Riley hisses. "No good can come from her dating an old fart like him, especially after the last guy cheated on her."

The thought of any man using Rowan in the way Nick did has me ready to bust my knuckles against his face. The thought of Rowan being with another man drives me insane, and it's something I try to ignore, though it's hard as hell. No one will ever be good enough for her. At times, I don't think even I can spoil and treat her the way she deserves, but I'd damn sure try.

He parks next to my Chevy and hops out, still thinking about Trace. "I'm lookin' quite good now, aren't I?" I waggle my brows, knowing I'm a better fit for Rowan than Trace or any man in a five hundred mile radius could ever be. "At least you know I wouldn't cheat on her."

With furrowed brows, he tenses. "No, because you don't date. You just bang 'em and bail. And I'd really hate to kick your sorry ass if you touch my sister. So, don't even think about it."

After I give him a cocky salute, I walk to my truck. Riley honks his horn, grabbing my attention long enough to see him shooting me the bird. He's more than amused with himself over it too. I expect nothing less from my best friend, an asshole extraordinaire who's determined to protect his little sister.

Riley Bishop has no idea how much I want and have always wanted Rowan, and I need to figure out how to keep that shit to myself, which may be more challenging than even I realize. Especially now that she's home, looking so goddamn beautiful, giving me all of her sass and side glances. It's not the attention I want, but hell, I'll take anything from her.

Flirting with Rowan might be a death wish from Riley, but damn, she's more than worth the risk.

CHAPTER TWO

ROWAN

Graduating from college was a dream come true, and I learned a lot that'll help with the family bar and ranch. It's been a week since I moved home, and I'm still trying to get used to it. It's been weird living back with my parents and staying in the bedroom I had growing up. The walls are the bright purple we painted them when I was thirteen, and all my old posters are still hung, just a tad faded by the sun. I'm temporarily brought back to being a kid without a care in the world.

While I've come home during my breaks to visit and help out, I wasn't here long enough to want to redecorate. Now that I'm staying with my parents until I get my own place, I might change it up a bit, make it more stylish. It'd be for no reason, though, because I won't be bringing a man home with me. My dad would murder him, and not to mention, I'm more single than a dollar bill.

My parents haven't enforced a curfew yet because I'm helping at the bar, which closes at two a.m. on the weekends, but it doesn't mean they haven't been in my business. While they mean well, I'm ready to have some privacy outside this house.

Mom knows Nick and I broke up, but I didn't give her the details about how dirty he did me. Cheating bastard. Just the thought of him has me raging all over again. I suck in a deep breath and exhale slowly, trying to calm down.

Nick never liked a woman who didn't know her place. I was always too much sass and dominance for him to handle, so he found a replacement—a woman who'd do whatever he said. The moment I caught them in bed together, it took everything I had not to murder them both. All I remember was walking across the room and pulling the bimbo by her hair before Nick hopped out of bed and rushed toward me. With all my strength, I pushed him, nearly knocking him down on his bare, cheating ass before leaving.

He immediately apologized, making up some stupid excuse for his mistake, but I told him to go fuck himself. I hate liars. A man who can't be truthful, especially one I loved and trusted with my whole being, has no business being in my life. I don't do second chances when it comes to cheating. After graduation, I was more than ready to come home even though I knew Nick was moving back to San Angelo, which is only an hour away. I'm grateful Dad made Riley and Diesel help me because I would've had to hire a company. It wouldn't have been cheap, but I would've paid any amount to get the hell away. Over the past four years of being in Houston, I've accumulated way too much stuff.

I look around my bedroom and see boxes stacked against the wall. Each one is marked with what's inside, but I'm not feeling motivated to unpack. I've put up all my clothes and attempted to go through my things, but I can't bring myself to do it. My heart still hurts from what Nick did a month ago and many pieces of our life together are packed in those boxes. I'd almost rather the memories of him stay there for eternity. While I'd love to forget about him, he's moving back to San Angelo to help with his family's business. Unfortunately, I won't be able to erase his dumbass from my life soon enough because he's literally forty-five minutes away from me. Running into him is still an unfortunate possibility.

A knock rings out on my door, and I roll over and check the time on my phone. It's nearly nine in the morning, and I've been up for a while, just thinking about how strange life is at the moment.

Another knock taps out. "Rowan?" my mother says from the other side.

"I'm awake."

The door cracks open, and I sit up.

"I made breakfast. Come eat before I put everything up." She gives me a smile, and I nod, twisting my hair into a high bun.

"You don't have to tell me twice." I put my feet on the floor and follow her into the kitchen. Mom doesn't disappoint and has a whole spread of food on the table. I know she probably got up early and had breakfast with Dad, then made this for me. After I fill my plate with bacon, eggs, and a biscuit with a huge scoop of gravy, I smile.

"You've outdone yourself, Ma," I tell her around a mouthful.

She shrugs. "I'm off work today, so I thought I'd spoil you a bit." She works as a nurse at the hospital in San Angelo, and her shifts are typically long.

Before I can say another word, Dad walks through the door. He goes straight to Mom and pulls her into his arms and kisses her. Their love is beautiful, and even though I've been burned, I hope one day I find what they have.

"Okay, gross," I say as the kiss deepens. "I don't want breakfast and a show."

Dad laughs. "You do know how you were made, don't you?"

I put my fingers in my ears. "I was delivered by a stork."

The last thing I want to think about this morning is my

parents doing it. That's a visual I can live without for the rest of my life.

Mom giggles, but I've known how babies were made since I was ten. Considering her job, she was determined to give Riley and me the sex talk as soon as puberty hit. Then we both proceeded to tell all the other kids at school, which got back to Grandma Bishop, who was ready to kick our asses. She was so embarrassed, but I've never seen Dad laugh so hard.

Dad talks about the ranch and his daily duties as I finish eating. "You workin' tonight?

"Mm-hmm." I finish chewing. "I'm supposed to meet Uncle John around five. I should be finished learning everything within the next month, and then he's gonna let me loose."

"Oh lord," Dad says. "Well just know if running the bar doesn't work out, you can always help Maize in the kitchen at the B&B." He grins.

"Hard pass. I didn't go to business school to cook. Not to mention, I'm horrible in the kitchen. Plus, Maize is a hard-ass perfectionist. One time, we made cupcakes, and she nearly had a hissy fit because of how I iced one. No thanks!"

Dad chuckles and shrugs. "Don't know where she would've gotten that trait from."

His sarcasm isn't lost on me.

"Not from Uncle John," I say, and we both laugh because Maize's exactly like him—meticulous to a T. He follows all the rules unlike his twin brother, Uncle Jackson. The two are complete opposites.

Mom fills a mug full of coffee and blows on it before taking a sip. "What are your plans today?"

I shrug. "Not much going on other than hoping Zoey has that baby before I have to go to work."

Mom and Dad both grin. We've been eager and waiting for Zach to be born, and after her last appointment, we were told it could happen at any moment. I'm just ready to become an aunt so I can spoil my nephew rotten. Grandma Bishop is growing impatient too because it's her first great-grandchild.

"Mama's been praying about it all morning," Dad says with a wink.

"You know when Grandma sends messages to God, things happen." I laugh, but I'm not wrong.

Dad checks the time and tells us he has to get back to work before anyone notices he's gone. We say our goodbyes, and I finish my bacon.

Once I'm done eating, I help clean the kitchen. Afterward, I hop in the shower and get dressed, then go to the B&B to see what's going on today. It's weird being home, and it'll take some getting used to after juggling a hectic schedule in college.

When I walk inside, Uncle John is sitting behind the counter and Maize is leaned over talking to him. Her dark hair is pulled back into a bun, which is normally covered in a hair net when she's in the kitchen. They're chatting about something and laughing their asses off. When I clear my throat, she turns around, and I smirk. They have a special connection, especially considering Maize's biological mother passed away soon after she was born, and he became a single dad overnight. John's wife, Mila, raised Maize as her own, and most don't know because they're so close.

"Hey, kiddo," Uncle John greets me just as Kenzie bursts through the back door being her usual loud self. She's majoring in education and is home for the summer. As soon as she has her degree, she'll be here permanently, following in Aunt Mila's footsteps—like mother, like daughter. She opened a daycare years ago, and it eventually transitioned to a private school. While our town isn't big at all, many of her students are from the surrounding areas. When more teachers are hired, they can accept more kids off the waitlist, so it's a big deal for Kenzie to get her degree.

"I'm starving," Kenzie says, glancing at her sister. "Did you make banana bread today?"

Maize gives her an incredulous look, narrowing her blue eyes. "Yes, for the *guests*."

"I'm a guest all summer," Kenzie quickly retorts.

When I chuckle, Kenzie just shrugs, then goes to Maize and wraps her arms around her and squeezes. "Come on, sis. You love me soooooo much. You can't deny my love for your banana bread."

Uncle John grins at his daughters the entire time. "She does have a point. It's really good."

"Fine!" Maize says, knowing she won't win.

"Well, if you're serving up slices, I want one too! And don't be stingy," I say.

"Same!" Uncle John adds.

Maize pretends to be annoyed, but I know how much she loves cooking and finds joy in us being obsessed with her food. Five minutes later, she's walking into the main area carrying three small plates.

"It's still warm," I say excitedly, noticing steam rising from the top. Kenzie doesn't wait before she's stuffing her mouth full. I take a bite, and it's so delicious that I quickly devour it regardless of the big breakfast I just ate. Maize happily snickers.

"So yummy and addicting. I think I need three more slices. How is this even legal?" I say, tempted to lick the crumbs from my plate. Kenzie and Uncle John nod in agreement.

"Y'all are just saying that."

I roll my eyes because she knows better. "Not many people can cook as good as Grandma. So shut the hell up."

That makes her laugh. "I mean, I don't wanna low-key brag or anything, but I know it's delicious."

"Of course you do," Uncle John says. "Good job!"

A guest walks up, and we move out of the way. I follow

Maize and Kenzie onto the back porch, giving the lady privacy to speak with Uncle John.

"So, next weekend is your twenty-third birthday…" Kenzie glances at me. "We're going out, right?"

"I'm sure I have to work." I walk to the edge of the porch and look out at the rolling hills.

Maize interrupts my thoughts. "Nope. I'll take care of Dad. We're celebrating instead. I mean, when's the last time the three of us got together?" She loops her arm in mine.

Kenzie comes to the other side. "It's been a while, Rowan. Let's drink and dance the night away."

"I honestly forgot about it. I totally would if I can get off work."

Immediately, Kenzie walks inside, causing Maize to shake her head. She turns to me. "You doin' okay with everything?"

A ragged breath escapes me because I know she's referring to the breakup. I texted her soon after it happened because while she's my cousin, she's also one of my best friends. Always has been. We're close in age, only a year and a half apart, and grew up doing all sorts of stuff together.

"I'm making it."

"You're better off without that douche in the long run. Seriously, I don't know what you saw in that polo-wearing pretty boy anyway. You need a *real* man. A cowboy. Someone who can fit in with the fam."

I suck in a deep breath, chuckling at her description of Nick. She's not wrong, though. "Sometimes love is blind."

"That's what they say," she sing-songs. Soon, Kenzie is bursting through the back door.

"You're off next weekend," she states matter-of-factly.

"Really?" I'm actually kinda shocked because I've only been home for a week.

"Dad was cool with it. You only get to celebrate your birthday once a year," she tells me. "I'm gonna get with Elle too and tell her to cancel all her plans next weekend and meet us. It'll be just like old times with all of us girls together!"

Maize squeals, and we're all giddy with excitement. I would love for Elizabeth to join us. Elle's in her last year of veterinary school and is interning at a local office, but she's been so busy with work this week, I've barely gotten to see her. Our schedules are completely opposite these days, but I hope that changes now that I'm here for good. Before I can say another word, my phone rings with a call from Riley.

"Zoey's going into labor!" he shouts, not even giving me a chance to say hello.

"OH MY GOD! Right now?" I yell.

"Yep, her water broke. No baby yet, but Zach will be here soon! We're going to the hospital. Gotta go. Calling everyone else."

He immediately hangs up, not waiting for a response. Maize and Kenzie impatiently wait for me to explain.

"I'm gonna be an aunt today! Oh my God! I gotta go." I give them both hugs.

"Should we come with you?" Kenzie asks.

"Only if you want to sit in the waiting room for hours," I say.

Kenzie laughs. "How about you tell us when Zoey starts pushing and then we'll come up?"

"Sounds great!" I'm overjoyed as I tell them goodbye.

I rush through the back door, letting Uncle John know the good news on my way out. He's just as ecstatic about it as I am. "I'll be up there later! Don't worry about going to work tonight. I'll get Ethan to cover for you."

"Okay! Thank you!" I yell through the common area and hurry home where I know Mom and Dad are eagerly waiting for me.

"Let's go!" Dad rushes as soon as I walk in. We're giddy as can be as we drive to the hospital in San Angelo. The hour drive feels like an eternity. By the time we make it into the parking lot, I'm ready to hop out before Dad parks the truck. Once we're inside, Mom leads the way to the delivery floor, and her co-workers congratulate her as we pass them.

"You're gonna be a grandma, River! Feelin' old yet?" Amelia asks.

They've been friends since Mom started working at the hospital after Riley was born. Mom laughs and tells me and Dad to stay in the waiting area as she checks on Riley and Zoey. We sit, and the anticipation nearly kills me. Dad's a bundle of nerves too.

Moments later, Mom returns. "They're checking to see how dilated she is. She's having some intense contractions already, so it shouldn't be too long."

I let out a sigh. "She needs to hurry up and push that baby out already."

"Rowan, it's barely been two hours since her water broke. They're not going to pull the baby out by his head. He'll come when he's ready."

Patience isn't one of my strong suits. I try to busy myself and play on my phone, and text Riley every twenty minutes until he tells me to stop bothering him. Instead of listening, I keep up my annoying little sister act that I've perfected over the years, but he straight up ignores me. It's deserved, though, because I'm sure he's helping Zoey with whatever she needs.

More family members arrive until the entire waiting room is full of Bishops. All I know is I'm going in and seeing my nephew first or I'll be throwing fists. After four hours, Riley comes out, and he's grinning wide. Pretty sure he's shedding some tears too. He tells us everything went great, and they've moved Zoey into a regular room so we can visit now.

I quickly text my cousins and let them know the baby is here. Riley's bombarded by everyone, but I hurry and follow my parents through the hall to see Zoey while he explains that all went perfect with no complications.

When we enter the room, she's nothing but smiles as she holds her little bundle of joy. I rush over to her, and my emotions get the best of me when I see Zach for the first time.

"Oh, Zoey," I whisper. "He's beautiful."

She sees my eyes well with tears and chuckles. When she looks down at his sweet little face, it's obvious how much love she already has for him. "Do you want to hold him?"

Mom and Dad stand behind me, and we all admire this adorable tiny human in my arms.

"Hey, buddy," I say. "I'm your aunt Rowan, and I'm going to spoil you so much."

Though I want to be greedy with him all day, I eventually pass him to Dad. Riley enters, and we're all beaming. Considering there are so many family members here, I give my brother a congratulatory hug, then tell Zoey and Zach how much I love them before leaving so others can visit. As soon as I make it to the waiting room, Grandma and Grandpa excuse themselves to go in next.

"So?" Kenzie prompts as Maize stands next to her. "How are they doing?"

"They're great! But I don't know how my brother made such a cute baby." I chuckle. "Newborns typically look weird, but not Zach. He's absolute perfection," I tell her. "Where's Elle?" I look around.

"She said she got stuck at work and would be here as soon as she could," Kenzie explains.

"You got baby fever yet?" Maize pops an eyebrow.

"You kinda need a partner to have baby fever," I retort.

"That is true," I hear a husky deep voice say over my shoulder. Turning, I see Diesel's wide grin. I give him my well-practiced groan and go to hell look.

"Mind your own business," I mutter and ignore him. Maize

tilts her head as Diesel moves closer to us, forcing himself into our conversation. I turn and look at him. "What?" I challenge, needing him to go away.

He shrugs and tilts his cowboy hat toward me. "If you really want a baby...I can help you with that. Big D is at your service."

I look at him like he's lost his mind, then roll my eyes. "What's wrong with you? Do you have brain damage or something? Eat too many paint chips as a kid?"

Kenzie snickers. "It's all the cow shit he's sniffed over the years. Affected his critical thinking skills."

Diesel arches a brow, smirking. "Man, are all the Bishop women this quick on their feet? Hopefully that means the same under the sheets." His eyes pierce through me, and I'm ready to clock him right in the jaw as a blush hits my cheeks.

Uncle John walks up, and my other uncles Evan and Jackson are behind him with their wives. Usually, when all the Bishop brothers are together, it means trouble or a celebration. Thankfully, this time, it's the latter. As soon as he sees all of my uncles, I see the fear of God in Diesel's eyes as he wonders if they overheard him or not. He quickly leaves and sits in a chair against the wall on the other side. It takes everything I have not to laugh at how quickly he cowered. My uncles are mighty intimidating, especially Uncle Evan, but I think it's because he's a doctor and has an arrogant air about him.

Kenzie and Maize go with their parents to see the new addition to our family, and I pull out my phone and sit, trying to busy myself while everyone takes their turn visiting. Diesel gets up and moves close to me, taking a seat next to mine. I ignore him the best I can, but it's nearly impossible when I can smell the fresh scent of his body wash and cologne. I've always enjoyed how he smells, even when I was teenager, but I'll deny it till the day I die. I try my damnedest to breathe in the other direction, but it's so obvious, he notices.

He clears his throat, trying to get my attention. Some things never change. I scroll through my social media to tune him out, but it's no use. Diesel's being so obnoxious as he shakes his leg and taps his foot. I turn my head and glare at him.

"What do you want?" I look into his green eyes.

He pops an eyebrow. His gaze meets mine, then trails down to my lips, my breast, and further before he shrugs.

"You're an animal."

When he leans over, his lips are mere inches from my ear, and his warm breath brushes against my skin. "Only in the bedroom. Care to find out for yourself?"

My mouth falls open, but I quickly close it. Swallowing, I try to force the images of him out of my head. Diesel is undeniably attractive and has muscles for days, but I also know his history. He's known for banging women's brains out and then not calling them the next day. While there have been times in my life when I may have gone for something like that, I don't find that appealing anymore.

After my heart was used and abused by a cheating bastard, I need something more than to be dicked down by a manwhore. I need someone I can trust and who will treat me right. I have more respect for myself than a one-night stand with someone like Diesel, who I'll have to see every day for the rest of my life. Plus, there's no doubt Riley would murder him. The thought makes me grin, and he notices.

"What?" he asks.

"Oh nothing," I sing-song and lean further back in my seat.

Seeing baby Zach, and my brother so happy with his family, I've realized that's what's really missing in my life. I want a forever relationship, not one that's just temporary, but after Nick smashed those dreams, I'm starting to think it's not in my future.

Almost as if it's a divine intervention, I get a text message from Trace, a guy I sorta dated for a short time two and a half years ago. When we first met, he'd just moved here because his job transferred him to San Angelo. He's older than me, nearly thirty now, but mature and well established in his life, which is a change from the guys my age. Things ended mutually when I left to go back to college, and we kept in touch as friends.

My smile grows even larger.

Trace: Welcome back to Nowhere, Texas! I didn't forget to text you when I got back in town, but wanted to give you some time to settle back home. Hope we can get together soon!

Rowan: I'm ready when you are! When are you free?

Trace: Next weekend?

I think about my plans with my cousins and know I can't cancel on them. I wouldn't anyway, especially not for a guy, but Trace is one of the good ones. He's also not bad to look at either.

Rowan: Dang! I'm busy next weekend. What about the one after?

Trace: I'll be traveling that weekend. Hmm…we'll have to reconvene again ;)

Diesel shifts in his seat. "Are you talking to that old asshole again?"

Frustration is written all over his face, and I find it adorable he's so damn jealous. When I first introduced Trace to everyone at the Bishop's traditional Fourth of July party, Diesel and Riley nearly lost their minds. They don't like the fact that Trace is so much older than me, but I am a grown ass woman and will do whatever I want. The last thing I need is their permission or approval.

"What's it to you, *Adam*?" I say his real name and watch him stiffen even more.

"It's nothing to me. When you're in public, though, everyone's gonna wonder why you're dating your dad. That's all." The snark in his tone isn't lost on me.

"My dad?" I laugh. "Trace isn't much older than us," I remind him.

"Nearly ten years, Rowan."

"Seven," I correct.

He scoffs. "You need someone who won't pull their back out to keep up with you." He tilts his head. "Someone who's used to working hard and not sitting behind a computer all day."

"Oh really? Someone like you?" I snort. "No, thank you."

"Don't knock it until you've tried it." He waggles his brows.

I think back to when he kissed me when I was thirteen, then I remember how he denied it, and I hated him for ruining the memory. All night I'd been rejected, and it was just another reminder that I wasn't good enough to be claimed by anyone, not even *him*.

My phone vibrates in my palm as I watch Diesel from my peripheral. He's trying to play it off like he doesn't care, but it's more than obvious he does.

I look around, making sure none of my family is close, and it seems most of them have cleared out. They're probably all stuffed in Zoey's tiny little room or waiting in the hallway to go inside. "I'd rather be alone for the rest of my life than *try it*. I don't want to catch a disease. I have no idea where you or your traveling dick have been."

"You can only deny me so much before you jump on board, Row."

I scoff. "I'm not jumping on anything, especially you."

"We'll see," he says confidently.

"Whatever. Shit in one hand and wish in the other. See what happens quicker." I shake my head, knowing he's trying to get under my skin. At times, I think he might really have a thing for me, but I'm convinced he flirts just to aggravate the piss out of my brother and me.

Instead of giving him any more attention, I unlock my phone and reply to Trace. We decide to play it by ear and plan something another time. A smile touches my lips, and Diesel tightens his fist as uneasiness drifts from him.

Knowing he's jealous as hell only encourages me to keep chatting with Trace because poking the beast and watching him squirm is fun. If Diesel wants to play games, maybe I'll appease him, but it doesn't mean I'll ever be crawling under the sheets with him. I don't care about his cute, boyish grin or how great he smells; he's off-limits. The last thing I need is my brother punching Diesel in the face, but I do smirk at the thought.

CHAPTER THREE

DIESEL

Two weeks have passed since Rowan moved back, and as much as I try, I can't seem to get her off my mind. It's nearly impossible, especially when she's working at the Circle B Saloon nearly every night. Hanging out at that bar is one of my favorite pastimes, and knowing I'll see her has me putting on cologne and taking showers twice a day. When I get off work, I just want to have a beer and relax, but now, I'm changing into nice clothes as if I'm going on a date. "Dress to impress" is one of my mama's favorite sayings.

After work, I do exactly that, then sit at the bar for hours. I was actually kind of disappointed when I arrived and didn't see Rowan there. Apparently, she had the night off, or at least that's what Kenzie told me after giving me shit for asking. They all think it's just an act, but I'm gonna prove to her and everyone else that it's not.

I've had a thing for her since we were kids, but knowing she was Riley's little sister has always deterred me. Thinking back on my past relationships, though, the reason I haven't settled down is because they weren't Rowan. The heart knows what it wants, and while Rowan's favorite hobby is pushing me away,

I'm confident that one day she'll see what's always been right in front of her.

Saturday's her birthday, and I got her something she'd never guess. She probably doesn't think I remembered, but I'll never forget her special day.

I thought she'd be working tonight, but she's spending time with her nephew, so I'll have to give it to her some other time. With her name on my tongue and thoughts of her dancing in my head, I start taking shots. It doesn't take long before I drink too much and have Grayson taking me home. He's a good, responsible sidekick while Riley's busy with his family.

"Want me to pick you up in the mornin'?" he asks, my vision slightly blurring.

"Yeah, don't be late, though, because Alex will chew me up and spit me out."

"Yep, will do, but remember all this when it comes time for a raise," he tells me, grinning. "Need help gettin' inside?"

"Imma big boy. I can handle it." When I open the door to the truck and step out, I nearly lose my balance and laugh. Grayson waits for me to make it on the porch before he backs out of the driveway and leaves. It's really dark out and idiot me forgot to turn on the porch light, so I end up tripping over the mat in front of the door. I catch myself before falling and lean against the wood for a second, noticing my mail haphazardly sticking out of the box. I reach over and grab it, then walk inside and plop on the couch.

Most of it is nothing but stupid fliers and junk, but one envelope grabs my attention. The handwriting is neat and is addressed to my nickname instead of my formal name.

I open it and pull out a single sheet of paper. The curly handwriting matches the front.

Diesel,
My sister, Chelsea, didn't want me to contact you, but I feel it's your

right to know that she gave birth to a little boy named Dawson, and I believe he's yours. She could really use your help right now. If you could, please call me.

-Laurel

There's a phone number and name at the bottom, and all I can do is laugh. I'm ready to throw it in the trash because this seems like something Riley would do, especially after I bragged about how cute his son is to everyone. Word around the ranch travels fast, and I wouldn't be surprised if he's trying to pull my leg or something.

I set it on the coffee table, kick off my boots, and end up falling asleep on the couch. Hours later, I wake up to pounding on my front door. Disoriented and a bit confused, I roll over and land on the hardwood floor, then look up and realize I'm home. When the knocking continues, I stand, unsteady on my feet, and open the door to see Grayson's smiling face.

"What?" I ask.

"It's time to go to work, ya big dumbass. It's five," he says, pulling his phone from his pocket and shining the bright screen in my face. "And you look like shit."

"I drank too much...*again*," I mutter, needing to brush my teeth because the nasty taste in my mouth makes me want to vomit.

"I know, I was there. You have five minutes. We gotta go, or Alex is gonna be pissed." Grayson snaps his fingers, and I'm two seconds from shutting the door in his face and going back to sleep. Instead, I get dressed and cleaned up, take some headache meds, and before I follow him out, I grab the letter from the coffee table and shove it into my pocket. I thought I'd imagined it all but guess not.

I need a gallon of coffee and a bottle of ibuprofen, and the sun hasn't even risen yet.

When we pull up to the B&B, I say a little prayer that today won't be too hard. I should learn my lesson about not going to the bar on a weeknight, but until I start dry-heaving next to the boss, I might not.

"Damn, Diesel. You sure you're okay?" Grayson asks, actually looking worried.

Wiping my mouth with the back of my hand, I suck in a deep breath. "Yep. I'm good," I lie. I feel like a giant sack of shit, and considering it's supposed to be well over a hundred degrees today, it's not gonna get any better. The heat always makes my hangovers worse.

Grayson pats me on the back, and we walk inside the shop. Alex is kicked back in a chair with his feet on the desk, sipping his coffee.

"Mornin'," Alex greets. He's had a permanent grin on his face since becoming a pawpaw. If I wanted to try to get away with anything, now would be the time because he's been in such a good mood. I break out into a cold sweat.

Alex notices as he goes through our schedule today. "You okay?"

I nod, walking to the fridge and grabbing a cold bottle of water and taking a long sip. "Yeah, I think I'm just hungry." I can't remember the last time I ate, which might legitimately be a part of the problem.

"Well shit, go to the B&B and eat. You know what needs to be done now."

Grayson agrees. "Yeah, and if you don't feel any better, I can take over and let everyone know."

"Hell no. Duties need to be done, rain or shine," I argue.

"Hungover or not." Alex shrugs. "Been there. Sucks, but all of our choices have consequences. I gotta hand it to you, though, at least you were on time."

Grayson looks at me. "You're welcome."

"Shut the hell up." I grunt.

Alex glances back and forth between us. "You better get

going before I change my mind and give you tomorrow's chore list too."

"Not needed," Grayson says as we leave.

When we get into the truck, Grayson cranks it and backs out. "Maybe next time you're on beer eight, you'll stop drinking before ordering two shots. Don't you know the rule? Beer before liquor, never been sicker."

I close my eyes. "Once I eat, I'll be good to go."

As soon as we arrive at the B&B and walk inside, I smell the homemade bread. My mouth waters as we help ourselves to the buffet. Before I sit with my plate stacked high, Maize comes around the corner glaring at me.

"That's for the guests," she says with her arms crossed.

"I'm a guest. I'm just visiting until my plate is empty," I taunt, shoveling food into my mouth like I'll never see a biscuit again.

Grayson doesn't say a word while she's around, and eventually, she walks off, muttering some cuss words. I shrug, completely unbothered by her. He picks up his fork and begins eating.

"So, boss, where do you want me to start today?"

We're digging a trench to place pipe so we can get water to a new area on the property that has more shade for the cows. It'll take us at least a week to complete, which is okay.

"I was thinking maybe a few of you can mark the area first, then half of you start on the east side. Eventually, we'll meet in the middle."

"Sounds like a good plan," he says. I've had some time to think about it because Alex had mentioned it last week in passing.

"You think you can get everyone started? I wanna go check on Riley after breakfast. I'll grab some keys to a side-by-side and meet you out there when I'm done."

"Sure thing," Grayson says around a mouthful.

Once we finish eating, Grayson sits back and pats his stomach. "Damn, that woman can cook."

"Right?" I grin. "She should open a restaurant, but this is much better because then I can eat for free."

Grayson chuckles. "If we keep eating triple amounts of food, she might start charging us or really kickin' our asses. The woman hates us."

"Comes with the territory." I shrug, not that worried. "But if she did that, I'd call her grandma and snitch because Mrs. B told me I could eat here anytime I wanted," I explain. "And no one crosses Grandma Bishop. Not even her own kids and especially not her grandkids."

I stand and pick up our extra plates and place them in the dirty dish tub. We say good morning to John and walk out the back door before he has the chance to give us a hard time.

"See you in an hour?" Grayson asks as I look out at the rolling hills, feeling slightly human again after eating some carbs.

"Yep, an hour should be good. Hey, after work, can you take me to the bar to get my truck?"

"Yeah, not a problem, boss." He nods, and we go our separate ways.

Walking to the shed, I grab the keys to a four-wheeler and climb on. It takes no time to get to Riley's house. Even though he's not working at the moment, he keeps his early morning schedule to help take care of the baby or spoil his wife with breakfast. We've been waking up at the butt crack of dawn since we were teenagers. Chores had to be done, which meant rising early, and it's hard to reset an internal clock after that long.

I lightly knock on his front door, and within seconds, Riley opens it and lets me in. He rushes back to the kitchen where he's cooking. I glance around and notice all the lights in the house are off except in this room, which means he's the only one awake. Every move we make seems amplified, or maybe that's just my hangover.

"So what's up? You're visitin' early," Riley says as he pours oatmeal into a boiling pot of water.

I pull the letter from my pocket, grinning like an idiot before I sit. "You almost got me."

Riley looks confused. "What're you talkin' about?"

I pick up the envelope and tap it against the table. "This."

His forehead creases. "I really don't know what that is."

Riley comes over, and I hand it over. He takes the paper out and reads it. "I didn't send you this."

"Shut up." I laugh. "You really don't have to keep up the act."

The look on his face is pure seriousness. "I swear to you on my great-grandfather's grave, Diesel. I didn't send it."

It only takes seconds for my smile to fade. Riley never jokes around about family like that. I take off my cowboy hat and set it down before running my fingers through my hair.

"You want something to drink?" he asks as the blood drains from my face.

"Is it too early for whiskey?" I glance up at him.

He pulls out a bottle of Jack Daniel's from the cabinet, and I shake my head, wanting to puke just from looking at the liquid. "I'll take some coffee instead."

A mug is set in front of me, and Riley hands the envelope back. "Did you call the number?"

"No, because I thought this shit was a joke," I admit.

"Chelsea. Chelsea," Riley repeats. "Wasn't that the chick's name from Vegas?"

I think back to my birthday nearly two and a half years ago and try to refresh my memory. "I don't remember." Sadly, I don't even remember what she looks like either, but I don't say that out loud.

He begins plating food. "Did you wear protection?"

"I always wear protection. There's no doubt about that."

Riley shrugs. "If you know for a fact you wore protection, then I wouldn't worry about it until she comes knocking on your door with a kid in tow. You know? If she'd have sex with you after one night, then you probably weren't the only person she slept with at the time she got pregnant. You weren't exclusive or anything. Hell, you didn't even exchange numbers."

"Right," I agree, tucking the letter back in my pocket.

"I'm sure it's nothing," Riley encourages. I push the thoughts away and refuse to give it any more of my attention.

"How's the dad life so far?" I ask with a grin, changing the subject.

"Feels like a dream," he admits. "I can't believe I have a son. It's everything I've ever wanted."

"I'm happy for you, man. And envious as fuck," I say, wishing I had what he has.

"You'll find someone. She might be an idiot for gettin' with ya, though," he teases.

"Shut the hell up. That's no way to talk about your sister," I add and then hightail my ass out of his house before he beats the shit outta me. I tell him goodbye and ask him to give Zoey and Zach my love before I hop on the four-wheeler and head to the east side of the land where my ranch hands are hard at work.

By the time I make it to where the guys are working, my stomach has settled. The food I ate and coffee I drank made me feel like a million bucks.

After parking, I walk toward them and look over what they've accomplished so far. The area where we need to dig is marked with spray paint, and they're spaced out in twenty-foot sections with shovels. Working with them makes my life easy because I don't have to micromanage anything they do, and they're self-sufficient.

"Make sure y'all are drinkin' plenty of water. Don't need anyone gettin' heatstroke out here," I tell them.

I look at Grayson, who's wiping sweat from his brow. "I'm gonna drive around to the other side of the property and check on the cattle we moved last week. If you need anything, call me."

He nods before going back to digging, and I make my way across the pasture on the four-wheeler. Though I run the cattle operation, we have to do backbreaking tasks at times so the cows will survive the intense heat waves. Making sure they get water is the number one priority in the hotter months.

It takes me nearly thirty minutes to drive to the far pasture. I go down a large hill and start counting the herd to make sure none are lost. There's a lot of land fenced off, so it takes me a while, but each one is accounted for. It's easy for them to get lost, and I've heard rumors of thieves cutting barbed wire and stealing entire herds at dark. It's one reason we spend weeks branding in the summer. If I ever catch anyone stealing from the Bishops, my fists would have a long conversation with their face.

By the time I make it back, it's well after lunch. They took a break to eat, but since I ate a large breakfast, I decided to skip. For the rest of the afternoon, I help lay the pipe and am sweaty and starving by the time our shift is over. Grayson and I decide to stop at the B&B to see what Maize cooked for dinner before going to get my truck from the bar.

As soon as I walk up the steps to the porch, Rowan, Maize, and Kenzie walk out dressed in short skirts that leave absolutely nothing to the imagination. My jaw hits the floor as my eyes trail up Rowan's long legs until I meet her gaze.

"Take a picture, why dontcha?" she barks, and her cousins laugh.

"Where the hell are you goin'? I ask. "Especially looking like *that*."

"We're going out," Maize says.

"For Rowan's birthday," Kenzie adds. The two of them look at me before walking down the steps in their high heels, but Rowan lingers for just a moment, and I notice she's wearing cowboy boots with her skirt.

"Damn. You look really nice," I tell her, smiling.

"Thanks, *Adam*. That was the goal," she gloats.

If she only knew what I really want to say to her right now, but instead, I keep my feelings for her tucked deep inside. I suck in a deep breath. "Stay out of trouble tonight. You need a real man to save you, call me."

She laughs. "Trouble's my middle name, and I'm more than capable of taking care of myself, thank you very much."

And I don't doubt her one bit. All I want to do right now is pull her into my arms and kiss the fire out of her, but the way she's looking at me tells me I'd only get burned.

"You got a designated driver?" I ask.

"Shit, you're worse than my parents."

"Rowan," I warn, crossing my arms over my chest.

"We're staying at a hotel all weekend. We don't need a DD. Any more questions? " She runs her fingers through her dark brown hair, and I watch her tongue dart out and lick her ruby red lips.

If asking her questions would keep her here all night, I'd keep going.

"Come on!" Kenzie yells from her Jeep.

Rowan looks at her, then back at me but doesn't say a word.

"Hope you have a happy birthday," I say, lowering my voice. She looks as if she wants to say something but doesn't. Instead, she walks away.

"And be careful," I say even louder. She glances at me over her shoulder and smirks.

"We'll see," she says. I swear Rowan's shaking her hips just to drive me fucking crazy. She climbs into the Jeep and mumbles something to Maize before Kenzie backs out of the driveway. The dust kicks up in the air, and I watch until they're out of view.

I'm half-tempted to go home, take a shower, and follow them, but I didn't ask enough questions. They could be going to San Angelo, or hell, knowing them, they might've even gone to the River Walk in San Antonio. The Bishop girls are unpredictable.

Though I'm full of disappointment because Rowan won't be here for her birthday, and I left her gift at my house, I push it away and go into the B&B with Grayson trailing me.

"What?" I look at him.

"Nothing," he says. "Just seems you've met your match."

"With who?" I ask and notice John's sitting behind the counter reading a magazine. Instead of giving me shit, he just throws us a head nod and a grin.

"Rowan. I saw the way she was lookin' at you."

I smile as I help myself to the beef tips and mashed potatoes they're serving tonight. Maybe I wasn't imagining the look in her eye, after all, or maybe Grayson is just fucking with me, but either way, I'll take it.

As I sit down and eat, Rowan's long legs fill my mind. After I get my truck, I'll be taking a cold shower with hopes of pushing the thoughts of her away. But I'll fail miserably because I always do when it comes to Rowan Bishop and what she does to me even if she doesn't realize it.

CHAPTER FOUR

ROWAN

KENZIE TURNS the volume up on the radio, and we blare Garth Brooks. We sing along about friends in low places like stupid teenagers as we make our way to San Angelo for the weekend. I thought it would be more difficult to get off work since I've only been back for two weeks, but Uncle John wasn't too much of a hard-ass about it. As Kenzie said, the four of us haven't been together in ages and deserve a girls' night out.

When we make it to town, I can't stop thinking about how Diesel looked at me. Not often do I catch the seriousness in his eye that says I'm more than his best friend's little sister. The reality is that line can't be crossed, even if Diesel was the first man I ever kissed. Not even my cousins know that secret.

"What's on your mind?" Maize asks me as we park and walk toward the entrance of the hotel.

I hurry and smile. "My eighth grade winter formal."

Maize laughs her ass off.

"Why?" Kenzie chuckles as she opens the door, allowing us past her.

"I dunno, just a random thought."

She looks at me as though I've lost my mind, and a part of

me thinks I have. Eighth grade wasn't that important. It's not like it was high school prom or senior formal. It was a stupid dance where the boys were too embarrassed to be close to the girls.

After we check into the hotel, the three of us wait for Elle to arrive. She's been super busy with work and assisting Dr. Wallen but said she could use some fun and decided to join us after her shift. I'm so damn excited to get to hang out with my cousins this weekend. The four of us used to get into so much trouble growing up.

A light knock on the door grabs our attention, and Maize gets up to answer it. Elle walks inside, looking pretty as ever with her dirty blond hair pulled up and bright green eyes behind black-rimmed glasses. She's all smiles as she gives us hugs.

"Look at you, birthday girl!" she says, noticing my outfit. "You're gorgeous as ever!"

I willingly take the compliment. It's the first time I've seen her since I moved back.

"We look like trouble." I giggle. We grab our purses and head to the Honkey Tonk bar down the road. Kenzie doesn't turn twenty-one for a few more weeks, so she's our designated driver, which is a good thing because honestly, getting drunk is the only thing on my to-do list tonight.

We immediately walk up to the bar, and I order a soda for Kenzie and three shots.

"To Rowan turning the big two-three and all of us celebrating together!" Maize says, and we all clink our glasses together. I smile wide, then shoot the tequila down. It's smooth and goes down like water, which is dangerous as hell. Moments later, Maize orders another round.

"I'm not going to have any more," Elle tells us after the second one. She's always been the responsible one and follows the rules. "I don't want to drive back home tomorrow with a hangover." She winks.

Once the liquor is flowing through my veins, we sashay onto the dance floor and shake our asses. Martina McBride blares through the room, and we sing along to an oldie but a goodie as loud as we can. The music fades, and a slow song comes on, and I'm brought back to being that girl who isn't asked to dance as Maize and Kenzie go off with two guys. Instead of letting it get to me, I go back to the bar with Elle and order a cocktail as I get lost in my thoughts on being single forever.

"How's work going?" I ask her.

She groans. "Busy, as usual. I work nonstop."

I chuckle. "Well, your boss is drop-dead gorgeous, so it can't be that bad to be around him all the time."

"True. He's a walking, talking wet dream. I think people feed their dogs chocolate just so they can get an emergency home visit from him. It's pathetic. I mean, I get the allure, but he's kinda an asshole, which is a total turn-off." She smiles, but there's something more behind her tone.

"Who's an asshole?" Kenzie walks up and asks as Maize continues dancing with this tall, good-looking fellow.

"Dr. Connor Wallen." Elle says his full name with an eye roll. "He's good with animals and turns on the charm with their owners, but behind closed doors, he's brooding and snappy," she explains. "And that's *after* he's had his morning coffee."

"Oh damn." I chuckle, thinking how it sounds like Dr. Wallen needs to get laid and how long it's been since Elle's been in a relationship. She could probably help turn his attitude around.

"The things I'd let him do to me." Kenzie releases a dreamy sigh, elbowing Elle in the arm.

"Before I forget, who's that guy who works with Diesel again?" Elle asks, noticeably changing the subject away from her boss. I glance out on the dance floor and notice Maize still's shaking her ass with a guy who seems super interested in her.

"You're probably talking about Grayson. A little shorter than Diesel, sandy brown hair," I describe him and watch as Kenzie tenses. We make eye contact, but she tucks her bleach blond hair behind her ear and pretends it's nothing, but I saw her reaction.

"Yeah, that sounds like him. Is he new? I saw Diesel with him the other day when I was dropping something off for Uncle John." Elle glances at Kenzie.

"What? I don't know anything about Grayson." Kenzie sucks on her straw, checking out of the conversation, which causes me to laugh. I've noticed she snaps at him any chance they're in the same room together, though she's never given us a reason. She only says he's annoying and leaves it at that.

"He's been around for five or six months. I think he's Kenzie's age," I tell Elle, glancing at Kenzie.

She shrugs with a look of indifference. "So? Doesn't mean I know anything about him."

I laugh at her expression, but I see something in her eyes. She's not telling us something, but I don't push her on it.

A few minutes later, Maize joins us and orders a drink too. We all turn and look at her.

"Please tell me you got his number," I say, looking past her at the sexy guy across the room she was grinding against the last few songs.

She shakes her head. "He didn't ask me for mine, and I wasn't gonna dare to make the first move. It's all the validation I need to know I'll end up a nun or single forever with forty-seven cats. There are no good-looking, single men around here."

I stand, lifting my hand, and Maize gives me a high-five. "Same, sis. Same."

A few more slow songs play, and eventually, the mood in the room changes as Shania Twain blasts out about men not impressing her very much. I'm pretty sure this is my theme song. One reason this country bar stands out above the others is they always play old-school country songs. It brings me back to being a kid and the music my grandparents always have playing in their house.

I know I need to stop drinking, or I'll be trashed before midnight. I order a glass of water and chug it so I don't have a hangover tomorrow. When I'd go out with my friends in college, it was the only way I wouldn't be sick the next day.

As soon as Rednex comes on, the entire room starts line dancing. I'm honestly having an amazing time with my cousins. The four of us can't stop laughing as we nearly trip on each other to "Cotton Eye Joe." Drunk people were not taken into consideration when this dance was invented, but it's another reason I love to wear my cowboy boots. Heels are just too dangerous. Kenzie and I stumble around and nearly take Maize and Elle down with us. We are those basic girls wearing skirts and being obnoxious at the bar, but I don't care what anyone thinks. Maize encourages me to take more shots with her and to keep dancing. She's the life of the party right now, and I'm living for it.

After we've nearly tired ourselves out, we find a table in the corner, then sit and catch our breaths. My face hurts from laughing so much, and I honestly can't remember the last time I had this much fun. Damn, I love being home. These girls are my best friends and practically like my sisters.

While I'm at the table, I pull my phone from my purse and ask the waitress to snap a picture of us. We smile wide, wrapping our arms around each other. Once we check the photo, I post it to Facebook with a sappy post about being out with my cousins. *Grateful these three are in my life. Happy Birthday to me!*

After it's live, I scroll through my feed, and that's when I see a picture of Nick and the skank he cheated on me with. She has a big diamond ring on her finger and looking at it makes me want to puke. The ring, the man, the future—all of it was supposed to be mine, but it was stolen from me in a blink from a man who never deserved me in the first place.

"What the fuck!" I shout and show Maize my screen. Immediately, her reaction changes, and she shakes her head.

"He's a bastard," Maize says.

Elle adds, "A *cheating* bastard, at that."

"I guess we'll join the convent together," Maize continues. "Won't be so bad if we're both there, right?"

I snicker, regardless of how frustrated I am. "You know what I want right now?"

All eyes are on me, waiting for me to continue.

"I want *revenge*."

Kenzie rubs her hands together. "Are you thinking what I'm thinking?"

By the evil look on her face, I'm not sure I am. "I'm scared to know what's going through your mind right now."

"Bishop women don't get back, they get even." Maize has always been Team Rowan, and even from the very beginning, she didn't like Nick that much. She said there was a *vibe* about him. I never saw it, but should have. I was blinded by his good looks and made excuses for his arrogance.

Never again.

Elle looks back and forth between us. "Oh lord. You're gonna make me be an accomplice, aren't you?"

"I just need you to drive by his place for me."

"He's back in town?" Kenzie asks.

I suck in a deep breath, then blow it out. "Yes, he moved back with his ho in tow last week. Trust me, I wasn't thrilled about it. Out of all the men in the entire state of Texas going to the University of Houston, I had to date some asshole who only lived an hour away from home."

"You were happy about that when you thought it was going to work out," Elle reminds me.

"Yeah, I honestly thought it'd be great because I always planned to come back after graduation. No man was going to keep me away from home. I don't care how sexy or rich he was. It was a compromise. Have a handful of kids. I'd work on the ranch and help with the bar, and he'd continue running his family's business. We'd had our entire future planned out," I explain with a frown. "Until he fucking ruined it. I'm not sure I'll ever be able to forgive him for what he did to me."

"I might become a nun with y'all," Elle says, causing the three of us to laugh.

"Are you sure about this?" Elle hesitates.

"Abso-fucking-lutely," I tell her and walk toward the exit, leading the way.

We hop in the Jeep. I sit in the front while Maize and Kenzie sit in the back. Elle starts the engine, and we turn out of the parking lot, then I give her directions to Nick's house. A part of me feels like a loser for keeping tabs on him, but we dated for a little over a year. I can't just snap my fingers and make my heart forget the way he made me feel when things between us were good. We shared some happy memories, but he was so willing to throw it all away.

Elle turns down his street, and my heart races a million miles per hour. My throat goes dry, and I'm unsure of what I'll see when we pass. Thanks to Facebook and his willingness to brag about everything, I knew exactly what house he'd bought. We'd looked at it together online once, but when I said we'd need to compromise and live between San Angelo and Eldorado so it'd be convenient for us both, he closed out of the webpage, then told me to forget about it and changed the subject.

She slows in front of the house, and that's when I see his Mercedes parked next to a Corvette. I bite my bottom lip so hard, I'm shocked I'm not bleeding.

"Stop," I tell her, my blood pressure rising as I think about everything that's happened over the past couple of months. I get out of the Jeep and open the back door to the hatch and find a tire iron. Before I even know what I'm doing, I'm marching down the driveway on a mission and take all of my frustrations out on his beautiful bright yellow Corvette. With every bit of strength I have, I swing the cool iron against the windshield. Watching it shatter gives me so much fucking satisfaction that I don't stop. I go to every side window and even the back before I take my anger out on the hood of the car.

Maize whisper-shouts my name. "Rowan, come on!"

Looking up at her, I make one final blow to the taillight. I'm sure if she wouldn't have stopped me, I'd have kept going too. Before walking back to the Jeep, I look at all the damage I've caused and don't feel an ounce of regret. Actually, I feel better. Though I'm still not over being cheated on, I'll sleep great tonight knowing tomorrow morning when that prick gets up to go to work, his prized possession won't be so immaculate.

I climb inside the Jeep, setting the tire iron in the back seat between Maize and Kenzie. They look at me with wide eyes and their jaws dropped.

"That was badass," Kenzie eventually says, breaking the silence.

"I'm in shock," Elle tells me, chuckling. "I can't believe you fucked up his car like that."

"Thousands in damage, without a doubt," Kenzie says.

"Yep!" Adrenaline rushes through my body as we head back to the bar. "Oh wait, can we just go back to the hotel? I think I've had enough fun for the night."

"Only if we can stop and get double cheeseburgers first. Do you know how badly I'm craving McDonald's?" Kenzie says. "Sometimes it's hard living so far away from greasy food."

"I'm convinced you're really a raccoon," Maize teases. "Mischievous, messy, and eats everything in sight."

I burst into laughter. "That's the best thing I've heard all day. Kenzie, the trash panda. I think we might've found a new nickname for you."

Kenzie rolls her eyes. "Oh my gosh, y'all. I'm not *that* bad!"

"You are," Elle speaks up as she pulls into the drive-through. "You totally are."

After she's ordered nearly four of everything on the menu, she pays, and then we're handed three bags filled with chicken nuggets, double cheeseburgers, and a ridiculous amount of salty french fries. Living in the country does have its disadvantages, but I'm grateful not to have any of this conveniently close to home. In Houston, there was a fast food place on every corner.

Kenzie has a bag opened and is stuffing her mouth before we even make it out of the parking lot. I honestly didn't realize how hungry I was until Maize hands me a box of chicken nuggets. I feel like I swallowed them whole and didn't even chew them. Elle drives us to the hotel, and once we're in our room, we finish eating. I continue to devour food until I'm stupidly full, then kick off my boots and lie back on the bed with a smile on my face.

While I may not have gotten completely even because bashing in a car doesn't fix a broken heart, damn, it felt good to get him back. If only I could see Nick's face in the morning when he notices his expensive toy is now damaged goods. I'd pay good money for that. I hope he learns his lesson, but men like him never do.

A part of me wonders if he'll even suspect it's me, but the other part doesn't care. He never could handle me, not when we were dating and especially not now. One thing's for certain, I might be a Southern woman, but I still have a temper at times. He's underestimated what happens when you cheat on a Bishop.

CHAPTER FIVE

DIESEL

I'M SOAKING WET, covered in nasty water from head to toe. A calf walked into the pond and couldn't get out because of the mud, which meant Grayson and I had to perform an impromptu rescue mission. There was no time to think about taking off our boots or anything before we were hopping into the water and walking through mush.

It's common for cows to stand in the bodies of water during the hot months since it helps them cool off, but the babies are sometimes the worst because they go out too far and can't get back to the bank. The little bastard was screaming at the top of his lungs, and we just so happened to be doing our afternoon checks. Together, Grayson and I carried the little asshole to the grass and made sure he was okay before driving off. Doesn't help our situation, though. We officially smell like cow slobber, pond mush, and sweat.

By the time we make it back to the shop, we both stink, my feet are soaked, and I'm ready for a drink.

"Wanna go to the bar tonight?"

Grayson looks at me. "Like this?"

"Hell no! I need a shower," I tell him, taking off my hat and setting it on my lap.

"I think I'm gonna take a rain check. It's been a hectic fuckin' day, and I'm exhausted. Gotta love Mondays."

I give him a smile and look down at my boots and pants. "Yeah, I totally understand. Never expected to be doing half that shit today. Every day's an adventure on the ranch," I remind him. The unpredictability is one of the things I love the most about my job. There's no monotony. Honestly, I don't know how people sit behind a computer at a desk all day. It sounds like eternal hell. I'd go crazy not being in the country.

We give Alex the rundown of what happened, then I hop in my truck and drive home. At times like this, I wished I carried an extra set of clothes around. I'm forced to drive back with the windows down because I can't stand the smell of myself. Once I'm home, I see Rowan's gift on the counter and smile before going to the bathroom. She's working tonight. I made sure to find out this morning from John. I've been waiting all weekend to see her to give her that present.

I take off my clothes and turn on the hot water. Stepping inside, I allow the warmth to soothe my sore muscles from carrying a one hundred pound calf today.

After I'm done washing every inch of my body, I brush my teeth and get dressed. I run my fingers through my hair and throw on a baseball cap, then spray on some cologne because I know it drives Rowan wild. It always has, ever since we were teenagers. She pretends to be immune, but I've noticed her reactions. The thought of seeing her tonight causes excitement to bubble inside me. No woman has ever made me feel like this, and as much as I try to shake it, I can't. Rowan Bishop has been in my veins since I was fourteen years old and tasted her lips against mine. Even though we were so young, I've never been able to forget the electricity that streamed between us. It's still there too.

Before leaving, I grab the gift along with my keys and head into town. I couldn't stop thinking about her the entire weekend. I saw a picture she posted on Facebook of her and her cousins at the Honky Tonk in San Angelo and thought about making the drive, but I knew better. The last thing I'd want to do is ruin her birthday by showing up unannounced. She looked beautiful as can be, though, and I know all eyes were on her at the bar. There's no doubt she was the prettiest woman there.

When I park in front of the Circle B Saloon, I see Rowan's car on the side. I sit and stare inside the building, watching as she pours a beer for an older guy and then smiles sweetly as she sets it down on a napkin. She laughs at something he says and just looking at her nearly takes my breath away. Without even trying, she's as pretty as can be with her hair pulled up into a tight ponytail on top of her head.

Knowing I can't watch her from my truck all night, I turn off the ignition, grab the present, and go inside. As soon as I walk in and sit at the bar, our gazes lock. I smile, and she narrows her eyes at me, then at the bright-colored wrapping paper. A moment later, she walks over, places a napkin in front of me, and treats me like every other customer.

"Hi, would you like a drink menu?" she asks, properly batting her eyelashes.

I snort at her sarcastic tone. "Give me a Bud."

She glances down at the box. "What's that?"

I push it toward her, grinning wide. "I got you something."

"Why?" She tilts her head. "Is it a gag gift?"

"You'll see," I challenge, moving it closer to her.

"I trust you as far as I can throw you, and we both know how much that is," Rowan retorts as she walks away and grabs a frosty mug from the cooler. She sets down an ice-cold beer in front of me before snagging the box.

I gently grab her hand before she can walk away and meet her deep brown gaze. "Don't open it around anyone."

"Oh God. Now I'm really scared."

I shrug and take a sip of my beer, the smile meeting my eyes as she walks away.

A second later, I watch a preppy ass guy enter and forcefully move the stool from in front of the bar next to me, making all sorts of noise. He stands tall like he owns the place, but everyone in here knows better. He's a puny little runt wearing a polo tucked into well-pressed khaki pants with a belt. Rowan notices him and tenses fiercely. Alarm bells go off in my head as he barks her name. Something isn't right with this guy, but he needs to watch his goddamn tone when speaking to her.

Rowan rushes over to him and lowers her voice, and I try not to pry. I try to keep my eyes locked on the TV on the back wall, but I can't tell what's on right now, though.

"What're you doing here?" she asks in a hushed tone, trying not to draw more attention.

"You know why I'm fucking here," he hisses.

I suck in a deep breath, trying to control my temper while staying out of her business. Truthfully, it's damn hard.

Rowan laughs. "Because you miss me?"

It takes everything I have not to roll my eyes because I know exactly who this prick is now—her cheating ex-boyfriend, Nick. Granted, the way he's looking at her, though, isn't with love but hate.

"Miss you? Miss *you*?" His voice grows louder. "Not quite. I'm here because you're a stupid bitch."

I jump to my feet so fast, the barstool falls to the ground with a loud crash. "You need to watch your language when speaking to a lady."

"Lady?" He snarls. "She's no fucking lady. She's a jealous whore who destroyed my Corvette."

Rowan pipes in. "I did not touch your *precious* car. Why

would I do that?" She crosses her arms over her chest, challenging him.

"Because you're a goddamn cunt," he snaps.

Taking a step forward, I'm mere inches from him and ready to punch his face in. "I've already warned ya once. Don't call her names again. I don't care what the fuck she did to your car. And trust me, it won't be anything compared to what I do to your goddamn face if you keep disrespecting her like that."

"You need to leave, Nick," Rowan demands, pointing at the door, but something in her expression tells me she really did fuck up his car.

"Leave? How about you make me?"

Seconds later, his stark white polo is in my fist, and I'm ready to beat his face in when Rowan quickly comes around the bar and breaks us up. She softly places her hands on my chest and begs me to calm down. "Please, Diesel," she whispers. "He's not worth it."

I take a step back and try to chill out. No one's going to talk to her like that in front of me—not an ex, not even a family member, and especially not in *her* bar while she's working. He's trying to humiliate her, and I won't tolerate it.

"You're gonna pay for this, Rowan," Nick threatens.

"For what, exactly?" she questions.

He takes his cell phone from his pocket and plays a video, turning it around for her to watch. Considering I'm so much taller than she is, I can see it perfectly. She's got a tire iron in her hand, and she's destroying his car. With every swing she takes, I can feel the anger buried deep inside her. Damn. Remind me never to piss her off. She's a goddamn savage. Without realizing it, I start laughing my ass off, which nearly makes her ex spontaneously combust. He's not stupid enough to threaten me, though he gives me a dirty ass look.

I hear Rowan suck in a deep breath and groan. "Cameras."

"You're a fucking idiot," he tells her.

I move Rowan to the side and step closer to Nick. "I warned you about your language," I tell him. Before he can move, my fist meets his nose, and he falls down hard on his ass as the other customers watch the commotion.

"Motherfucker!" He covers his face with his hands.

"I think it's time for you to leave," I demand, pulling him up by his shirt and pushing him toward the door.

"You're gonna pay for every fucking dent and scratch you made," he shouts at Rowan, spitting out blood. "I'll be back if you don't."

"You're done, asshole," I tell him, basically throwing him outside. I stand in front of the entrance with my arms crossed over my chest and watch him storm off to his sparkly Mercedes. If he doesn't watch out, she might destroy that one too.

After he peels out, kicking up dirt and rock, I go back inside. Rowan is nowhere to be found. Kenzie is helping customers and refilling drinks. Honestly, I didn't even notice she was here until now. She helps at the bar but assists her mom at the daycare during her college breaks. She has a couple of years left before she graduates. Though she plans to work with kids, she does a good job bartending too. That natural people-person personality comes in handy in a small town like this. I sit and finish my beer, hoping Rowan returns soon. I order another drink and bide my time, but I still don't see her. Soon, it's closing time, and Kenzie locks the front door, then proceeds to clean. Considering I'm kinda part of the family, she doesn't force me to leave but rather lets me sit there even though I'm stalling.

"Hey, is Rowan still here?" I ask as she grabs her purse from under the counter.

"Yeah, she's in the office. You can go back there if you want. I won't tell anyone." Kenzie shoots me a wink. I walk her to the door, let her out, then relock the entrance.

When I go to the back, I see Rowan sitting in the office with her head down on the desk.

"Rowan?" I ask softly.

"Yeah?" She turns around, and I can tell she's been crying by how puffy her eyes are. It hurts my heart to see her like this.

"You okay?"

She nods and forces a smile, wiping her cheeks. "I'll be fine."

Shaking my head, I walk toward her, and she stands.

"Thanks for sticking up for me. I appreciate it."

"I'd punch him for you any day of the week," I tell her with a grin.

A chuckle escapes her. "You'd protect any woman who was being called names like that. He's such a dick."

I shrug. "Not sure what you saw in him, honestly."

"Me either." Rowan glances at me before moving past me. "I need to close out the drawers."

I follow her, going behind the bar as she takes out the money. "So…" I laugh, trying to lighten the mood. "I didn't realize you were the batshit crazy ex-girlfriend type who seeks revenge on luxury cars."

She eyes me. "It was a moment of weakness."

"Didn't look too weak to me with the way you were swinging that tire iron. I guess all those years of playing softball in high school did you some good."

Rowan grins, then scoffs, trying to blow me off, but I'm standing way too close to her to be ignored. I can tell she doesn't want to talk about this, but something in the way she looks at me says more than her words ever could. That familiar spark I saw when I kissed her the first time returns and dances behind her eyes.

As she sucks in a ragged breath and her lips part, I have the urge to kiss her again. We're too close, and I can smell the sweetness of her skin and the flowery scent of her shampoo. Loose strands of her dark hair fall from her ponytail, and I reach over and tuck them behind her ear. Her chest rises and falls when I place my thumb under her chin, hoping she gives me permission to move in.

The world around us seems to fade away as I lean closer. My heart is galloping in my chest as Rowan's eyes flutter closed. I lick my lips, and then as if someone turned on the lights, she moves away from me and denies our kiss. Shattered is the only way I can describe how I feel, but it also gives me hope. We were so close, but I understand her hesitancy.

She just went through a major breakup, one that had her beating the shit out of his car, so it might seem too soon. Having her almost give in to me, though, is all the encouragement I need to know that not all hope is lost between us. That fire is still burning bright, and I'll do whatever I need to help it blaze.

"You should open your gift," I say, swallowing hard around a large lump in my throat.

"Okay." She nods.

I gain my courage after being rejected and follow her back to the office. She rips off the paper on the small box and looks at me with happiness as she holds a mood ring between her fingers.

"Where did you find this?" she asks, grinning.

I lean against the doorframe, soaking in her beautiful features. "You lost it when we were younger."

"Yeah, I remember. Me, you, Riley, and Elle were playing tag, and it fell off," she reminds me.

I nod. "I spent an entire week looking for it out in the pasture."

"And you actually found it?" She seems shocked.

"I refused to give up because I knew how much you loved it," I admit.

"Why didn't you give it back to me then?" Rowan's eyes meet mine as she adjusts the sizing and slips it on her finger.

"Because you hated me, and I didn't want you to think I was weird or something."

She lets out a holler of a laugh. "You'll always be weird to me, Adam. But thank you. It really means a lot."

"So what color is it?" I step inside the office and look down at the ring.

"Pink," she says, and I watch her cheeks heat.

"Which means what exactly?" I'm actually curious. She had all the meanings for the colors memorized when we were younger.

Rowan shakes her head and playfully tucks her plump bottom lip inside her mouth.

"Come on, tell me," I urge. "I promise I won't laugh."

She sighs, inhaling a deep breath. "Fine. It means feeling flirty or romantic," she tells me with a chuckle, and my eyebrows rise.

"I think it's spot-on," I tease, and I'm damn happy about that.

CHAPTER SIX

ROWAN

It's been two weeks since Nick showed his ugly face while I was working and threatened me. I know I acted irrationally, but considering he's stupid rich and doesn't need the money, it grates on my nerves. He could easily afford to pay for the damage or report an insurance claim, but to appease him and save my ass from him reporting me, I'll pay to get him out of my life for good.

The way Diesel stepped in and protected me hasn't left my mind either. We shared a moment and almost kissed, but I got cold feet and turned away. He's always been that annoying brother type who picks on me and drives me crazy for shits and giggles, but that doesn't mean I haven't noticed how he's changed over the years. He's huge—muscular and tall—dark and handsome. It'd be impossible not to notice.

Although it's Friday and Ethan doesn't normally work, he'll be here tonight for a few hours. Kenzie is coming in soon to help with the late rush. Once the ranchers finish their shifts and have dinner with their families, they'll come down and drink for a few hours. The weekends are definitely busier, and having an extra set of hands is always nice so I can focus on manager duties too.

"Another cold one..." George holds up and waves his empty beer bottle at me. In his mid-fifties, he's one of our regular customers and drinks like his stomach is never-ending. At least he's a decent tipper, though.

"Coming right up," I tell him, walking toward the cooler to grab him a new one. His wife, Mary, comes in with him sometimes, but he's riding solo tonight. "Where's the missus?" I ask when I swap out the bottles.

"Her sister is visiting this weekend. Hence why I'm here and not at home." He tilts the corner of his lips before taking a sip.

"Ah..." I say with a smirk. "Not a fan, huh?"

"Oh, they cluck like hens all night long. It gives me a headache, so I come here to look at your pretty face instead."

"Be careful now, George. Your compliments might go straight to my head."

"And trust me, she doesn't need a confidence boost," Ethan adds, coming up to my side. "She's already full of herself."

I jab my elbow into his ribs, causing him to let out a harsh breath. "Look who's talking, Mr. Suave. I could smell your cologne the second you walked in. Who're you tryin' to impress?"

"The ladies, duh." He chuckles, moving around me.

"You mean Harper." I cackle, and he gives me a dirty look. They've been best friends since they were in diapers, but he'll never make a move. She's the daughter of my dad's best friend, Dylan. We're all friends and grew up together, but she's currently dating some asshole they went to high school with. "Stop being a chickenshit," I tease.

"Look who's talkin'." He gives me a pointed look, then flashes a cocky smile. "Plus, I'm too young to settle down. Gotta play the field a bit."

Shaking my head, I hold up my palm toward Ethan and

look at George. "See? This is why I'm single. Men are just too annoying and full of themselves."

Speaking of which…

The door opens, catching my attention, and Diesel walks in with Grayson and Wyatt, one of his townie friends. He laughs and playfully pushes Wyatt before our eyes lock, and his smile deepens.

"You were sayin'?" George taunts, chuckling around the neck of his beer before he takes a long sip.

Blinking, I clear my throat and grab a rag, needing to stay busy. It's not uncommon for Diesel to hang out and drink after work, but ever since he put Nick in his place, I can't stop thinking about him.

"Hey, *Row*," he says, taking a seat next to George, and the other two follow suit, sitting down on the other side of Diesel. He knows I hate that nickname, yet he says it to annoy me anyway.

"Hey, *Adam*." I flash a smug grin, knowing he hates it when people use his real name especially in public settings.

The corner of his lips tilts up into a shit-eating smirk. "You know, it only makes my dick harder when you call me that."

I gulp, then glare at him as I shake my head. "Pretty big talker there."

He winks, then continues, "Didn't know you'd be workin' tonight."

Liar. Yes, he did. With the exception of my birthday weekend, I've worked every Friday night since I moved back a month ago.

"Yep, I'm closing. Putting my big fancy finance degree to work." I chuckle because this was the plan after graduation. Maybe not bartending per se but being involved in the family's businesses and training to handle all the financial accounts. It'll be a while before I completely take over, so I'm managing the bar for now. "What can I get y'all?"

Diesel looks at them before glancing back at me. "Three beers to start. We'll save the shots for right before I kick their asses in pool."

"Pretty cocky for someone who almost broke their neck earlier," Grayson teases.

"Cocky is his middle name," I interject before I grab their drinks and set them down in front of them.

"Got that right," Wyatt adds.

"So how were you a dumbass today?" I ask, holding back my worries.

"They're being dramatic," he states calmly before bringing the beer to his mouth. The mouth I shouldn't be fantasizing about.

"This motherfucker..." Grayson starts, shaking his head. "He's on a tractor, and instead of parking it where it *belongs*, he wedges the damn thing between two others with no space to actually get down. So he decides to *jump* to the one next to him and nearly misses. Then he does it again and falls on his damn head."

"It was my shoulder," Diesel corrects. "And I'm fine, by the way. Thanks for your concern." He narrows his eyes at them, and I snort at their interactions, shaking my head at the way they give him shit. It's too easy, though. Diesel's a big kid in a grown man's body.

A really sexy body.

"You poor thing," I sing-song, resting a hand on my chest. "I'll keep you in my thoughts and prayers."

He cocks a brow. "I like you thinkin' about me."

My eyes slide to George, who's shooting a half grin. "Told you," I tell him.

George laughs, and Diesel furrows his brow, clearly not amused he's not in on the inside joke.

"Told him what?" he asks. "That I'm charming? Good-looking? Your future baby daddy?"

I nearly choke as a blush creeps up my neck and cheeks.

"That men are annoying. You just proved my point."

"You wound me, Row." Diesel sticks out his lower lip, pouting.

"Sorry to burst your *enormous* ego, but men like you are the worst ones out there," I say matter-of-factly.

"Gentlemanly? Kind? Willing to punch an ex-boyfriend for their best friend's little sister?" he challenges, raising his eyebrows and clenching his jaw. The scruff on his face is a little thicker than usual, and a fantasy of his facial hair brushing against my inner thighs emerges into my head. I immediately blink the vision away.

"He's gotcha there," Grayson chimes in.

I roll my eyes, no longer wanting to give this conversation any more attention. Luckily, more customers enter and order drinks.

Ethan and I take turns with the customers, mixing cocktails while making sure the place stays clean. Kenzie shows up for her shift and replaces Ethan, and before long, it's nearly closing time. Diesel, Grayson, and Wyatt played pool and darts, taking shots after each game. I watched them silently, forcing my eyes away before Diesel could catch me staring, and have started wondering what the hell's wrong with me. Diesel's been like an annoying brother to me most of my life, and now whatever is sparking between us is freaking me the fuck out. I know I'm not imagining it.

"Diesel, we're heading out," Grayson says.

"You better not be driving," I tell him sternly.

"They're not," Diesel reassures me. "We're staying at Wyatt's apartment tonight. It's just down the block. We walked."

"Ah, okay. Good," I say as I turn toward the register to grab their tab so they can cash out.

"I'll meet you guys there in a bit," Diesel tells them after they pay.

Grayson and Wyatt stumble out, leaving Diesel and me alone with a couple of regulars on the opposite end of the bar. Kenzie is busy wiping down tables and sweeping, not paying any attention to anything else.

"Here," he says, grabbing my attention with his signed receipt.

I grab it from him and go to input it into the system when I read the tip amount he wrote.

"Diesel, I think you made a mistake and added too many zeros," I say, chuckling and glancing over my shoulder at him. He looks sober as hell, which is crazy, considering the amount he drank tonight. His lips are in a firm line, and his eyes pierce through me.

"No, that's right."

My face falls, and I think I'm in shock. "You don't have to tip me that much."

"I know, but I wanted to, so let me."

"No."

"Yes. I'm the customer, and I'm *always* right," he fires back.

I snort, shaking my head. "I can't allow you to do that."

"And why not?" he challenges.

I slump my shoulders in embarrassment. "Because I need to earn the money to pay Nick back without it being given to me. You did enough, and I already feel guilty you got involved."

"It's not a handout. That tip was hard-earned."

"You're full of shit, and you know it."

"Just take it, Row. It's not like I have a wife and six kids to support. I can afford it."

"I wasn't saying you couldn't," I quickly defend. "I just don't want your pity."

"I'd never pity you, Rowan," he says sincerely.

"Fine," I say in defeat, but quickly add, "Just this once.

Don't get used to me giving in so easily when you try to overtip again. Got it?"

He chuckles, enjoying this way too much. "Sure, whatever you say."

I groan with a smile. He's so damn stubborn sometimes.

"Do you remember the night of your eighth grade winter formal?" he asks after I input the tip amount and take out the cash, stuffing it into my apron.

"What?" I ask, scrunching my nose. "That was like…ten years ago. Why do you ask?"

"Because I remember it like it was yesterday and wondered if you did too."

I swallow hard because I *do* remember and even found myself recalling it not too long ago. How could I forget my first kiss? Or that it was with Diesel.

"Um…yeah, kinda. I guess." I blush, thinking about it.

Before he can continue, Kenzie comes up to me. "All done. Chairs are up, floors are swept, garnishes are stocked. Do you need me to do anything else?" she asks.

I think about the closing checklist, but I can't really concentrate on anything other than the fact that Diesel has chosen tonight to bring up a memory that's haunted me for years. "Nope, I think that's all. Once I cash those guys out, I'll just have receipts to go through, and then I'll close up."

"Do you mind if I go? I know I'm supposed to so you aren't alone, but—"

"I'll stay with her," Diesel interjects. "That way you don't have to wait, and Rowan doesn't have to close alone."

"Are you sure?" Kenzie asks eagerly. She must have plans, but it's almost two a.m., so I can't imagine she'd be doing anything this late. Then again, she is almost twenty-one and on her college summer break, so anything's possible.

"I was gonna stay anyway, so go right ahead," he tells her. The two of them don't even ask what I think about it, but honestly, I'm glad they don't because my throat has suddenly gone dry.

The final patrons pay their bill, and I follow them to the door so I can lock it and flip over the *open* sign. Nerves tickle my skin as I walk back around the bar and feel his eyes on me. We've been around each other for most of our lives but hardly ever alone. And never in this kind of situation.

Honestly, most of my memories with Diesel are of him aggravating the shit outta me. He finds ways to tease me, and I always ignore him the best I can. But ever since I've moved back and he threatened Nick, there's been a shift between us.

An indescribable one.

"I remember the exact dress you wore that night," he says, my back turned to him as I print out the end of day reports. "Probably makes me sound like a creep, but—"

"A little." I chuckle. "But I remember the song we danced to, so it's not any less creepy than that, I suppose."

Turning around, I see his intense gaze on me. Butterflies swarm my stomach as I watch his expression.

"Why are you asking about that night?" My voice is soft.

Diesel shrugs. "I actually heard that song on the radio recently, and it reminded me of my first kiss."

I blink hard and retreat a step. "Wait, what?" Tilting my head, I study his face and then my eyes lock on his. "That...that wasn't your first kiss."

The corner of his lips tilts, amusement written all over his face. "Actually, it was." He furrows his brows. "Why's that so surprising?"

"Well, considering your history..." I chuckle anxiously. "I just assumed you started kissing girls in kindergarten or something."

He laughs, his shoulders relaxing. "I probably did, but those don't count. Our kiss that night..."

"That counted?" I ask, my cheeks flush by the direction our

conversation went. Diesel's rarely serious, and things feel different with him tonight. That kiss affected me, more than I was willing to admit at the time, but nevertheless, it sparked numerous fantasies as I bloomed into a teenager.

"It did," he states honestly. "But I thought maybe it didn't mean as much to you since you seemed to hate me after that."

"I didn't *hate* you," I blurt out. "I was thirteen and…awkward."

"Then why'd you lash out at me after I took you home?"

"I don't know." I suck in my lower lip, shrugging. "After Riley suspected us, I guess I figured that if I pushed you away first, then you couldn't reject me." I shrug again, embarrassed. "Teenage girl insecurities."

Narrowing his eyes, he rests his forearms on the bar. "You're the one who called me gross," he reminds me. "I denied it so Riley wouldn't punch me in the face, and afterward, you avoided me like a bad haircut."

"It was *ten* years ago, Diesel," I emphasize. "We were kids."

He leans back against the stool and stares at me before speaking. "I guess you're right."

Needing to end this unpleasant conversation, I grab my store keys from my pocket and shake them in my fingers. "I better close up."

Diesel nods, staying silent as I walk to the office. My nerves are in overdrive, like I'm thirteen all over again, and it takes me three times to input the right safe code before it successfully opens. I grab the log notebook and sit at the desk, writing in the total amounts for the day. Once I'm done, I walk back to the register and take out the cash to put in the zipper pouch for a bank drop afterward.

One of the reports I printed calculates our inventory and how many cases I need to restock, so I do that next.

"Can I help with anything?" Diesel asks when I return in front of him.

"Sure." I smile and hand him the list of what I need.

He follows me to the stock room, and we make trips back and forth until the beer fridges are stocked full. I look around a final time, double-checking Kenzie's work and wiping down a few stools before I spot clean behind the bar. She took care of most of it, but missed some small things.

"Would you mind wiping down the liquor bottles while I finish up in the office? I have just a couple more things to do," I say.

Diesel nods with a grin. "Can do."

"Thanks."

We've been working in silence, the tension between us thick and electric. I input some information into the computer, then sign off. I tidy up the desk and double-check the safe is locked. I'm stalling, too nervous to face Diesel, and I hope he doesn't call me out for my weird behavior.

The sound of glass breaking draws my attention, and I shoot out of the chair, then rush to the bar. "Are you okay?" I ask when I see a shattered beer mug on the floor.

"Don't come over. I'll sweep it up." He walks around the mess. "Where's the broom?"

"It's in the storage room. I'll grab it."

"No, let me. You finish what you're doing." He walks toward me, closing the gap between us. I swallow hard as my gaze lowers down his body, taking in how good he looks in his tight jeans and boots.

"If John asks, tell him Kenzie did it," he teases, and we both laugh, which eases the tension some.

"She dropped an entire bottle of tequila once, so trust me, one mug doesn't even put a dent in the amount of shit workers have broken around here," I reassure him.

Diesel walks around me to get to the cleaning supplies, and I head back into the office, needing the space to clear my head for a moment. I don't know what's happening right now, but

I've never felt this nervous around him, and now suddenly, I'm worrying if I have food in my teeth and if I remembered to pluck my eyebrows this morning.

I leave myself a few Post-it reminders, then do one final glance around the bar. Closing never takes me this long, but Diesel has me completely distracted and on edge. But I need to face him, lock up, and get out of here. I square my shoulders and walk out to where he's waiting.

"All good?" I ask casually.

"Yep, everything on my end anyway."

I snort. "Thanks for your help," I tell him, swallowing down the large knot in my throat. "Although you *did* volunteer so…"

He chuckles, nodding. "That I did." Then he walks toward me with a shrug. "Hope you didn't mind the company?"

Diesel searches my face as the space between us gets smaller and smaller. "Uh, no. Not at all. You're a lot easier to boss around than Kenzie," I tease, taking a small step back.

"I don't know about that…" He lifts his baseball cap, an old one he's worn for years, and brushes a hand through his messy hair.

"I think that hat is on its last leg," I say, dragging out the conversation for whatever reason I can't figure out yet.

"You think so?" The corner of his lips tilts into an amused smirk. "I've had this since I was—"

"Fifteen," I answer without thinking. I'm not sure why I just blurted that out or how I even remember, but the memory resurfaces of the first time he wore it. He'd been working on the ranch all summer, which meant I saw him almost every day. I was horseback riding when he and Riley drove up on a four-wheeler, and I couldn't stop staring at him. The boys typically wore things to keep the sun out of their eyes while working—either their Stetsons or baseball caps—but this one fit him like a glove, and it stood out to me for some reason.

He puts it back on his head and nods. "Yeah, a gift from my grandfather."

It's a beaten-up bluish gray color with a silver embroidered Texas state on the front. Nothing fancy, but I always liked the way it looked on him.

"I can't believe it hasn't unraveled yet, honestly." I lick my lips, willing myself to stop talking. This is the most normal conversation Diesel and I have had in ages, maybe ever. He's usually poking fun at me, and I'm typically telling him to fuck off.

Get out! Time to leave! Walk away and drive home!

Diesel chuckles, nodding in agreement. "Same. It's my favorite one, though, so hopefully it'll last forever." He takes a step toward me, nearly caging me in against the bar top. "So, I have another question for you."

"Okay." I swallow hard.

"About that night..." he reiterates.

"What about it?"

Diesel's in front of me, our bodies so close our feet touch. "Was it your first kiss?"

Inhaling a sharp breath, I can't seem to get enough oxygen. Why is he asking me this?

I remember how he asked that night too.

Blushing, I nod. "Yeah, it most definitely was."

He cocks a brow, entertained. "Really? Because I remember a sassy brat who told me 'yeah, right' and then stomped away."

My chest deflates as I exhale. "Like I said, thirteen-year-old insecurities...I wasn't exactly an expert on boys. Hell, I didn't even have a *real* boyfriend until my junior year of high school."

"Chad was a tool bag," he states. "Edward too. Your history ain't lookin' too good."

"*Mine?*" My voice raises an octave. "Let's discuss your lineup of Southern belles then, shall we?"

"Actually, I was hoping to have a repeat of our first kiss instead." He leans down, pinning me with his hard stare.

The casual way he throws that request out has me blinking, slow and hard. "What?"

"Can I kiss you, Rowan?" His deep Southern drawl sends shivers right between my legs.

What the hell is happening?

Swallowing hard, I inhale a deep breath, trying to find my courage. "You didn't ask that night so…"

"I'm a gentleman now," he retorts with a cocky grin. "Do I need to ask a second time?"

Biting my lip, I chew it for a moment before releasing it and sliding my tongue across it. "Yes."

"Yes, I need to ask again, or yes, I can kiss you?"

The smug look on his face tells me he knows exactly which question I was responding to. He's such an arrogant jerk sometimes.

Deciding to give him a little taste of his own medicine, I wrap my arms around his neck and pull his face to mine but not all the way. I stop when our lips are merely centimeters apart, and I can feel his ragged breathing against my mouth.

His strong hands grip my waist, and he squeezes my hips, waiting for permission. "Yes," I whisper. "Kiss me."

CHAPTER SEVEN

DIESEL

As soon as the words leave her mouth, I wrap my hand around her neck and pull her lips to mine.

Sweet and soft.

Just as I remembered.

But this kiss is electric. Intense. A decade in the making.

My other hand squeezes her hip, and she arches her back, pressing herself into me. Rowan moans when I slide my tongue inside and taste her deliciousness. My fingers grab her two french braids, and I roughly pull on them like I used to when we were kids. Her head falls back, and our kiss deepens; our tongues fight for control as eagerness takes over.

"Fuck, Row," I growl, sweeping my tongue along her bottom lip. "I've been waiting ten years to do that."

Her breathing is ragged as we make eye contact. "I was only thirteen. That would've been highly inappropriate."

"Most of my fantasies about you were," I admit, shrugging.

"Oh really?" She cocks a brow. "Care to elaborate?"

My eyes gaze down her body, admiring every curve. "Hell yeah."

Before she can protest, I grab under her ass and lift her. She squeals as she locks her hands around my neck and wraps her legs around my waist. I walk us around the bar and set her down on one of the stools so we're eye level. Cupping her cheek, I bring our mouths together and savor her taste.

"I always liked when you did your hair like this," I taunt, pulling on one of her braids again. "You have no idea what they did to my teenage boy hormones. Then you'd put on a cowboy hat, and I'd nearly nut in my jeans at the thought of how I'd yank on them as I bent you over."

Rowan bursts out laughing, tightening her thighs around me. "That's quite the imagination for a teenager."

I flash a half grin. "That was in my thoughts just last week."

She swats at my chest, but I grab her wrist, pulling her closer. "Did you wear them for me?"

"Do you think everything is about you?" she retorts. "How does that ball cap even fit with that big head of yours?"

"Answer the question, Row."

"I've been fixin' my hair like this for years," she tells me. "You'd chase me and pull on them, then tease me and say I looked like Little Red Riding Hood."

I chuckle at the memory and shrug. "Well, your hair does have a red tint in the sun."

"And you'd say how you were the Big Bad Wolf, and that if you caught me, you were going to eat me," she adds, unamused.

I burst out laughing again. "I was a little shit."

"So I'd run, and of course, you were always faster than me," she deadpans, tilting her head. "Now I remember why I hated you so much."

My mouth tips into a grin. She's trying so hard to be upset with me, crossing her arms and putting space between us. After a decade, I finally kissed her again and am not wasting another opportunity.

"That was just foreplay," I taunt, leaning closer. "All these years of pent-up sexual frustration…stop fightin' it, Row."

"And what were all the one-nighters and hookups? Practice?"

I arch a brow. "Were you jealous?"

She gives me her famous eye roll. "No."

I tilt her chin up until our gazes meet. "Let me kiss you again."

"You gonna ask every time?" I can tell she's holding back a smile.

"You gonna stop being stubborn?" I counter, plucking her bottom lip from her teeth. "Because I have plans for this sassy mouth."

"Is that how you win all the girls over? Skip over the dating and get-to-know-yous and go straight for the panty-dropping one-liners?"

"I know everything about you, Rowan. At this rate, we've been datin' for years because there isn't anything I don't already know or haven't observed."

She scoffs. "You don't know *everything*."

I close the gap between us until my mouth hovers over hers. "Try me," I challenge. "I bet if I slid my hand between your legs, you'd be wet. Am I right?"

She swallows. "Wrong."

I smirk. "And I bet if I rubbed my thumb over your nipple, it'd be hard."

"It's chilly in here."

"That right? So I have no effect on you? Is that what you're sayin'?"

Rowan shrugs, unfazed.

"You're bruising my heart here, woman. Throw me a bone or something," I plead. "I won't kiss you again until I know where your head's at."

I refuse to screw this moment up by thinking with my dick.

As much as I want her, I won't go into this one-sided. She'll have to tell me she wants me just as much, or she'll need to stop this before it can even start.

"Alright," she says, sitting straighter. "Can I show you?"

I wave my hand out, motioning for her to proceed.

Rowan grabs my wrist and places my palm against her chest. "You feel that?" she asks. I close my eyes and feel her heart rapidly pounding.

"Yes," I tell her.

"That's *you*," she says softly. "Something changed between us, and now when you're near, my body reacts to your presence." She exhales sharply. "Even more with your touch."

"What changed?" I open my eyes and ask, sliding my hand up to her face.

"I started seeing *you*." Rowan looks up at me, her expression soft and vulnerable. "You still annoy the shit outta me, but now I see a man I want to spend more time with than away from."

Chuckling, I brush my thumb over her flushed cheek. "Took you long enough to get here." I cover her mouth with mine, sliding my tongue between her lips, and give in to the desire I've held back for so long.

We battle with our bodies, touching, sucking, pushing, pulling. I can't get enough of the woman I've wanted since I was a teen, and it feels too good to be true.

"What does this mean for us, Row?" I ask, leaning my forehead against hers. "The ball's in your court."

I watch as she licks her lips and blows out a shallow breath. "I think it'd be best if we just take it slow and see where things go before announcing anything."

"You're afraid of what Riley will do?" I cock a brow.

"Well, yes," she admits, then smirks. "Plus, sneaking around could be kinda fun. Gives us a chance to explore our feelings before the whole town's in our business. Because they will be."

She's right. The moment the news is out, everyone will have an opinion about it. "Alright, I'm good with that."

Rowan smiles, then nervously chews on her bottom lip. "Now what?"

"Now I walk out of here with blue balls, and we try this secret dating thing until we're ready to tell people, which means we have to keep up the act of only being friends in public."

"Does that mean you'll be dating other people in the meantime?" she asks. "You know...to keep up *appearances*."

"Hell no and neither will you. I'm not screwing up the best thing to ever happen to me."

Rowan's who I've always wanted anyway, and I'll do everything I can to prove that to her.

She chuckles, then nods. "Okay."

"Rowan Bishop, are you blushing?" I tease, pulling on one of her braids.

"Oh my God, I hate you!" She punches my arm, laughing.

"See? People will be none the wiser that we're dancing between the sheets behind closed doors." I waggle my brows, and she pushes me back, jumping off the stool.

"I'm already regretting this decision," she states, walking away, but I quickly grab her arm and pull her back into my chest.

"I've always adored that smart mouth of yours," I tell her, bringing my lips to hers. "I can't wait to see what else you can do with it."

Diesel: You're lookin' pretty sexy in those jean shorts. Especially when you bend over.

Rowan: Stop staring at my ass.

Diesel: Never. I've been staring at it since I was ten.

Rowan: OMG! You were a little perv.

Diesel: Says the girl who wore bikinis around all summer. Would you rather I stared at your chest?

Rowan: I'm almost certain I did catch you looking a few times…

Diesel: Well, I only had so much willpower. Teenage hormones won nine times out of ten.

Rowan: Go away.

Diesel: Come home with me tonight.

Rowan: I can't. I'm trying to work, and you're distracting me.

I chuckle, unable to hide how happy bantering with Rowan makes me. She's working till close, and I've been here for two hours, purposely ordering expensive beer that she has to get from the bottom of the cooler. Though she's trying to act unaffected by me, she's doing a shit job with her hidden glances and flushed cheeks. We're supposed to be acting normal so no one notices, but considering Riley and Grayson both asked why I've been smiling all day, I know I'm not doing a great job at it either.

So far, we only get moments together at closing time when I stay behind and help her. Once her duties are complete, we make out in the office until she tells me to go home. I've been fucking exhausted for four days, but it's been so goddamn worth it. However, I crashed right after work tonight so I didn't get to the bar until ten. Staying up until three a.m., then having to be up at six to work a nine-hour day is quickly catching up to me. Rowan's told me I don't have to come in and visit every night, but it's the only time we get between our work schedules. I have off on Saturdays, so I'm hoping she'll have some time to spare for us to really hang out privately.

My place is still being fixed up, but we can still hang out in my living room. Of course she's hesitant because Riley or any of the other ranch hands could come over and bust us being together. Keeping our relationship to ourselves isn't an ideal situation, but it's what we have to do right now until we figure out this new territory together.

Diesel: You should meet me in the equipment barn tomorrow during my lunch break.

Rowan: What time? I have a couple of errands to run for my dad in the morning.

Diesel: I'd make any time work for you.

Rowan: I should be done by noon.

Diesel: It's a date, baby. Wear your hair in those braids I like.

Rowan: Get your mind out of the gutter! No getting handsy.

Diesel: Absolutely no promises…In fact, wear a skirt too.

She knows I'm joking, but just to be sure, I send her a winking emoji. We're taking things slow, something I'm constantly having to remind myself, but it's for the best. As much as I want to explore every inch of Rowan, I want to give this a real shot. No hopping into bed and screwing shit up. Though I know a lot about her, she's slowly been opening up, and I've seen another side of her. Rowan confessed last night that she's hesitant about jumping into a relationship after the way her last one ended. I assured her we'd go at her pace, and I'm not pressuring her to do anything she doesn't want to. I'll be one hundred percent patient for her. I've waited this long, and I'll wait as long as needed until she's ready to take a leap.

Rowan: SMH. You're relentless.

Diesel: I can lift it again like I did at the church picnic when everyone saw your Barbie underwear.

Rowan: Another reason I hated you growing up.

Diesel: Lies. You adored me.

Rowan: That really was a cruel prank. I should get you back for that.

Diesel: What'd you have in mind? Handcuffs? Blindfolds? Maybe a whip?

Rowan: That's a GREAT idea! Once you're all tied up, I'll take a picture and send it to all your exes, and they'll realize they dodged a bullet.

Diesel: Man. You're evil. Pure evil.

Rowan: You started it!

Diesel: I was eight!

I hear her cackling in the office and know she's laughing at our conversation. She pretends to be annoyed by me, but by the way her mouth attacks mine, it's more than obvious she's putting up a front. Whether she's holding back because she's worried how everyone will react once we announce it or that she'll get hurt, my goal will always be to make her laugh. I'll prove to her I'm nothing like any man she's ever dated, especially her douchebag ex-boyfriends. I'd take a gunshot to the heart before I hurt Rowan.

She returns to the bar moments later and tells Claire, one of the other bartenders, to start on some of their closing duties. There's two hours left, but it's been slow, which means she might actually be finished earlier than usual.

"I can start grabbing cases and restocking for you," I tell her before finishing off my beer.

She rests her arms on the bar and leans close to me. "You should go home and sleep. Those bags under your eyes make you look old."

"I hear chicks dig older guys." I shrug.

"Really? What chicks are you referring to?" She makes a show of looking around at the near empty room. George is on the far end of the bar, and another couple are on the other side.

"The only chick I care about is right in front of me." I smirk, knowing that'll get me an eye roll because if I mention Trace, I might get slapped upside the head.

"Are you always a smooth talker, or do you just turn it on when it suits you?" she taunts.

"Oh, always. You were just too busy being a brat to notice."

"A brat?" She scoffs, pulling back. "You constantly picked on me!"

My face splits into a knowing grin. "Because I liked your attention."

I see the way her cheeks tint, and I crave more of it. Before I can open my mouth again, the door opens, and we both look.

"Uncle Evan," Rowan says, surprised to see him here this late. We both are. I notice he's still wearing scrubs too.

"Hey, kiddo." He gives me a firm nod when our eyes meet. "Diesel."

"What's up, man? You're comin' in late."

He takes a seat next to me. "Just getting off a thirty-six-hour shift."

"Geez," Rowan says. "Want a beer?"

"Yes, please, and an inventory report when you get the chance."

"Sure thing."

Evan and his wife, Emily, are both doctors and work in San Angelo an hour away, but he's always found a way to stay involved as much as he can with his hectic schedule. John handled the bar between his duties at the B&B, but now that Rowan is back for good, they're handing her the reins.

I'm proud of her because I know how hard she worked in school. She loves numbers and accounting, which is great for staying involved in their family businesses. Though we didn't talk much when she was away, I always made it a point to see her when she was home for breaks. She was smart in high school too, and I had no doubt she'd make perfect grades in college.

"You're here late," Evan states when Rowan heads to the office. "Don't you work in the morning?"

I nod, unsure how to approach this conversation. Most

ranch hands don't drink or party during the week, considering we have to be up early and work long hours, so he'd be suspicious no matter what I tell him.

"Yeah, but I thought I'd keep Rowan company since it's a slow night," I say, but he doesn't look convinced. "Everyone else was busy," I add.

"Hmm," he says, then takes a long sip. Thankfully, Rowan returns with the reports he wanted, and his attention turns to the papers in front of him. "Thanks. I'll bring these back in a day or two." He stands, puts a ten on the counter, then says goodbye.

"Now you should really go home," Rowan tells me once he leaves. "There's no way he's going to think you're just keeping me company for no reason."

I know she's right, but I argue anyway. "Well, he already saw me, so what's the point of leaving now?" I flash her an arrogant smirk.

"Then go home and sleep so you don't break your neck for real by being too exhausted tomorrow. If something happens to you, I'll have to find someone else to annoy me at work all night."

"Aww...you worried about me, Row?"

She groans. "George keeps me plenty company, so *go*," she urges, giving me a pointed look.

Claire returns, so I can't be sneaky and kiss Rowan goodbye even though she's not paying any attention to us. I take Rowan's hand in mine and bring it to my mouth, pressing my lips to her knuckles. "I'll see you tomorrow. Noon. Barn. Skirt and braids." I flash her a wink before standing and pull my wallet from my back pocket.

I set down two twenties and tell her to keep the rest. I only had a few beers tonight, so I know she's going to give me the death stare about over-tipping.

"Good night, Cowboy." She slaps her hand over the money and drags it off the bar. "Sweet dreams."

"Don't you worry about that." I waggle my brows, then reluctantly turn and walk away.

Tomorrow can't come soon enough.

CHAPTER EIGHT

ROWAN

My heart hammers in my chest at the reality of what I'm doing.

What *am* I doing?

I never thought in a million years I'd be sneaking into the barn to meet up with Diesel. If we'd been friends, it wouldn't look so suspicious, but everyone on the ranch knows I'd never give him the time of day.

Now, he's consuming my every thought, and it scares me. But his confessions, the way his smile gives me butterflies, and the nervousness I suddenly feel when I'm around him confirm that something has drastically changed between us.

And I don't want to ignore it. I can't.

After Nick left my heart in shambles, I should be running the other way at the prospect of dating another man, but I've known Diesel my whole life. He's not just a random guy I met at a bar, and I know the true intentions of his heart aren't to hurt or use me. If we're going to see where this goes, then I need to put in the effort and give it my all.

Goose bumps cover my arms as I make my way from the B&B where I stopped to meet with Maize for a quick chat and walk over to the equipment barn. It takes me a good ten minutes to get there, but since I don't want anyone to see my truck, I have to be sneaky. I could take one of the four-wheelers, but if someone catches me, I'd have no excuse as to what I was doing.

I step inside, looking around for him, but it's dead quiet. Perhaps he's not here yet, so I decide to text him.

Rowan: I'm here. Where are you?

After two minutes and no response, I'm ready to call his ass for not being on time, but before I can, a hand wraps around my mouth and I'm being hauled into a hard chest. I immediately know it's him when his lips brush against my ear.

"I missed you," he whispers.

Spinning around in his arms, I glare at him. "What the hell?"

He puts a finger to his lips, motioning for me to be quiet. "C'mon, I'm taking you somewhere."

Diesel grabs my hand and leads me around the tractors and gardening equipment until we're at the back of the barn. "What are you doing?" I whisper-hiss as he opens the side door.

"Sneaking you into my truck." He looks back at me and smirks. "Stay down."

I see his Chevy close by, and we quickly run together toward it. He helps me into the passenger side and then rushes to the other.

"Crouch down," he orders, then hits the gas.

"Where are we going?" I ask, feeling completely out of the loop.

"It's a surprise."

"This can't be good." I laugh. "I thought you only had a half-hour break?"

"I'm taking an extended lunch." He chuckles, making a sharp turn. "Don't worry, they won't even notice I'm gone."

"Mm-hmm, right." I lick my lips as I lower my eyes down his body. Even after working all morning, he still looks good enough to eat. "Can I sit up yet?"

"One second…"

I feel the truck drive up a hill and look through the window. Trees and overgrown brush line the dirt road.

"Okay, you're good to go now." He gives me his hand, and I grab it, hoisting myself up in the seat.

Looking around, I notice we're on one of the trails leading to an area we sometimes partied in high school and have the occasional bonfire.

"What do you have up your sleeve, mister?"

He waggles his brows with a mischievous smirk on his face. "I packed us a lunch."

My eyes widen in surprise. "Really? You packed us *edible* food?"

He rests a hand on his chest. "Why are you so shocked? I'm very capable of asking Grandma Bishop to make her famous chicken and biscuits."

I snort out a laugh as my head falls back against the seat. "You're slick, I'll give you that."

Diesel drives us to a place that's been named the "Bishop spot" over the years. Apparently, my uncles brought their dates up here, and they'd party and drink. It became something rather special and meaningful for a lot of them and even for Riley and his wife, Zoey.

"You know everyone who brings their crushes here end up married," he tells me smoothly as he parks the truck.

"I've heard," I say, fighting back a smile. "Except I'm pretty sure my uncles and even Riley brought a lot of women they ended up not marrying here too. Even you, probably."

"Nope. Been waiting for the right one." He flashes me a

shiver-inducing wink, and I'm nearly melting in my seat before he rounds the front and escorts me out. He grabs the cooler, then takes my hand to the back of the cab.

There's a sleeping bag unzipped and spread out with blankets and pillows all around. It looks cozy, and I'm shocked as hell he thought of something this sweet.

"Wow…" I say when he helps me up, and he makes his way to my side. "You've never done this before?" I ask.

"Never had a relationship, Row," he says.

"Seems you know what you're doing," I tell him when he hands me a plate covered in foil.

Diesel shrugs as if he doesn't agree. "Guess we'll see, huh?"

I smile when he does, and it warms my entire body. Adam Hayes is someone I never knew I needed.

We talk and laugh all through our lunch. The food is delicious, no surprise there, but the company and scenery are even better. Once we've finished, he wraps me in his arms, and we lie on the blankets.

"You can see the stars out here for miles at night. It's my favorite part of living on the ranch. You don't get that in Houston," I say as I wrap my arm over his chest and hold him close to me.

"There's just something special about living out here, and I'd never want to be anywhere else." His arm is around my shoulders, and he tightens his hold, sending warmth all down my body.

We continue talking and admiring the view for over an hour. Much longer than Diesel is allowed to take for his break, and after his phone starts going off, I know our time is over.

"Shit," he hisses when he pulls it from his pocket and sees all his missed calls and texts.

"You're gonna get in trouble," I tease.

He leans in and presses his lips to mine. "It'll be worth it."

"You better go back."

"But being here is *so* much better." He turns so we're face to face and lifts my chin. "I feel like I'm dreaming."

"And what are you gonna tell them when they ask where you were?"

"Tell them to mind their damn business." He flashes an evil grin. "Or that I had some hot chick in the back of my truck I was trying to seduce."

"Oh God." I groan. "Please don't tell them that. I think Uncle Evan is already suspicious now."

"Nah. If he mentions anything, just say he was sleep deprived and has no idea what he's talking about."

I snort, lifting myself on my elbows. "That'd go over well, I'm sure."

I'm close to all my uncles, but Evan is the most protective over me. I spent a lot of time at Emily's and his house hanging out with Elle. She's over a year older than me, but we were close growing up until she left for college. We always stayed in touch, but between me moving to Houston and her demanding job, it doesn't give us time to hang out as much.

Grabbing the cooler and blankets, we finally get into the truck and make our way back to the ranch. He manages to bring me back without anyone noticing.

"Thank you for lunch," I tell him before he leaves. "I could get used to that kind of company."

"You're very welcome." He lowers his eyes down my body, not even trying to hide his gawking anymore. "I could get used to the view."

"At least you're persistent," I say, laughing. "As usual."

"But now I can be even more so without you threatening to cut off my balls." He wraps his arms around my waist and snuggles me against his chest.

"Don't get cocky." I pull his face down and cover his mouth with mine. His tongue slides between my lips, and soon, we're panting for air as we battle with our desire for more. He slides his hands down to my ass, then back up to my neck where his fingers tangle in my hair. Every spot he touches burns with an intensity I hadn't known existed. I want more of it, more of him, and I'll take anything he's willing to give.

"Okay, now you really need to go," I say against his lips, neither of us moving. "Text me later, okay?"

"You workin' till close?"

"Yep. But maybe bring Wyatt this time so it doesn't look suspicious." He doesn't work on the ranch and has no idea we typically didn't get along.

"Damn. I was hoping to have you all to myself." He smirks.

"In a bar filled with drunks? Good luck."

Diesel pats my ass one more time and presses a quick kiss to my lips before he takes off and runs to his truck. "Dammit, now you got my dick all worked up!" he yells from the window, and I see him adjusting his jeans.

"Sorry 'bout that!" I chuckle, waving him away.

It's been a week since Diesel kissed me in the bar office, and it's been the best seven days I've had in a long ass time. We sneak around to find time to hang out, even if it's for thirty minutes or during my shift at work. He comes in every night and then stays late until I'm done. I know he's tired as hell, so on our days off, I make him sleep in or tell him to take a nap so he doesn't end up killing himself on the ranch equipment.

My adrenaline high crashes and burns the moment I wake up to a text from Nick the Asshole.

Nick: You better get me that money, or I'm taking the security footage to the cops.

Rowan: I told you I was working on it. I don't have a million-dollar trust fund like you to just write a check.

Nick: Should've thought about that before you took a crowbar to my car, you bitch.

Rowan: Wow, do you feel like a man calling me that?

Nick: Better watch that filthy mouth of yours, unless you want me to report you for vandalism? I wonder how your hick family would take that kind of news?

Rowan: Kiss my ass, you dickless cocksucker. I said I'd get you the money, and I will.

Nick: You better.

I'm on the verge of tears by the time I read his final text, then toss my phone aside.

God, what I ever saw in him is beyond me. He's such an arrogant tool bag, and I wish I'd never given him the time of day. I know he's probably already gotten the stupid car repaired and is just using this opportunity to have something to hold over me and piss me off. He didn't like that *I* broke up with him after he cheated.

Instead of eating my feelings like I want to, I take a thirty-minute hot shower. Though it feels good, it doesn't stop my anger from brewing over. Knowing Maize is probably working at the B&B, I decide to head over there after I get dressed and ready for the day.

"Oh my God! We should've cut him when we had the chance!" she squeals after I read her the texts.

I snort at her dramatics. "You and me both."

"Who are we cutting?" Elle walks into the kitchen with a perched brow.

"My stupid ex-boyfriend. Look what he sent me this morning."

She looks over my shoulder as I show her the screen and scroll down.

"Wow. Douchebag needs to get the stick out of his ass." She leans down and grabs a muffin, then stuffs it into her mouth. Maize doesn't say a word surprisingly.

"Tell me about it. *Why* did I date him?" I groan, collapsing on top of the counter with my head in my hands.

"You don't always see someone's true colors until it's too late," she tells me, rubbing my back. "The important thing is that you learned before you got in too deep."

"And even that was too long. I want that time back." I growl.

"You very well coulda married the dickwad. Yikes! Thank the Lord ya didn't," Maize says.

They both chuckle, and we end up hanging out for the next hour before Elle has to go back to work. She stops in from time to time like most of my family does. The B&B's a social spot for us to eat and gossip.

After saying goodbye and walking out of the kitchen, I head through the main sitting area and wave at the guests. Most are regulars who come every year, but some are new and just driving through, needing a place to stay for the night. Some love the atmosphere so much that they book a room to stay every few months. Can't say I blame them, though. The ranch offers horseback riding, four-wheeling adventures, trail walking, and true Southern meals. We host weddings and honeymoons here too.

Diesel: You okay? Grayson said he saw you at the B&B looking like someone kicked your dog.

I snort. We have lots of dogs on the ranch, but none that stay in the house.

Rowan: You two always gossip about me?

Diesel: Only every day of my existence. Don't you know by now my world revolves around you?

Rowan: Stop being overly sweet.

Diesel: Can't help it, baby. Charming is my middle name.

Rowan: It's Christopher, but close enough.

I giggle because our conversation easily puts me in a good mood again.

Diesel: So c'mon, tell me. What's going on?

I get into my car, then text him back.

Rowan: I woke up to a very nice message from my ex who reminded me that I'm under the gun to pay him back, and that if I don't soon, he'll report me for vandalism. I told him I was working on it, but he was being his normal asshole self.

Diesel: Let me take care of him and pay your debt so he goes away for good.

Rowan: No and definitely not! I'm not allowing you to get involved any more than you already have. I'm saving up and will give it to him.

Rowan: But thank you for offering. I do appreciate you wanting to help.

Diesel: Should let me punch his face in again to send him a not-so-nice message in return.

Rowan: Then he'd probably sue you for wrecking his pretty boy face.

Diesel: It'd be worth every penny to smash it in, though. ;)

Rowan: Okay, Cowboy. Hold back before you get arrested for assault. We can't sneak around when you're behind bars.

Diesel: You're right. I'll just have to be smug in the fact that I have you now, and he doesn't.

Rowan: Works for me :)

Diesel: Why don't you come over tonight since you work a short shift, and I'll show you all the ways I can console you?

Rowan: Hmm…you paint a tempting picture. You think that's a good idea?

Diesel: Park at the B&B and take a four-wheeler over to the equipment barn, and I'll pick you up there.

Rowan: Okay, I'll be done here in two hours and will text you when I'm leaving so you can meet me.

Diesel: I'll be waiting!

His eagerness always makes me smile. It'll be the first time visiting his house, and I'm not quite sure what to expect. I know he's been fixing it up since he basically got kicked out of the cabin he and Riley shared. Once Zoey came to town, and they decided to try to make things work, Diesel moved into one of the ranch hand cabins that needed a lot of work. I know he's been remodeling it in his spare time, which I'm learning isn't very much. Probably even less now that he's spending it with me instead.

Ethan's working till close tonight and knows how to do the reports and safe, so I don't worry about it when I decide to dip out early. Claire will arrive at eight, and since we aren't that busy, I decide to leave a half hour early.

I take the extra time to freshen up and change before heading to Diesel's. Before I can leave the house, my mother walks in the door and asks where I'm going so late. I hold back any comments on how it's barely dark outside, and that I'm twenty-three years old.

"Maize and I are meeting up for a girls' night. Nothing special." I smile, hoping she believes me. I hate lying to my mom. We're close, and she trusts me, but I can't tell her this secret. At least not yet.

"Oh, alright. Tell her I said hi. You two have fun." She gives me a kiss on the cheek and a hug, and my soul dies a little at how easily the lie spilled from my lips.

By the time Diesel picks me up, I'm in a sour mood, and I

hate that I can't be more excited to see him tonight. My eyes water, and I wipe away the tears before they can fall.

"Looks like someone needs cheering up," he says, guiding me through the front door. "Wanna start with a tour?"

"Sure." He takes my hand and shows me around, telling me how he plans to fix it up. Some of the things include: knocking out walls to open up the living room, adding a kitchen island for more storage space, replacing a window with patio doors, and then building on a huge deck.

"Wow…that all sounds amazing. I bet it's going to be gorgeous once you're done." I look around and see empty spaces with tarps and paint cans. He's done some stuff already but has quite a bit to finish.

"I hope so. Riley was supposed to help me, but now that he's on permanent Dad duty, I may have Grayson and Wyatt help too. Maybe Ethan."

I snort at the mention of my cousin. "Ethan barely wants to get his hands dirty as it is, so good luck." His parents are both doctors so he was never forced to do chores until my other uncles got a hold of him and basically threw him in the dirt. So now he's going to school for agricultural science and has one year left, but since he's home for the summer, he helps at the bar or anywhere he's needed on the ranch. Once he graduates, he'll work on the ranch full-time and plans to help find ways to expand.

"Maybe I'll bribe him with a few beers to help." He grins. "Maybe I can bribe *you*?"

"That wouldn't look suspicious at all," I mock.

"We'll say you owed me."

My jaw drops. "Owe you for what?"

"For kicking your ex's ass," he states proudly.

"Mm-hmm, right. Not sure what I can do anyway, besides paint maybe."

"Perfect. Sounds like a date."

"You really are relentless, aren't you?"

"All part of my charm."

When I smile, he lifts my chin and softly presses his lips to mine. "There's that gorgeous smile I love so much. My plan worked after all."

Nick is officially off my mind, and all I can think about is Diesel.

"Guess it did." I fist my hands in his shirt and bring his mouth back to mine, and soon we're making out like a couple of teenagers who have a curfew.

Diesel leads me to the couch and sets me on his lap without even breaking the kiss. His fingers thread in my hair, cupping the back of my head and pulling it back slightly so his tongue can slide in deeper. Hot electricity sparks between us, and it takes all the energy I have to pull away.

"If you don't stop doing that, we're going to violate our 'going slow' rule," I tell him.

He squints one eye and tilts the corner of his lips. "Pretty sure that was just your rule."

I playfully smack him and get off his lap, then sit down next to him. "I had to lie to my mother tonight, and it sucked."

He reaches over and grabs my hand. "We don't have to, you know? I can take care of whatever backlash Riley gives me. Or hell, your father. They'll probably both want their turn to knock me on my ass individually, but it'd be one hundred percent worth it."

Groaning, I throw my head back on the couch. "Don't say that. I'd just like to explore this without everyone's comments. I recently got out of a relationship, and I'm sure my mom and cousins will have something to say about it."

"What are you afraid of?"

"I'm worried they'll put doubt in my head about dating someone so soon, being with you, or that we're moving too fast."

"Okay…" He nods, then brings our hands up to his lips and sweetly kisses my knuckles. "Then we'll keep it our secret for now. I'm sure it's not the worst thing you've lied to your mother about." He flashes a devilish grin, knowing damn well he's right.

"Well, no. But that's besides the point. I don't like violating the trust between us."

"I'm sure once it's out there, she'll understand why you did."

I inhale slowly and sigh. "I hope so."

"Until then, we'll secretly make out in the back of my truck."

I laugh at how smooth he tries to be, but I don't exactly hate the idea either.

"So I know I wanted to take your mind off your ex, but can you tell me what happened between you two? How long did you date? How'd you meet?"

"You really wanna know that stuff?"

"Only if you feel comfortable telling me, but I want to know everything about you. The good, the bad, and even the ugly."

"And Nick is definitely the ugly part."

He chuckles, brushing his hand over his scruffy chin. I love that he leaves it just long enough for me to scratch my nails through it.

"We met at a college party and were actually friends for a few months before he asked me out. We dated for a total of fourteen months. It was after I hung out with Trace a few times."

Diesel audibly groans, and I smirk at how jealous he gets.

"Do you still talk to him?" he asks.

"Just as friends," I reassure him. "That's all we ever were, so don't get your panties in a bunch."

"He sure as fuck didn't look at you like y'all were only friends."

"You met him one time," I remind him, smirking. "Calm your tits."

"As long as when our secret is out, he knows it too."

"It's a small town. Everyone will know within twenty minutes."

He grunts, squeezing my hand tighter. "Good."

"Anyway…" I grin. "When I found out Nick had cheated on me, he apologized and begged me to give him another chance. He promised over and over he'd never do it again and tried to win me back. I told him there was no chance in hell because he'd broken our trust, and I couldn't forgive a man who did that to me. Being honest and having open communication are two of the most important things to me, and he violated them both."

"Well, I'm truly sorry he did that, but I'm also thankful as fuck because it brought you to me."

Diesel and I talk for hours. Even though we seem to know a lot about the other, we share more intimate and personal things. We laugh and tease each other, and before the night is over, I feel closer than ever to him.

It's just what I needed after the shitty way my day started.

CHAPTER NINE

DIESEL

Ever since that night a week ago when Rowan came over almost in tears, we've grown closer both physically and emotionally. We're still taking things slow and sneaking around, but after years of pining for her, it feels amazing to have my feelings for her reciprocated. Though I'm not getting much sleep, every second I spend with her is well worth the three hours I do get.

"You wake up gettin' your dick sucked or something?" Riley taunts as we walk out of the shop.

"That or he's gettin' it regularly," Grayson adds.

"How about y'all mind ya damn business," I say smugly, flashing my teeth.

"Shoulda seen him in Vegas," Riley tells Grayson. "Could barely handle himself around all the blondes."

"Look who's talkin'? You married one of them."

He points at me, smirking. "True, but she wasn't blond."

Riley's back to working full-time, which means he's returned to giving me shit as much as possible. Baby Zach was born over a month ago, and even though he was a little early, he's doing great.

"Probably some town skank," Grayson adds.

"Don't worry, I was thinkin' about your sister the whole time," I spit out and immediately move out of Riley's punching range. Rowan made a good point the other day that it'll raise red flags if my normal teasing about her disappears. She insists that we need to keep arguing around people.

"Dude, I swear to God," Riley growls, running after me as I rush toward the B&B and fly up the steps. He knows once we're inside, he can't try to kick my ass around the guests. As soon as I whip open the door and go in, he pushes my back and has me nearly flying into John. And he doesn't look happy.

"Guys." He steadies me, then steps back. "Behave or leave."

"Sorry." I swallow hard and hold back my smile. "I tripped."

John snaps his eyes to Riley who's giving him his best innocent look while Grayson covers his mouth with his hand, trying not to laugh.

"Hurry and eat so you can get out," John tells us before walking away.

The three of us make our way to the breakfast buffet and fill our plates full before taking a seat at one of the tables. We're chatting about what we need to do the rest of the day when Maize, Kenzie, Elle, and Rowan all walk out of the kitchen.

Shit.

"Oh, if it isn't the morning freeloader crew," Maize says smugly as she holds a plate of fresh muffins.

"Got a blueberry one?" Grayson asks, ignoring her snide comment.

"Not for you, asshole," Kenzie replies before Maize can.

Riley and I burst out laughing as Grayson narrows his eyes at her. "Pretty sure I didn't ask you."

"Okay, children. There are guests around." Maize grabs one of the muffins from the tray and hands it to Grayson. "Can I personally serve anyone else?" She flashes a condescending grin, unamused with us being here.

"Well, if you're offering—" I grin, knowing it'll piss off Riley or Maize.

"Not that kind of serving," Rowan interrupts, flashing me a glare that could kill. I know she's not really mad, but she's damn good at putting on an act.

"Shit." Riley shakes his head, stabbing his fork into his eggs. "How you two manage to always piss off all the Bishop chicks is beyond me."

"I'm pretty sure Diesel's been doing it since I was born." Rowan rolls her eyes, then stalks away.

"I think she likes you," Grayson mocks, and I kick him under the table.

"Don't worry, Diesel. I don't hate you," Kenzie says with a cheeky grin, then adds, "as much as Rowan."

"No, you just act like a spoiled brat," Grayson mutters.

Before Grayson can react, Kenzie grabs the muffin from his hand and smashes it against the table, digging her palm into it. The thing is nothing but a pile of crumbs.

Riley and I are nearly doubled over at Grayson's shell-shocked expression.

"What the hell?" He scowls at her.

"Enjoy your breakfast, *boys*," she says sweetly before walking away.

"You better clean that up," Maize tells him before leaving.

Grayson grunts, wiping up the mushy mess.

"You two need to just fuck it out, for Christ's sake," I tell him. Their rivalry started months ago, and no one really knows the reason. "Why does she hate you anyway?"

"Good fuckin' question."

"Probably calling her a brat doesn't help your case," Riley taunts.

"Well, am I wrong? Look at what she just did!" He holds out his hands, motioning to the table.

Laughing, I shake my head and continue eating. I'm almost

certain there's gonna come a time when they finally bang it out. It makes me think about Rowan and how far we've come in such a short amount of time. It gives me hope that someday we'll be able to tell everyone, and they'll support us being together.

Once the three of us are done eating, Grayson and I go off to work in the cattle barn while Riley does other maintenance shit.

"So, tell me honestly," Grayson says when we're knee-deep in cow shit. "You've been different the past week or so. What's goin' on?"

Fuck my life. He chooses to ask me this now?

"Nothing's goin' on," I lie, shrugging so he doesn't notice any of my tells. "Can't a guy just be in a good mood?"

He narrows his eyes as if he's trying to read my mind. "I don't know. Something is up with you, and I'm gonna figure it out."

Laughing, I keep my eyes down and continue shoveling to avoid his hard gaze. "Why don't you worry about yourself instead of me? Actually, go figure out why Kenzie hates your guts so much."

"Dude, she's hated me since the second I got here, I swear. I breathed, and she decided I was the devil."

I snort at his remark. Kenzie wouldn't just hate someone for no reason, but honestly, there's no telling. She's three years younger than me, and I didn't talk to her a lot in high school. It wasn't until I started working here full-time that I did.

"I'm sure there's a reason you haven't thought of yet. Did you run over her dog or something? Call her ugly? Fuck her best friend?"

He pinches his lips, shifting them side to side. "Not that I can recall." Then he shrugs and drops the conversation.

Thank fuck.

After three hours, we're finally done in the cattle barn and stop at the shop for a quick water break. I check my phone and see a message from Rowan.

> **Rowan: Sorry about earlier. My cousins are all getting suspicious and keep asking me why I'm so happy lately, so I was trying to keep up appearances. I wish I could tell them, but I keep denying anything's going on. Well, now they're certain it's because of Trace, because they know he's been texting me. But even though I tell them we're only friends, they don't believe it.**

I groan, hating that they're thinking she's with that tool bag. I don't think keeping this from everyone will get any easier.

> **Diesel: Don't worry, baby. I figured as much. In fact, the guys have been on my ass about what's going on with me all day. Guess it's been a little obvious how happy you make me ;)**
>
> **Rowan: Did you just call me baby?**
>
> **Diesel: Yes?**
>
> **Rowan: That's kinda…sexy. I like it.**
>
> **Diesel: Is that so? I'll make sure to whisper it in your ear later.**
>
> **Rowan: Did we have plans for…later?**
>
> **Diesel: Damn right. I'll come in tonight around 10. That okay?**

Rowan: That's perfect. Ethan's shift ends at 9:30, and Kenzie's off. Claire works with me, and she won't know any better.

It's a weekday, so it'll be slow after ten anyway, which means I might actually get to sneak her into the office and kiss her for more than five seconds. Claire isn't from around here and doesn't know our history, so it's a little easier to talk when we don't have to worry about prying ears.

Diesel: It's a date, baby.

"We're supposed to get some heavy rain and wind tonight," Riley says as he walks into the shop with Ethan. "I need all hands on deck to bring in the horses."

"Don't you work at the bar tonight?" I ask Ethan, curious as to why he's here.

"Yeah." He tilts his head. "How do you know my work schedule?"

Fuck, fuck, fuck. That slipped out way too easily.

I shrug, trying to act indifferent. "Just a guess. You work most weeknights, don't you?"

Ethan blinks, then nods. "Yeah, I gotta head in soon but thought I'd help before I go."

We pile into the back of Alex's truck, and when I look up, I notice how dark one side of the sky is already. We can always use the rain, especially in the middle of summer, but it sucks when we have to rush around the ranch and do things around the weather's schedule.

An hour later, I'm drenched with sweat and cussing out Riley for making me tag along. They could've handled it, but he has learned I won't say no and enjoys making me do extra shit.

"Quit scowlin'," he blurts out when we ride back to the shop. "Doesn't look good on your ugly mug."

Ethan and Grayson laugh at my expense, and he's damn lucky I hold back on pushing him out of the cab.

"Pretty cocky there, Bishop," I taunt. "You've gone soft since you became a dad, so I wouldn't poke the bear that's already bigger than you."

Riley laughs, kicking his foot out toward me. "I don't know. Those dark bags under your eyes imply you ain't gettin' much sleep, so I think we're pretty equal in that department."

"The difference is, my lack of sleep isn't due to changing dirty diapers and spit up." I flash a cocky grin.

"So it *is* a chick keeping you up," Grayson adds with satisfaction. "I fuckin' knew it!"

"Yeah right," Riley drawls. "He's drinking alone and jerking off to fetish porn."

Ethan chokes out a laugh. "Huh. What's your fetish?"

I grin, knowing Riley's about to kill me. "Best friend's little sisters."

"Goddammit, Diesel. That's getting old." Riley rolls his eyes with a deep groan. "Like ten years' worth old. Time to find a new fantasy."

"No can do, Daddy."

Alex parks the truck, and we all haul out.

"Told ya I'm gonna marry her someday."

"Not on my watch. You don't settle down for shit. You'll get your fix, then leave her brokenhearted like you do every other woman you bang." He pushes his finger into my chest. "Back off already."

"For your information, the last one-night stand I had was in Vegas," I tell him, reminding me of the letter I received weeks ago, but then I immediately push that thought away. Her name was Chelsea, and the only reason I remember that is because of Riley. Not my proudest moment, honestly.

"Oh, my bad. You buy them dinner and drinks first, then wait until after the second date to ghost them."

I shake my head, my jaw tensing as my anger rises. He's wrong.

"Actually, the last chick I took on a date told me she didn't see us having a future together, and we mutually broke it off before the second date ended." Which is true. We met through a friend and didn't even sleep together. My dating life has been pretty much nonexistent.

Riley slow claps as if he's supposed to be impressed, and it pisses me off further.

"Whatever." I walk away, finished with this fucking conversation.

"Yeah, whatever. Stay away from my sister!" he howls at my back.

"I'm pretty sure Riley's gonna kill me," I tell Rowan, then chug my glass of whiskey. "Like actually stab me, cut out my heart, and then display it on a wall like a deer head."

Rowan looks at me wide-eyed in horror. "That's quite graphic."

"I know he's been telling me for years that you were off-limits, but he's been extra asshole-ish about it lately."

"He's also sleep deprived and taking care of a newborn. He's probably just edgier because of that," she explains with a sad smile. "At least, let's hope that's what it is."

I take off my cap, brush a hand through my hair, then replace it. "I don't know. It's like he's determined to make my life a living hell right now." I rub my eyes, inhaling slowly as I think about the consequences of Riley finding out the truth. It'd suck if being with Rowan ruined my lifelong friendship with him.

Thankfully, Riley hasn't come in the bar since Zoey found out she was pregnant, so I know we're at least safe in here for now. But if he catches us even remotely being friendly, there's no way he won't figure it out.

"Well, I think we both need to get better at hiding our happiness so everyone stops asking. It'll calm down, and we can just go back to hanging out without guilt." She refills my glass.

I pick it up and take a sip. "Do you feel guilty?"

She shrugs, lowering her eyes before meeting mine again. "Only about lying, not that we're dating."

That makes me smile. "Good. Because even with all the outside noise bullshit, I've never been happier."

Rowan leans against the bar, placing her hand over mine. "Me too."

I could stare into her gorgeous brown eyes for hours. "I wish I could kiss you right now…" I whisper.

The corner of her lips tilts up mischievously as she looks around the bar and checks to make sure everyone's drinks are still full. "Come to the office in one minute."

She tells Claire she's going on a short break and then walks away. Luckily, she's been too busy to notice how close the two of us have been all night. I'm completely under her radar when I follow Rowan to the back a moment later.

As soon as I shut the door, I pin her against the cool wood and bring my mouth to hers. I wrap my arms around her body and hoist her closer as she loops hers around my neck. She slides her legs around my waist, rocking against the hard-on I can't contain.

"Fuck, baby," I whisper. "You're driving me wild."

"Mmm…that sounds even sexier in person."

"Yeah?" I slide my mouth against the softness of her neck

Rowan releases her thighs and lands on her feet. "We have at least fifteen minutes before Claire even notices I'm still gone." She locks the door, then gives me a devilish look.

"What're you up to?" I taunt, watching her and admiring how beautiful she looks. Some strands of her reddish brown hair have fallen loose from her half ponytail, and she tucks it behind her ear. Her jean shorts show off her long legs, and her band T-shirt hugs her in all the right places. Rowan's curves are what my wet dreams are made of.

"Let me fix that problem for you," she says confidently, tilting her head toward my groin. "You want to stand or sit?"

I blink. "*What?*"

She asks so casually as if we're talking about the weather.

"I want to get on my knees for you." She licks her plump lips.

My eyes widen in shock, certain she's joking. "Here? Are you serious? Don't fuck with me."

She chuckles, then nods eagerly. "Yes and we're gonna run out of time if you don't tell me. So sitting or standing?"

"I-I, uh…" I'm tripping over my words like a teenage boy about to get head for the first time. "Baby, you don't have to. Not here."

She comes closer, moving her hands to my belt buckle. "Adam…" She says my name seductively, and I melt into a puddle. "Let me suck you off and send you home a happy man, okay?"

"Jesus fuck, Row." My throat goes dry. She's the only chick who's ever managed to nearly put me into cardiac arrest. I must hesitate too long because she drops to her knees in front of me and torturously unzips my jeans.

The moment I feel her hand around my shaft, my eyes roll to the back of my head. I can hardly believe this is happening. I've fantasized about it a million times but never dreamed it'd be a reality.

Forcing my eyes open because I don't want to miss a second of this, I look down and watch as she peeks up at me like a seductress eating her last meal. The moment her tongue glides from the bottom of my cock to the tip, I'm about to explode.

"*Christ*, baby." I lean against the door and wrap my fist around her long hair. "This room soundproof?" I half-tease, though I really wish we could be loud without the entire bar hearing.

"No, so keep it down." She smirks before wrapping her lips over the crown of my length and sucks hard.

Fuck. She nearly swallows me whole, and when she pulls me to the back of her throat, I'm five seconds from prematurely shooting my load. Though I don't want to rush, we can't take our time like I'd want to.

"Rowan, shit." I cup the back of her head and help guide her mouth deeper and harder. She rotates and strokes her hand on the base of my cock as she continues sucking on the tip. Her hot mouth feels goddamn amazing, and when she blinks up at me again, my balls tighten, and I know I'm close.

Groaning, I watch as she pumps me faster, and then I quickly pull out and release in my palm. I stroke myself as she leans up, and I grab her chin, fusing our mouths together.

"You didn't have to do that," she says as we break apart. "I wanted to taste all of you."

"Then I'll have something to look forward to next time." I flash her a wink, then help her to her feet with my free hand.

"Let me grab you some paper towels." She snickers when she sees my mess.

Rowan goes to the storage closet and returns within a minute, and once I'm fully clean, I zip my jeans and redo my buckle. "You think anyone heard us?"

"Nah, the TVs are on, so if anything, they'll just think it's from the show," she explains, but I know she's full of shit.

I pull her into my arms and smile. "I'd stay and help you close tonight, but you've made me quite relaxed now."

"That was my goal the whole time. You need to get some sleep."

"Mm-hmm. I know, but I can't help wanting to spend all my time with you," I admit. "Does that scare you?"

She licks her lips before biting on her bottom one. "A little, but not because you want to be around me. Rather, it's how much I want to spend time with you too."

"You're not used to being on this side of things, are you?" I flash her a smug grin. "You're too used to running away while calling me an asshole."

She groans as her head falls back slightly. "You better pull that ego back, or I'll go tell Riley right now that you touched his little sister."

"Is that supposed to be a threat? I can take him." I puff out my chest, which causes her to laugh, and seeing the way her cheeks heat causes intense electricity to shoot through my body.

"Well, you just might need to start honing your fighting skills. I have no doubt Riley's gonna think you corrupted me."

"He thinks I'm going to use you, that I can't manage a real relationship, and that I'll break your heart."

Her face drops. "Are you?"

I tilt her chin up to look at me so she can see how serious I am. "Not a chance in hell, Rowan. I'm risking everything because if I lose you, I lose a best friend and a family I've known my whole life, too. I've waited for you, and I'm not gonna fuck up this chance you're giving me. Don't think for one second I don't know how lucky I am. I'm not taking a second of it for granted. You hear me?"

"You are risking a lot," she says softly. "It's only been a couple of weeks, and I'm already losing sleep thinking about you. The last thing I want is for our relationship to break apart friendships or cause any awkwardness in my family."

"I'll do whatever it takes to make this work, and if sneaking around is the only way I can have you right now, then I'll take it. We'll wait until you're comfortable or when you think everyone else can handle the good news."

She gives me an expression that makes me laugh. "We might be sneaking around a while then. Riley might never be ready."

"Maybe after we move in together, get hitched, and you get pregnant with my baby, he'll finally accept it. We wouldn't have to make a big ordeal about it then because everyone would eventually just figure it out." I shrug nonchalantly.

She snorts, laughing at my antics. "The *never announcing it* method. Sure, that oughta work. After the third baby, they might start putting the puzzle pieces together."

I brush the wild strands of her hair off her face and tuck them behind her ear before leaning down and kissing her forehead. "We'll figure it out."

Rowan reminds me that she has to get back to work before Claire comes looking for her. We kiss goodbye, then I casually make my way out the side door. I wish I could stay and talk to her all night, but we both know I need the sleep.

Hopefully one day—one day *soon*—I'll be able to go to bed and wake up with her in my arms, and we won't have to hide our relationship. I'm falling harder for her every day, and it almost doesn't seem real how strong my feelings already are. Then again, they've been lingering for years, waiting to be unleashed when she finally saw who was right in front of her the whole time.

CHAPTER TEN

ROWAN

I ACTUALLY HAVE the day off, so I'm killing time at the B&B with hopes to see Diesel later. Three weeks have passed since we've started sneaking around, and as much fun as it's been, I'm constantly on edge and worried we'll get caught.

It still doesn't feel real. These feelings seem as if they've come out of nowhere, but Diesel acts like he's been waiting his whole life for me. All the shit I used to give him now makes me feel guilty, though I keep telling myself it's just a part of our history. Perhaps if I had seen him differently years ago, we wouldn't be where we are now. I know us being together is still so new and early, but the timing seems right, and everything is so good. Trying to navigate a long-distance relationship while I was at college wouldn't have been ideal for either of us. We both had some growing up to do.

"So how's it feel to be back for good? Think you'll miss going to Houston?" Maize asks as we hang out in the B&B kitchen. She's making one of her Southern specialities for the guests and putting her amazing cooking skills to good use. Maize graduated from culinary school a couple of years ago and became the head chef at the bed and breakfast. It happened at a good time too since the previous cook in charge was retiring.

"Nah, I don't think so. Actually, it's not as bad as I was anticipating," I say honestly, reaching for one of the paninis. "After Nick the Dick ruined my life, I thought life would suck."

She perks up a brow, knowing there's more to the story. *More* that I can't tell her. "But it doesn't?"

I shrug, purposely not making eye contact with her. If I do, she'll know I'm keeping something from her. She's two years older, and we've always been close. She knows all my tells, and I hate having to lie to her.

"Nah, I guess not. It's nice to be back home and working for the fam. At least I'm not having to help with ranch chores." I chuckle with relief. When I was still in high school, I would do whatever was needed during weekends and summers, which meant a slew of bitch work. Didn't matter that I was a girl and half the weight of the guys, my dad made sure I had a good work ethic.

"You have been in a pretty chipper mood," she states as if she's implying there's a reason, but I play dumb.

"I'm not gonna let some cheating asshole bring me down." I take a large bite of my sandwich so I can't speak.

"Too bad there are no men around here for you to rebound with," she taunts, waggling her brows. "In fact, there are no men here period. We're all gonna be alone with a handful of horses. Horse ladies."

I snort and cover my mouth with my hand to prevent food from spewing all over her. After I chew and swallow, I laugh. "Well, you need to get out of the kitchen every once in a while to find someone. All you do is cook."

She shoots me a deadpan expression. "It's my job, brat."

"I'm working tomorrow night. You should stop in. It'll be busy," I tell her.

"And do what? Be the loser in the corner drinking alone?"

"Well, with that charming attitude, I'm shocked you're still single!" I gasp dramatically, placing a hand over my chest.

She grins and throws a piece of bread at me. "I hate you."

I scoff, waving her off. "There are like two dozen ranch hands. Pick one and make him your sex slave for the night."

Maize makes a gagging noise that has me doubling over. "Oh my God. I'm related to like half of them. Plus, I don't shit where I eat, okay?"

"Gross." I stick out my tongue.

"You don't mess around with men you can't escape from, which means all guys on the property are off-limits. That's my one rule," she explains.

"Oh really? So if a superhot and charming cowboy starts working here and is sweet-talking your panties off, you'd still say no?" I challenge, raising a brow.

"Well…" She hesitates a moment. "I didn't say it was a *hard* rule."

We're both laughing when my mother walks into the kitchen wearing her scrubs. She must be heading into work soon. "I thought I heard some giggling in here." She smiles, then comes over and kisses my cheek. "What're you girls talkin' about?"

"Boys," I tell her.

"Or lack thereof," Maize adds with a groan. "We're staying single forever and joining a convent."

"That is not going to give me or your mother—" She points at Maize. "Grandchildren."

"Riley and Zoey just gave you a grandson!" I remind her. "Shouldn't that hold you off for a while?"

"Nope. He only made me want more," she retorts with a smug grin.

"Well, don't look at me!" I tease. "I'm not like Riley who just goes out for a weekend and finds someone to marry."

My mom snorts, shaking her head. "Your father too," she reminds me. I think it's adorable how they met, but that'll never be me. "It's the Bishop male gene. Too bad you weren't a boy. You'd be married with a baby already. Maybe even two."

I roll my eyes. "Thanks for the reminder that my biological clock is ticking, Mom."

"Oh, you have time, sweetheart. Ten years or so. But the sooner, the better." She shrugs. "Especially if you want more than one."

"Alright, got it. Find a husband, then get knocked up ASAP."

"Your words, not mine." She smirks. "But your grandmother did say she was hoping to have another great-grandchild before she kicks the bucket."

"Oh my God, Mom!" I scowl at her. "Grandma isn't dying for a long, long time." Although she is in her mid-seventies, she still has a lot of life left in her. She's too stubborn. The woman will probably live until she's a hundred and twenty.

"Okay, girls. You two be good. I gotta get to work." She gives me a hug, and we say our goodbyes.

Once she's out the door and out of earshot, Maize speaks up. "Guess you better find yourself a ranch hand to procreate with very soon." She smirks.

I narrow my eyes at her and walk toward the door, flipping her the bird. "Fuck off." Then I turn around before leaving. "Tomorrow night. Come and hang out. Drinks are on me."

Maize breathes in sharply through her nose, then exhales. "Fine. But you promised me fresh man meat, so you better deliver."

I snort and wave goodbye.

Checking my phone as I walk to my car, I shoot Diesel a text.

Rowan: My mother wants more grandchildren.

Diesel: Now? Meet me in the barn. Haystacks.

Rowan: OMG, you animal!

Diesel: Only for you, baby ;)

Rowan: You're lame.

Diesel: You adore me.

Rowan: Sometimes.

Diesel: You gonna come visit me or what?

Rowan: Where are you?

Diesel: Just got out of the shower.

Rowan: You're done with work?

Diesel: We had extra hands on deck today, so I bailed early since someone's been keeping me up all hours of the night.

Rowan: Then you should take a nap. I can come over later since I have the day off.

Diesel: Hell no! Get your luscious ass over here right now.

Rowan: On one condition…

Diesel: …what?

Rowan: You actually go to bed early. No more working on three hours of sleep.

Diesel: I'd sleep a helluva lot better if you were in my bed with me.

Rowan: Play your cards right, Cowboy and MAYBE.

Diesel: DEAL.

Though we're not rushing into sex, there are times I'm tempted to rip off our clothes and give in to the emotions swirling between us. I gave in to my desires last week when I got down on my knees in the bar office. It was hot as hell and perhaps a little reckless, but the memory of it makes it hard for me to continue to take things slow. It's not that I don't trust him or my feelings, but once we cross those lines, there's no going back. If something bad happens, and we break up, it'd be impossible to be just "friends" and pretend nothing ever happened. I know I'm over Nick, but it doesn't mean I'm over how he violated my trust. Diesel would never intentionally hurt me like Nick did, but I still need to be cautious. My heart is still fragile.

I also know the moment Riley finds out, he's going to be red-hot angry. Even though Diesel's reassured me he'll get over it, I don't want to be the reason their friendship blows up. Since we were younger, Riley's been clear about me being "off-limits" to his friends. While I'm not a child anymore and can make my own decisions, I only hope he's not as mad as I think he'll be when he finds out.

I drive toward Diesel's house but don't park in front of his cabin. Instead, I leave my car near one of the barns, then walk the rest of the way. Before I go up his porch steps, I look around and make sure none of the ranch hands are working close and can see me. There's no doubt it's weird for me to be at his house.

Once the coast is clear, I knock, and within seconds, he whips it open.

"Hey—" Before I can finish my sentence, Diesel has me wrapped in his arms and shuts the door behind me. Then he pushes me against it and covers my mouth with his. After a moment, I suck in a breath and laugh. "What the hell was that?"

He flashes a lopsided grin. "Didn't want anyone to see you."

"I checked before I walked up the porch," I tell him, smiling. "Mmm...you smell good." I clench my fingers in his shirt and pull him closer, inhaling his scent. *Really* good."

"Fresh outta the shower." He winks, sliding his hand down to squeeze my ass. "I missed you today."

"You just saw me last night," I remind him.

"With a bar between us and a dozen pair of eyes on you." He growls. "I hate that all the guys stare at you."

"They do not."

"Trust me, they do. I want to go all caveman on their asses and claim you publicly so they know you're mine." He holds me tighter.

"Oh yeah? And then what?"

"Then we get hitched, knock you up, and raise our ten kids on the ranch."

My eyes go wide at the seriousness of his tone. Pulling back, I look at him wide-eyed. "Okay, that's my cue..."

He grabs my wrist before I can slide out of his grip. "Okay, fine. I'll compromise. Five kids." Then he winks, and I burst out laughing.

"Why do I feel like you're actually serious but downplaying it for my sake?"

"I don't wanna scare you off, so..." He casually shrugs.

"Have you ever done this before?" I ask as he leads me into his living room. It's half covered with tarps from his remodel.

"Done...what?" he asks, pulling me onto his lap when he sits on the sofa.

"A relationship. Commitment. Dated someone longer than one night," I reiterate.

"Well, there was Billie Sue in fifth grade. She told everyone she was my girlfriend and made me hold her hand at recess."

I arch a brow, amused. "That skank. How dare she!"

"I broke it off during the second recess."

Chuckling, I wrap my arms around his neck as I straddle his lap. "So what makes you think you know how to be a boyfriend?"

"Is that what I am?"

"I don't know. Do you wanna be?"

He blinks hard. "You have me going in circles here."

We both laugh, and I blush at the direction this conversation is going.

"What if I said I've considered it?" I shyly admit.

"I'd say...is it too early to propose?"

I throw my head back with a groan. "How can you just throw those kinds of lines out when you've never had a girlfriend before? Aren't you like, terrified of commitment and shit?"

"Nope," he says immediately and with certainty.

"You're strange." I lean in closer. "You've pushed my buttons for as long as I can remember, and then you'd hook up with my friends." I pop a brow, waiting to hear how he explains himself.

"You—" He punches the word, gripping my hips tighter. "Wouldn't give me the time of day."

"That's your excuse?"

"If memory serves me right, and I'm sure that it does, you weren't so nice to me either. *Even* when I was nothing but sweet to you." He tilts his head, daring me to argue, but he's right. We've been going back and forth for years.

"You're obnoxious sometimes!" I admit, chuckling, then biting my lip. "I could never take you seriously, and you liked making me uncomfortable. Or like last month…" I throw up my hand. "You went through my boxes and brought up my red thongs in front of my brother!"

His head falls back with loud laughter, and I swat his chest. "See!"

"Alright, so I'm not the subtle type." He shrugs unapologetically. "Most chicks dig that, by the way. In fact, a lot of girls in high school always commented on how much attention I gave you, but you wouldn't have any of it. Instead, you found ways to get rid of me."

Rolling my eyes, I shake my head. "Not true. You're so full of shit."

"Right. So me going out of my way to do things for you was for what? Shits and giggles? Boredom? It's not like I had any motive to be nice to you unless I wanted to be."

His words hit me hard as I think back to all the ways he did do things for me during middle and high school. "I thought it was because Riley told you to," I admit. "Or you had some best friend's sister code."

"The only rule he had was not to touch you, so…"

"So I was the shiny forbidden toy that made you want it even more?" I mock.

"If you mean the smart-mouthed, sassy pain in the ass, then yes." He wraps an around my waist and hoists me up higher until I feel his erection between my legs. "You gonna be my girl, or do I need to get a plane to spell it out in the sky?"

I arch a brow, confused.

"You're not as subtle as you think you are, Rowan Bishop. I knew exactly where this conversation was going, and if you need to throw a bunch of questions at me to make sure I'm ready to be in a relationship with you, then go ahead because I've been waiting years for this. I'm not gonna be the dumbass who lets the girl of his dreams slip through his fingers."

My breathing quickens at his unexpected confession, but it's one I'll replay in my head over and over again. Adam Hayes officially has my heart.

"Okay," I whisper, then bite my lip. For whatever reason, my nerves are shot, and I can feel my cheeks heating.

"Okay what?"

"You're gonna make me say it, aren't you?"

The smirk on his face tells me his answer.

"I'm gonna need to hear you say it just so there's nothing lost in translation," he states, clearly loving how nervous I am. I rock my hips against him, and he groans. "Better stop that."

"Or what?"

"Or you better be prepared to finish what you start, sweetheart."

My eyes lower down his sculpted body. He's large, and I feel small next to him. Everything on him screams man—his large hands, long legs, and toned arms.

"You're the one who pulled me onto your lap," I remind him.

I screech when he shoots off the couch and lays me down on my back, then towers over me. "Answer my question, Row. Are you mine?"

Licking my lips, I nod. "Yes, I'm yours."

He grins, shaking his head in disbelief. "About goddamn time."

Diesel crashes his mouth to mine, sliding his hand up and around my neck. My legs wrap around his waist, wanting him against me. I grind against his obvious erection, which causes him to growl against my lips. "Fuck, don't do that. I only have so much willpower when it comes to you."

"I said I wanted to go slow, not that we had to withhold from *everything*," I reiterate, grabbing his hand and placing it on my breast.

Without another word, he leans back, then lifts up my shirt until it flies off. He presses kisses on my chest and wraps a hand around my back to unclasp my bra. I flash him a suspicious look. "Did you just undo my bra with one hand?"

He shrugs, undoing my bra and flinging it off. "I'm good with my hands, baby."

I roll my eyes and laugh. "I'm sure you are."

He cups my breast and wraps his lips around one of my nipples. My eyes close at how good it feels. His hot mouth and his eager tongue have my entire body on fire.

"Adam," I cry out, arching my back to give him more of me.

"Jesus fuck," he hisses. "I love hearing you moan my name."

He moves his mouth to my other breast, giving it the same amount of attention. I'm smacking myself in the face for telling him we needed to go slow because right now, I'm craving more of him.

Diesel has wedged himself into my head and heart so quickly that if I'm not careful, I'm gonna get whiplash. All of my assumptions about him hit me in the gut because I was so damn wrong.

"I'm sorry," I tell him softly, and he lifts his eyes up to mine. "I never should've treated you the way I did growing up."

He brings his finger up to my face, brushing back the strands of hair that fell from my ponytail. "Don't be. It's a part of our story."

"I don't deserve you."

"I've told myself that for so long, and I started to believe it, but you know what? It didn't stop me from going after what I wanted anyway. And now look?"

"Your persistence paid off," I say, chuckling at his honesty.

"Damn straight." He smirks, bringing his mouth back to mine. "You have the sexiest tits, by the way."

I snort, blushing. "Wow. There's that romantic side of you."

"I'm romantic as fuck! Just wait until I can take you out on *real* dates."

"Oh, really? What would a real date with Diesel be like?" I

taunt as my fingers play with his belt buckle. The damn thing must come with a combination because it's impossible to undo with one hand.

"You will find out *very* soon, sweet Rowan. Now get your hands away from my dick before I throw your rule out the goddamn window and fuck you against my couch."

I groan loudly, tempted to rub my thighs together for relief. Sticking out my lower lip, I give him my best pouty look. "That's not fair. You took off my shirt."

"Okay, fine." He leans back and wraps a hand behind his neck, pulling off his. "There, we're even."

"Hardly," I say with a deadpan expression. "Now, your pants."

"No, ma'am." He swats away my eager hands. "I'm not just a play toy."

I scoff, chuckling at him feigning offense. "Then tell your cock that because it's begging to come out and *play*."

Diesel chuckles, leaning over me. He tilts my chin up and brings our lips together, soft and slow. "Let me take you out. We'll leave town and see where the night goes."

"You really take this whole dating thing seriously, don't you?" I tease, capturing his bottom lip with my teeth.

"I take you being my girl seriously."

We continue making out, his rough hands massaging my breasts while heat pools between my thighs. He's working me up but not willing to do anything about it.

"You need to stop, or I'm going to combust." I grind against him, needing the friction to relieve myself.

"Let me help with that…" He shifts our bodies so we're chest to chest. Sliding his hands down my body, he slips beneath my shorts and into my panties. His fingers find my clit, and soon, he's rubbing circles, and I'm gasping for air. "Better?" His voice is taunting, but I nod, arching my hips for more.

"Don't stop," I beg. I wrap my hand around his bicep,

squeezing hard as he increases his pace. "Oh my God…" My eyes roll to the back of my head as he slides two fingers inside me while his thumb rubs against me.

"You have any idea how many wet dreams I've had of this exact moment," he murmurs against my lips, and I can tell he's smiling. "So fuckin' many, Row."

"Sounds like you needed a hobby," I tease, bucking my hips.

He chuckles. "I did. You're it now."

As I get closer to the ledge, his mouth sucks on my neck, and he kisses my jawline before sliding his tongue between my lips. The heat between us is so intense, and I know I'm about to explode at any moment.

"Let go, sweetheart. Come on my fingers," he demands. "I wanna taste you."

My legs shake, my back arches, my spine tingles. So. Damn. Close.

"Diesel!" Two hard knocks sound at the door, and we both freeze. "Open the door!"

"You gotta be fuckin' kidding me." He growls.

The doorknob jiggles, and that's when I push him off me. "Shit, I need my bra and shirt!" I fly off the couch, gathering my things, and once I cover myself, I rush toward the bathroom.

Diesel grabs my arm and stops me before I make it down the hall. "Stay in there, and I'll come get you when they leave."

I nod. "Don't forget your shirt." Then I lower my gaze to his groin. "Might wanna adjust that…"

He curses under his breath, then walks back to the living room while I go and hide.

Like a dirty mistress.

After ten minutes of waiting, I start to worry. I heard voices at the front, but he didn't let them in. I don't know what excuse he gave them, but after a while, it goes eerily quiet, and I worry he left me in here.

Another five minutes pass, and I grow more annoyed. "Fuck this shit."

Slowly, I undo the lock and poke my head out. I don't hear a thing and decide to chance it.

The moment I open the door wider and step out into the hallway, a hand covers my mouth, and I'm slammed into a hard body.

"Shh…" Diesel whispers into my ear, then pushes me back inside the bathroom. After he shuts the door, he twists me in his arms, then lifts me up under my thighs.

"What the hell are you doing?" I squeal and wrap my arms around his shoulders as he carries me to the sink counter. "Who's here?"

"Your dad."

My eyes widen. "What? Why?"

"And Riley."

"Oh hell. That can't be good." My head falls back against the mirror.

"Nah, it's fine. They were looking for something I had in my truck. They're gone now."

I straighten and look at him. "Then why did you—" I wave my arm out. "Basically shove me back in here like we were gonna get caught."

The corner of his lips tilts up. "To fuck with you."

I narrow my eyes at him and growl. "That was mean! Asshole."

He laughs, showing off his perfect white teeth. "I'm getting revenge for all those years you tortured me with these delicious tits and long, tan legs you always showed off but never let me touch. And now that I know what they feel like against my skin and tongue, don't expect me to be able to keep my hands off."

I can't even be mad at his little stunt because hearing those words from him—a guy who annoyed me for years but managed to turn what I thought about him around—changes everything. I love that no one knows about us, and we can be completely honest with one another without any outside noise.

"Not sure I can get used to this charming side of yours…" I lift a brow. "But I kinda adore it."

He presses a hand to his chest. "Because I'm fuckin' adorable."

I shake my head. "You're too much sometimes."

"And I'm all yours, baby."

CHAPTER ELEVEN

DIESEL

IT'S BEEN two days since Rowan came to my house and we almost got caught by her brother and dad. Luckily, they didn't ask to come in, and they only talked to me for a few minutes outside, but it was another reminder of how careful we have to be.

Grabbing Rowan's arm before she walks past me, I guide her into one of the tack rooms in the horse barn and bring her against my chest.

"Jesus!" she whisper-hisses. "You're gonna give me a heart attack one of these days." She playfully swats at my chest. "Why can't we sneak around without you scaring the shit outta me every damn time?"

I cup her face and lower my mouth, brushing my lips against hers. "I like getting your blood pumping." Waggling my brows, I slide my other hand down her back and squeeze her ass. "Now let me do dirty things to you."

Rowan's eyes widen, pulling away. "What if someone walks in?" she asks as I slowly move her backward until the saddle stand stops her.

"They're free to watch me pleasure you." I flash her a cocky smile as I grip her hips. "Everyone went to the diner for lunch today," I tell her. "We have an hour, at least."

She perks an eyebrow. "And you didn't go with them? Aren't you hungry?" The way she so sweetly asks gets my dick hard.

"Oh, sweet Rowan." My gaze rolls down her tempting body. "Starving."

My fingers reach for the top of her jean shorts, and she watches as I slowly unbutton them, then lower the zipper.

"What are you doin'?" she asks with a grin.

"I told you...I'm hungry." I throw her a wink, then drop to my knees. "And you're just what I'm craving."

As I slide her shorts down, my cock throbs at the sight. I look up as Rowan snags her bottom lip between her teeth while keeping her hands steadily planted on the saddle behind her.

"You okay with this, Row?" I ask, digging my boots into the floor as I balance my weight in front of her.

She nods with a half-smile. "No one's ever..." Rowan nervously clears her throat. "But I want you to."

I tilt my head at her, wondering if she's fucking with me or not. "What do you mean, no one's ever...?"

"The few guys I've dated didn't do *that*."

"Wait. Are you kiddin'? That's what they told you, or they never offered?"

"Both." She shrugs as if she's embarrassed.

Standing to my feet, I hold her face in my hands and press my lips to hers. She melts against me, wrapping her fingers around my wrists as I slide my tongue inside her mouth.

"That's because before me, you were with *boys*, not a man." I smirk, excited I'll be the first and *only* to taste her that intimately. "Another first kiss of yours I get."

Rowan chuckles, then nods. "I'm glad it's you."

I press a quick kiss to her mouth before lowering my body

again. Not knowing how soon the rest of the workers will return, we don't have a lot of time to waste.

When I brushing my lips to the inside of her thigh, she shudders. I've barely touched her, but she's so goddamn responsive; it won't be long before she's coming on my tongue.

"Widen your legs, baby," I tell her. She obliges, and I tease her first, kissing her skin and sliding my tongue on her clit over her panties.

She arches her hips toward me, groaning and holding my head in place. I love how vocal she is, and the way she responds to my touch sends a jolt of electricity through me. I want to please her more than anything, but I also want to taste her.

Pulling back slightly, I gaze up at her and watch as she licks her lips. Her eyes burn into mine, and I know she's ready.

I slide her thong down, and she steps out of it, baring herself for me. She watches as I tuck it into my pocket, giving me a teasing side-eye.

"What do you think you're doing with that?"

"Keepin' my prize."

"And what do you plan to do with it?"

I lean in close, then rub the tip of my nose along her thigh, inching toward her pussy. "Savor it till the day I die."

She chuckles, spreading her legs in response.

"Fuck, Row." I slide my tongue up her slit and circle her clit. "I can't get enough of you."

"Mmm..." Her sweet voice vibrates. "More. We're on a time limit here," she reminds me.

I laugh at her urgency, then dive in.

Licking, sucking, fucking her with my tongue.

It's better than I could've ever imagined.

Her moans echo through the room, burning a fire within me so deep, I'm not sure how to control myself when I'm this worked up around her. The desire to be near her, touch her, kiss, and love her hits me so strong, I want her to feel me for days.

Gripping the back of her thighs, I squeeze hard as I feast on her like my last meal. Sliding a finger inside her tight cunt, I thrust in and out as I suck on her clit. She grinds against my tongue as she throws off my hat and digs her nails into my hair. I smile in amusement as I feel her buildup start to soar.

"Oh my God. I'm so close."

"Yes, baby. Just like that." I flick my tongue and increase my pace, finger fucking her harder and faster until she jerks her body and shakes against me. She unravels, hissing through her teeth as I relentlessly taste her.

I adjust my body between her legs and spread her pussy wider, not wanting to let her go just yet.

"Adam..." she whispers. "You're going to get us caught."

Sliding my tongue up her slit, I taste her arousal, sucking on her clit. Rowan rides my face as I drive her to another orgasm. Her hands shake as they rest on my shoulders, and she's only seconds away from giving me more of what I want.

The moment she claws her nails into my skin, I know she's there. Her body jerks as I release her clit, then press a kiss above it.

"I'm a selfish man. I wanted more." I wink, licking my lips.

With a satisfied smirk, she shakes her head at me. "That was...crazy."

Knowing I was her first fills me with pride and possession. I want to be the only one to ever touch and taste her down there forever.

"Best damn lunch break I've ever had," I tease. "Same time tomorrow?"

Rowan laughs, then rolls her eyes. "I need to get out of here before someone catches us."

I help her back into her shorts, then stand. "You should let me take you out this weekend. I'm off on Saturday and work

Sunday evening. We can plan a sleepover since I know you're not working," I tease.

She retreats a step and side-eyes me. "Take me out? Like on a *date*?"

"Yes, ma'am. Dinner, dessert, a walk under the stars."

She snorts. "You and me?"

Tilting my head, I hold back a smirk. "You gonna make me beg, woman?"

"I'm just trying to imagine *you*, Adam Hayes, taking a girl out on a romantic date, and…I'm just not seeing it." Rowan shrugs with a grin.

"That's because you haven't experienced it yet." I pull her back to me, wrapping my arms around her waist. "So whaddya say? We'll go into San Angelo and stay at a hotel. It'll be romantic as fuck."

She laughs, and I beam with excitement when she finally agrees. "Okay, I suppose I could spare a night."

"And the morning after." I wink.

Before Rowan leaves, I peek outside the barn to make sure the coast is clear. The guys aren't back yet, but our time together is coming to an end. They'll be here any minute.

"Alright, I think you're good to go," I tell her, then give her one last kiss.

"Text me later tonight."

"What are you talkin' about? I'm gonna text you in five minutes."

She chuckles as she walks backward out of the barn, looking at me, then spins around and goes out the side door.

I wait a few minutes before leaving, staring at my phone at a text Riley sent, then stop in my tracks when I see Rowan and Maize are talking outside.

They both stop and look at me.

"What?" I blink.

"What are you doing?" Maize asks.

"Going to my truck. What are you doin'?"

"I meant, what are you doing in there?" She points at the barn behind me.

"I was putting some shit away. That okay, nosy?" I taunt, walking toward them while trying to act normal. "What's it to you?"

"Because I watched Rowan coming out of there, and when I asked her if she saw you, she said she hadn't..." Maize looks at Rowan, then to me.

I shrug. "I was in the tack room."

"Hmm." She folds her arms, narrowing her eyes.

Glancing at Rowan, I can see her cheeks heat and her nostrils flare, which means she's nervous.

"Why were you lookin' for me anyway?"

"Oh, right." She clears her throat. "I need some muscles to help me lift a large box of flour, and it looks like you're the only one around. Literally everyone's gone."

I chuckle and raise my arm, showing off my bicep. "By help, you mean, do it for you?"

Maize rolls her eyes. "Never mind. Put your ego away. I bet Rowan and I can handle it."

Shrugging casually, I walk around them. "Alright." Then I look over my shoulder and grin. "Remember to lift with your legs."

"Asshole," I hear Rowan mutter, then smirk when Maize looks away.

Diesel: Are you packed?

Rowan: If by packed you mean a bag of Starbursts and my cowboy boots, then I'm good to go!

Diesel: Well, darlin', you won't be needing much else anyway :) I'm almost to Wyatt's. You leaving soon?

I'm driving us to San Angelo, but since her parents think she's staying with a friend, she can't leave her truck at home or anywhere they'll see it. But since Wyatt lives in Eldorado, he's letting her park it in his garage. He's the only person who knows about us, and I trust he'll keep it that way until we're ready to announce it.

Rowan: Be there in 10! Had to find my lucky thong.

Diesel: The red one, I hope?

Rowan: You'll have to wait and see ;)

I love the way she always makes me laugh. Chuckling, I shake my head and park my truck on the street outside Wyatt's apartment. I send him a text so he knows I'm here and can give me his garage opener.

"You two gonna finally bang tonight?" he asks the moment he comes up to my window.

"Shut the hell up and give me the opener," I say, holding out my palm.

"I've had to listen to you talk about Rowan Bishop for months, so the least you could do is give me the details."

I roll my eyes, ready to sucker punch the idiot. "Not happenin'. Go back to your Pornhub."

"Just fuckin' with ya. Relax." He digs into his pocket, then hands it over to me. "Tell her to park it in nice and slow…"

"For fuck's sake, don't make me kick your ass."

Wyatt laughs, and when I try to smack him, he retreats. "Okay, for real, though. Have fun. Wear a condom."

He waves when Rowan's car comes into view, and I open the garage for her. She turns in, and I go and meet her.

"Hey, Cowboy." She hops out and immediately wraps her arms around me.

"Hello, yourself." I pull her closer and press my lips to hers. "I'll grab your stuff so we can get outta here."

I put her bag in my truck next to mine, then open the passenger door for her.

"So gentlemanly," she teases as she sits and fixes her sundress.

"My thoughts are anything but *gentlemanly*." I waggle my brows as I stare at her bare legs. "Especially with you wearing that."

She blushes and shakes her head at me.

"Ready?" I ask after I get in the driver's side.

"Yep! If anyone asks, I'm visiting my friend Camila this weekend."

"Camila? Got it." I smirk.

"Do you remember in high school when Thomas Blake asked me to junior prom?" she asks as I turn on the main road that leads out of town.

I look at her confused. "Huh?"

"Thomas Blake," she repeats. "The quarterback of the football team," she clarifies, though I know exactly who she's talking about. The asshole I nearly punched in the face after I found out he'd asked her.

"What about him?" I tighten my grip on the steering wheel, hoping she's not about to confront me about something in the past.

"I've just been doing some thinking lately and wondering why no guys asked me out until my senior year because the day after Thomas did, he canceled."

I feel her staring at me.

"Huh. Weird."

"Yeah," she draws out the word. "*Weird.*"

I finally look at her. "You think I had something to do with it?" I lift a brow, feigning innocence.

"I'd be willing to bet money you did." She crosses her arms, glaring. "I started to put it together the other day, especially when I asked Riley about it, and he looked at me like I'd grown a second head. So that only leaves one other option…"

"That you just weren't that nice in high school, and no guy wanted to date you?"

She smacks my arm so hard, I actually groan and pull away from her. "See?"

"Don't play dumb!" She points her finger and narrows her eyes at me. "I know you must've said or done something to make sure no one ever asked me out. It's no coincidence that once you graduated, a few guys finally did."

I inhale a deep breath and readjust myself in the seat. "It was for your own good, Rowan."

"Oh my God!" she screeches. "I knew it!"

"Okay, geez. Take it down an octave, babe."

"I can't believe you…" She pouts and looks out the window.

Reaching over, I grab her hand and thread my fingers through hers. "You can't be mad. That was years ago, and we're together now, so…you're welcome."

Slowly, she turns her head toward me as though she's possessed. Her eyes are squinted so tight that I'm waiting for her to blow me up with her lazers.

"You're really mad I told some punks to stay away from you?" I pop a brow.

She continues glaring, but it's so damn cute, and I can't help but laugh at how adorable she acts when she's upset.

"This isn't funny!"

"Alright, fine." I bring our locked hands to my lips and press a kiss to her knuckles. "Let me make it up to you this weekend, and you'll be glad I kept those little dickheads away. Otherwise, the alternative would've been you dating some tool bag who would've broken your heart. And you were going off to college anyway." I flash the most charming smile I can.

"Well, we could've gone to the same college together..." she counters.

"Name one guy in our high school who went to the University of Houston," I challenge.

"If I had dated someone, and it was serious, he might've followed me. Or I could've followed him to another school. You don't know!"

I snicker at how serious she is about this. "But aren't you glad you came back to me?"

Rowan rolls her eyes as she struggles to fight a smile.

"You forgive me?"

"No," she says dryly. "But maybe you're right about the long-distance thing. Nick and I went to the same school, and it still didn't work out."

The corner of my lips tilts up. "That's because he's a fucking asshole. It's no coincidence y'all broke up before you moved back home. It just allowed me to give you everything you've ever dreamed of having in a man."

"Don't be smug! This doesn't mean you're off the hook."

"I'm about to romance your pants off this weekend, and you'll forget all about those lame high school boys."

She snorts, then starts chuckling. The sound is contagious, and soon, we're both laughing our asses off.

"I really should've suspected something when no one would dance with me in middle school."

"Exactly!" I say proudly. "Now we can tell our kids we were each other's first kiss."

Rowan blushes, then smiles. "You got lucky that after years of tormenting me, I actually did end up liking you." She pinches her thumb and finger together. "Just a little."

"I think you mean a lot," I mock.

She shrugs casually. "Nothing else to do, so…"

My eyes widen.

She bursts out laughing. "Relax, geez! I'm kidding."

"Now you have to make it up to *me*…" I tell her. "I expect full service treatment too."

"You ruined all my teenage dating opportunities," she reiterates. "You have *years* of making it up to me."

"Oh, sweet Rowan. Don't fuckin' tempt me."

CHAPTER TWELVE

ROWAN

ARGUING and laughing with Diesel makes the drive to San Angelo fly by. A part of me worried that if we weren't sneaking around, being alone would be awkward, or that our relationship was only built on the excitement of hiding, but it's not been the case at all. If anything, I've felt more comfortable with him, and it makes me want to tell the world that somehow, someway I'm falling for Diesel.

I'm falling hard and fast for him.

This weekend, we won't have to hide, and in some odd way, it feels so damn right.

We'll get to hold hands and have dinner in a restaurant and act like a normal couple out on a date.

"Wow...this room is so nice," I say, noticing how fancy our hotel room is.

Walking in farther with Diesel behind me carrying our bags, I spot a large bouquet of roses on a table, an ice bucket with a bottle of champagne, and a platter of chocolate covered strawberries. He wasn't joking when he said he'd pull out all the stops to make this romantic and perfect for us.

It's a scene straight from a Hallmark movie, but I love it all the same. So very *not* Diesel, but very much him trying to be sweet.

"You planned quite the night," I hum, turning around with a smile.

He drops our bags, then pulls me into his chest. "I told you I was turning on the charm."

"I'm gonna be really mad if there isn't a violinist at our table or it doesn't rain when you kiss me outside," I tease, biting my lower lip. The anticipation of what's to come gives me butterflies.

"You don't give me enough credit," he mocks with a wink.

"It's very sweet," I tell him. "Thank you for doing this."

"I would've done it much sooner, but you were too busy hating my guts."

"That's because you were too immature to tell me you liked me."

He chuckles, and a grin spreads across his face that has my entire body fluttering. "Well, you calling me an asshole every other day didn't convince me you'd reciprocate the feelings…"

I roll my eyes and squeal when he lowers his hands and smacks my ass. "But we're here now, so let's not waste another minute…"

Before I can respond, Diesel lifts me over his shoulder caveman style. I squeal as I hang down his back, yelling at him to put me down.

He smacks my ass before tossing me on the bed. "You still think I'm *sweet*?" he mocks.

I laugh, wrapping my legs around his waist and pulling him on top of me. "I didn't mean it as a bad thing."

"Mm-hmm…" He smirks before cupping my face and pressing his lips to mine.

Arching my back, I lean my hips into him, feeling how hard he is against his jeans. Grinning, I inhale the scent of his cologne and groan at the anticipation of getting to be with him all night long—without worrying we'll get caught.

"I don't want to wait, Adam," I tell him, sliding my hands up his chest and undoing a button. "I'm dying and want you inside me."

"Fuck, Row," he growls against my mouth. "I have a whole night planned out for us…but shit."

I chuckle, and when he leans back, we lock eyes. Sucking in my lips, I reach for his belt buckle and zipper. He's hard, and when I slide my hand into his jeans, I wrap my palm around his cock through his boxers.

Stroking him, I watch as he unbuttons his shirt as we keep our gazes on one another. My heart pounds hard in my chest as the reality of what's about to happen seeps in. Even though he's been "Diesel" to me my whole life, Adam makes me anxious by how quickly we're growing close. I want to give him all of me, but I'm so scared of giving my heart away again.

Once his shirt is off, I help him remove my sundress and bra. "You're so beautiful, Row. I'm one lucky man."

I swallow hard and smile. "You're not so bad to look at either."

"I've caught you checking me out a few times." He winks with a smug grin. "Drooling over the eight-pack."

"Oh my God!" I burst out laughing. "Just like when you drool over my ass."

"Damn straight!"

I wrap my legs around his waist and move his lips back to mine. Rocking my hips against his, I moan at the friction our bodies create, so damn eager for more.

Diesel pushes his cock against my pussy, and I'm desperate to tear off our remaining clothes and climb him like a damn tree. "Boxers. Off. Now," I demand, panting.

He moves back slightly, grabbing both of my wrists and putting them above my head. "Not so fast, baby."

I'm seconds away from begging. "What? Why?"

"Because I've been waiting years for this, and I'm not about to rush my time with you." He wraps one hand around both my wrists and moves his free hand down between my breasts. "I'm taking it nice and slow. Gonna devour every inch of your soft skin and make sure I mark every part of you properly."

Shivers run down my spine at the anticipation and desperation for everything he's willing to give me. I want it all.

"Adam...don't tease me," I plead.

"Oh, I'm going to have you beggin', sweet Row." The corner of his lips tilts up in a cocky, assured smirk as he circles my nipple with the pad of his finger. "It's the only way I'll know you really want me as much as I want you."

"You know I do," I tell him. "I'm going insane!"

"Let me taste you first."

He guides himself down my body and widens my legs as he settles between them, peeking up at me with a knowing grin. Then he kisses the sensitive part of my thigh, and my eyes roll to the back of my head.

Switching to my other thigh, he does the same and shoves his hands under my ass, pulling me closer to his mouth.

"Fuck," he mutters as he nuzzles his nose against my clit. "Hope you aren't attached to this."

Before I can respond, he grabs both sides of my thong and rips it completely off my body.

Holy. Fucking. *Shit*.

My eyes widen in shock, and without another word, he slides his tongue up my slit and buries his face in my pussy. I don't have anything to compare his skills to, but he's a fucking pro. His mouth and tongue feel amazing as he drives me closer to the edge.

"Adam...*yes, yes, yes*," I pant as my fingers tug his hair, and my back arches. "Don't stop."

He pushes a finger inside, and when he sucks my clit, I

unravel against his mouth. It's intense, and I'm still flying high when he adds a second finger.

Diesel's groans are such a turn-on. Knowing he's feasting on me like his favorite meal, I want more of him, and I don't ever want him to stop.

My hands fist the blankets as I jerk my hips up and down, so close to another release. My body responds to him so strongly and it drives me wild every time he touches me.

"That's my girl," he praises as another orgasm rocks through my core.

"Please don't stop," I plead. "I want you inside me, *now*."

"Patience…" He presses his lips to my stomach. "I'm just getting started with you."

Diesel's hot mouth kisses up my body and cups my breast before sucking on my nipple. He gives them equal attention, massaging and licking each one. Every inch of me is on fire, desperate and greedy for all of him.

My arms wrap around his body, being as close to him as I can. He's muscular and hard, but he touches me so softly and sweet.

Diesel roll his hips, grinding his dick harder against me, and I groan. "That's not fair." My head falls to the side as he kisses up my neck.

"This is what you do to me, Row," he whispers in my ear. "You make me crazy. For *years*. I couldn't stop wanting you even when I fuckin' tried."

"*Adam…*"

He moves his mouth to mine. "I tried to get over you. Tried to date other women. Tried to have feelings for someone else so I could erase the ones I had for you."

My eyes water at his confession. "I'm so happy you didn't…" I say softly.

"It never worked anyway. My heart is yours. Always has been. I was just waiting for you to catch me."

I palm his cheeks and hold his face. I never thought I'd say these words to him, but I mean them wholeheartedly. "You have mine too. I'm falling for you faster than I could've ever imagined, but I'm not going anywhere now that I know these feelings are real."

"I've been falling for you for years, baby, but harder than I could've predicted."

Diesel kisses me passionately, pressing our bodies together as our hands explore each other. He pulls back and stands, removing his jeans and boxers. My breathing increases as I watch him grab a condom from his wallet, then strokes himself and slides it on.

He stares at me, moving his eyes down my chest, stomach, legs. Then he meets my gaze with a smirk. "So fucking gorgeous."

"You better get over here before I do the job for you…" I tease, sliding my hand down to my clit. It's been throbbing since the second he touched me.

"Like hell you will, woman." Approaching the edge of the bed, he wraps his hands around each of my ankles, then gently yanks me down until my ass is nearly hanging off the mattress.

I squeal, hanging onto the covers. "What're you doing?"

"Making sure my hands are the only ones pleasuring you."

He strokes his cock a few times before lining it up to my entrance. My chest rises and falls faster; the anticipation mixes with desire as he pushes inside.

Diesel grips my thigh and pulls it up around his waist as he goes deeper. He feels so thick and hard as I widen my hips and take all of him.

"Oh my God…" My head rolls back, the sensation already too much.

"Jesus, Row," he groans, slowly sliding out before returning. I dig my nails into his biceps, enjoying how tight he feels inside me. "So goddamn wet."

My other leg wraps around him, and I lock my ankles behind him. He places a hand on the bed next to me while his other cups my breast and squeezes. "You feel amazing."

I can't even form words around my heavy breathing and moaning, but I smile when our lips meet.

As I rock my hips against him, our bodies form a perfect rhythm as our hands and lips touch and kiss everywhere we can. Diesel increases his pace, grabbing my waist and controlling the speed. He's sculpted to pure perfection, and I could stare at him all day as he drives us further to the ledge.

He brings his hand between us and rubs my clit. It's the sweetest torture I've ever felt, and even though I'm close, I don't want this to end.

"That feels so good," I moan, pinching my nipples. "I'm so close…"

"Yes, baby. I wanna feel you come on my dick," he says, his voice rough and deep, almost sliding all the way out before he drives back in. He's so deep, my legs shake at how hard he's fucking me.

Diesel continues circling my clit, and when my back flies off the bed, he slows his pace and whispers sweet things as I ride out my climax.

"Not gonna lie, that was fuckin' sexy."

His cocky smile makes me laugh.

Pulling out, he nods toward the headboard. "Scoot up."

Once I'm settled in the middle of the bed, he climbs up my body and lifts my leg to his shoulder. When he's back inside me, I gasp for air as he thrusts harder.

"Faster," I beg.

Moments later, my body tightens and shakes as another orgasm rocks through me. I've never had more than one during sex, but Diesel's changed the game for me in more ways than one. He's changed *everything*.

It's not long before Diesel's groaning out his release and burying his face in my neck.

"Jesus fuck," he grunts with a laugh. He falls to my side, and we look at each other with big, satisfied smiles on our faces. Leaning in, he brushes the hair out of my face with a grin. "Wow. That was…incredible."

"My thoughts exactly." I chuckle while trying to catch my breath. The way he looks at me has my heart pounding, but not because of what we just did. Diesel stares at me as though he actually sees the real me.

I wish I knew where we go from here, how we'll announce the news, and what it'll mean for his friendship with my brother. Diesel's been a part of my life for years, and I can't imagine him not in it.

Leaning forward, I brush my lips against his, and we kiss slowly. He lets me take the lead as I slide my tongue inside and capture his with my teeth, smiling as his hand moves down to my ass, then smacks it.

"I think we're gonna be late for our reservations if we don't get out of this bed," I tell him after twenty minutes of us making out and teasing each other. He got up to dispose of the condom, but then climbed right back into bed next to me.

"Probably," he says, shifting our bodies until I'm straddling and leaning over him. "But knowing how you look underneath me will distract me too much, so you better ride me to help me focus."

"I don't think that's how that works…" I mock, grinding my pussy against his bare cock between us.

"Or we could just order room service and stay naked the rest of the night," he counters.

"Now that's a deal I'm willing to accept."

By the next morning, my entire body feels like I've run a marathon. Every inch of me is sore but in the most delicious way. Knowing it's from having sex with Diesel all night and into the early morning has me smiling like a damn fool. The man is insatiable, and I've never experienced anything like it before.

After I rode him for our second round, we ordered food and ate while talking and laughing in bed. It was actually quite sweet how attentive he was and all the memories he recounted of us as kids.

Our third round was him bending me over, but when my legs gave out, he slid behind me so my back was to his chest, then fucked me until I nearly went blind.

We finally passed out sometime after three a.m., and our fourth round was in the shower before we had to check out at noon. The entire night feels like a dream come true, one I wish didn't have to end, but when Diesel drives us back to Wyatt's house, I know we're back to hiding and sneaking around.

"Say something to piss me off," I tell him after he opens the door to my car.

"What?" He laughs, putting my bag inside.

"If I go back all euphoric and happy, my cousins and parents will start asking questions. So I need a reason to wipe this smile off my face," I explain, knowing how ridiculous I sound, but it's true. "They're already suspicious, and I won't be able to hide the way I feel unless I lock myself in my room all week."

"Guess that makes two of us. The guys will be all over my ass. You're better at telling me off, so you say something to piss me off instead."

I groan. "We're not gonna be convincing at all."

He closes the gap between us, brushing his finger over my cheek to fix my hair. "It'll be alright. If they find out, they find out. I can handle Riley."

"And my dad?" I add.

"He loves me!" We both laugh because it's true. My dad treats Diesel like a second son, but he wouldn't think twice about hounding Diesel for dating his only daughter.

"And my grandma, my cousins, and my uncles. All their opinions and comments."

"Don't care." He shrugs. "I've been telling them for years I'd finally get you."

Wrapping my arms around his waist, I rest my chin on his chest. "That's true, you did. Kinda like a stalker."

He kisses the tip of my nose. "Stalkers need love too."

I snort, and we break apart, knowing I have to get home before my mom and dad send out a search party for me.

"I'm gonna hang out with Wyatt for a bit so we don't arrive at the ranch at the same time," he tells me as I sit in the driver's seat of my car. "Text me when you're back home."

"I will." I start the engine and stick out my lower lip, pouting that our weekend's over.

"Don't be sad. I'll see you soon," he promises. Then he kisses me one final time before I leave, my heart racing as I think about what an amazing night we had and how I hope this never ends.

It's one thirty when I finally make it home. I missed church and know my mom is gonna give me shit for it, but luckily, no one's at the house yet. Diesel and I showered this morning, but I go ahead and take another one with my fruity body wash to make sure his scent doesn't linger on my skin. Though I love the way he smells after he showers.

Once I'm dressed and make a cup of coffee, I check my

phone and see a message from him and a group text message from Elle and Maize.

> **Diesel: Confession: I stole your ripped thong for my spank bank.**
>
> **Rowan: You're really adding to your stalker resume.**
>
> **Diesel: I'm also sniffing them while picturing your tits bouncing in my face.**

My cheeks heat at his words. He's so blunt, and it turns me on. I've not really sexted before. Nick could hardly perform in the bedroom, and his skills didn't land in texting either.

> **Rowan: Oh yeah? I'd shove them into your mouth while riding your cock so you could taste and feel me at the same time.**
>
> **Diesel: Jesus, now I'm hard as fuck again. Which is really awkward with Wyatt playing video games next to me. He's already giving me shit for looking like a stoned-out rodeo clown.**

I giggle as I imagine how uncomfortable he must be not being able to take care of himself right now.

> **Rowan: It wasn't awkward before with you sniffing my panties?**
>
> **Diesel: He wasn't looking then.**
>
> **Rowan: Mm-hmm. Well, good luck with that. It's safe**

for you to come back now and touch yourself in the shower.

Diesel: Don't give me any more ideas...though I've been jerking off to thoughts of you since I was a teenager, so it'd be nothing new.

Rowan: You just went from sexy stalker to weird creeper.

Diesel: So I shouldn't tell you about the love letter I wrote you when I was in eighth grade?

Rowan: You did not!

Diesel: I swear! I was infatuated with you. Still am ;)

Rowan: Stop being so damn sweet when I was such a brat to you. I feel so bad when I think about all the times I was mean to you.

Diesel: Don't worry...I took it as flirting. You just weren't very good at it :)

I snort, chuckling in relief. He's the easiest person to talk to and always knows what to say to keep me laughing.

Rowan: Har har. You're seriously ridiculous sometimes.

Diesel: You've always adored me, admit it.

Rowan: Ha! Gotta go! Elle and Maize want me to hang out, so I gotta put my game face on.

Diesel: If it helps, I'm picturing you naked right now.

Rowan: That absolutely does not help. Asshole.

I click to the group message so they don't think I'm ignoring them.

Elizabeth: I gotta help birth a calf. The mama is having some complications. You two wanna come and help?

Maize: Where's Dr. VetDreamy?

Elizabeth: On another job, which is why I gotta go solo.

Rowan: I just took a shower…

Maize: I'm hungover from last night.

Elizabeth: OMG you guys suck! I just need some extra hands.

Maize: Take Ethan.

Rowan: Or Kenzie.

Elizabeth: Meet me at the B&B in 10 minutes. Both of you!

I laugh because Maize and I were only joking. She knows we'll come. Grabbing my rubber boots and keys, I head to my car and drive over.

"You nervous or something?" I ask when I see Elle in her truck. "You're sweating."

"It's hot."

"Mm-hmm." I snicker, hopping into the passenger's seat. "Maize coming?"

Before she can answer, we see her walking down the steps of the B&B porch looking like she got hit by a bus.

"Oh my God…" I laugh when she opens the back door. Turning, I raise my brows at the dark circles under her eyes and the messy bun on top of her head. "What the hell happened to you?"

Elle starts driving, and Maize groans at the bumpy road.

"I went to the bar last night to keep Kenzie company, and well…" She sighs. "Do either of you know a Gavin?"

I purse my lips, thinking about all the regulars and townies who come into the bar. "No, doesn't ring a bell," I tell her.

"Thank God. I hope he was just passing through."

"Maize…" The corner of my lips tilts up. "What'd you do?"

"I think the question is *who* did you do?" Elle mocks.

"You hooked up with a stranger!" I laugh, shocked and kinda impressed. Maize doesn't do hookups.

"Don't talk so loud!" she scolds. "My head's still pounding."

"Go figure, the one night I'm not working you find a hottie to bang. What'd he look like?"

"Like all the other cowboys in this damn state. Ugh, fuck my life. I'm gonna be so embarrassed if I run into him again after being a sloppy drunk and probably a horrible lay." She hangs her head in shame. Elle and I try to hide our laughter, but it doesn't work.

"Stop worrying. I doubt he's from here."

"So…how was it?" Elle asks.

"Yes, do tell."

She rolls her eyes, but I see a half-smile on her face, which is enough for me to know she had a good night.

"Even drunk, he was good. Like *really* good."

"Did you get his number?" I ask.

"No! I didn't even get his last name. And to make matters worse, I left before he woke up."

"What?" I screech. "You didn't!"

She buries her head in her hands. "I was embarrassed! I didn't want to be the one he bailed on, so I got dressed and got the fuck out."

Her face is so red, I'm tempted to ask if she's running a fever, but then I think better of it when she smacks her forehead against the window.

"I can't believe you left…" I chuckle to myself.

"I wanna meet this guy," Elle adds. "He's got you all kinds of flustered."

Maize turns and glares.

"Do you remember anything else about him?" I ask as Elle turns into a gravel driveway.

"I think he mentioned something about bull riding…like he used to or something."

I snap my fingers. "I bet that's why he's just passing through town. Probably on the way to a competition or something."

"Wait, where did y'all hook up?" Elle asks.

"At some apartment but he said it wasn't his."

"So he must be visiting a friend," I say, trying to put the pieces together. "Did you see anyone else there?"

"No, but it was like two in the morning, and I was on the tipsy side," she states dryly. "This is humiliating. What was I thinking?"

"You were thinking you needed some dick." I snort.

"I hate you. If you'd been working, you could've stopped me from making a fool out of myself."

"Oh, this is *my* fault?" I ask, amused.

"Yes," she states firmly. "Where were you anyway?"

"Visiting my friend, Camila," I tell her, the guilt immediately creeping in as I lie right to her face.

"Alright, we're here. Think you two can manage to help me so I don't fuck this up?"

"You've done this dozens of times. Why are you so nervous now?" I ask as we all get out of the truck, and she grabs her bag of supplies.

"Connor made it very clear these were very close friends of his and to treat them well." She shrugs when I pop a brow at her, not buying it. "I don't want to disappoint him, okay?"

"Because you *love* him," Maize teases. "I wouldn't mind having one night with him."

"Alright, drunky, you stay in the truck," Elle orders.

"Oh c'mon, I'm fine! I just know you have a thing for your boss, and you're too chicken to tell him."

"How could you not, though? He's ridiculously sexy!" I fan my face when Elle glowers at me.

"You two are hopeless." Elle starts walking toward the barn, and Maize and I follow. "Y'all gonna get me fired."

CHAPTER THIRTEEN

DIESEL

I'VE HAD a permanent smile on my face ever since I got back from San Angelo with Rowan. Being with her has been a dream come true and something I've always fantasized about but never imagined would happen. After I got home, I almost told her we needed to just tell her family. I'm tired of hiding the way I feel, and considering the way she looked at me when we last saw each other, I know she is too. Riley would get over it, and then she could move in with me. Every night and morning, I'd make sure to pleasure her in all the right ways. I'd treat her like the queen she is and prove to her I was the right choice.

"What the hell are you smiling about now?" Riley looks at me as he stuffs his face with sausage. I actually didn't realize I was cheesing so much. It's hard to hide happiness like this.

"Just thinkin' about your sister," I tease, but I'm being truthful, which is even more funny to me. If only he knew I wasn't joking this time. Rowan. Damn, just thinking about her causes my temperature to rise as memories of this weekend cause heat to shoot through my veins.

A biscuit flies toward my head, and I quickly move out of

the way only for it to swiftly hit one of the guests. Riley immediately stands and goes to her.

"I am so sorry, ma'am. I was just horseplayin' and didn't mean to hit ya," he tells her.

She smiles. "It's okay, honey. I have grandkids your age, so I understand."

A clearing of a throat comes from the doorway, and I see John looking at us incredulously. "Riley!" he snaps, curling his finger. "Come over here, boy."

I snicker and pull my phone out of my pocket to see a text from Rowan.

Rowan: I miss sitting on your face in the mornings.

I swallow hard.

Diesel: And I miss having you for breakfast. I mean, Maize's cooking is great, but it's nothing compared to eating you.

Rowan: You're bad, but in a way I love, Cowboy.

Diesel: Did you just say you love me?

I smirk, knowing it's way too early to exchange those words, but there's no other way to describe the way I've always felt about Rowan Bishop. Now that I have the chance of a lifetime with the woman my fifteen-year-old self jerked off to nearly every night in the shower, there's no way in hell I'm fucking it up.

Hurrying, I send another text, not wanting to put her on the spot.

Diesel: I'm just kidding.

Rowan: Shut the hell up.

Diesel: Why don't you make me? I can think of a few ways.

Riley returns, and I tuck my phone in my pocket and stuff my mouth with food so I don't have to talk. The smirk isn't lost on him, though.

"You're a dickhead," he murmurs, keeping his head low.

"Surprised John didn't murder you back there," I tell him.

Riley glares at me. "If I wasn't family, he probably would've. Just picked up extra chores for hitting a woman with a biscuit because you don't know how to shut the fuck up."

I shrug. "And you don't know how to control your temper."

A few seconds later, Riley takes his attention from his plate and glances behind me. I turn around and see a blonde walking toward us, but I don't recognize her, so I go back to my breakfast.

"Diesel?" she asks when she gets closer, looking directly at me.

"Howdy," I greet. "Can I help you?"

I wonder if I've met her before, but she doesn't look too familiar, so I'm fairly certain I haven't.

She looks at me, then at Riley. "Is there any way we can chat in private?"

Riley shoos me away.

"Sure, no problem." Though I'm curious as to what she has to say.

Looking around, I lead her out onto the back porch because it's fairly empty. Once we're outside, she turns to me.

"I'm sorry for showing up unannounced." She hesitates as if she's waiting for a reaction.

I give her a grin and shrug. "It's no problem, ma'am. What can I help you with?"

She sucks in a deep breath, and I can tell she's nervous. I wish she'd just spit it out, though. "I wrote you a letter a couple of months back…"

It takes me a minute to comprehend what she's talking about. "Letter?"

…but I know exactly what she's referring to.

"Yeah, my name is Laurel. You didn't call me even though I left my number so you left me no choice but to come here. My sister, Chelsea, needs your help, even if she's too proud to ask for it."

I blink hard. "Chelsea?"

She nods. "Chelsea's my sister. You two hooked up in Vegas three years ago. She gave birth to your son nine months after." Laurel grabs her cell phone and swipes through her photos, then turns it around and shows me the screen.

"There he is. Just look at him. There's no doubt he's your son. I knew the moment I saw your Facebook photos that you were his daddy."

I look down at the picture of the beautiful boy who's a spitting image of me when I was that age. He has my mouth, nose, and even my green eyes. Learning I have a son that Chelsea never told me about makes me sick to my goddamn stomach.

"Why would she keep this from me?" I search Laurel's face. Her cheeks flush, and her pink lips tuck inside her mouth.

"I have no idea. Anytime I brought it up, she'd tell me to mind my own business. But now—"

"But now you're not?" I stare at her.

She shrugs, unapologetically. "Not when it comes to my nephew. I love him more than anything."

My heart races, and I don't know how to feel or what to think. I take one last look at the boy's photo, a toddler at this point, and allow the image of him to burn into my memory. Then I walk off the back of the porch.

"Where are you going?" she asks, trailing me.

"I got some thinkin' to do," I tell her without turning around. Right now, I need to be alone, but she doesn't take the hint. The only thing that stops me is her grabbing my hand and spinning me around.

"Can you at least give me your number? I want to stay in contact with you."

I study her, then swallow hard. "Tell me what you hoped to accomplish by coming here, Laurel. Chelsea obviously doesn't want me involved so what can I really do?"

She tilts her head and looks at me. "You can be a father to your son. It's your right." She digs in her purse and hands me a business card. "My cell is on there. If you change your mind about wanting more information, call or text me. I did my part. I can't make either of you do the right thing for Dawson, but I can sleep better at night knowing I told you. The ball's in your court now."

After she's finished, she turns on her heels and walks toward the B&B. Once she's out of sight, I go to my truck, crank the engine, and mindlessly drive around.

Never would I have imagined that today I'd wake up and discover I'm a dad. This news was so unpredictable, I feel as if I'm living in an alternate universe. Of course, it'd come when Rowan and I took the next step in our relationship.

This could change everything.

The plane lands on the runway in sunny Phoenix with my heart lodged in my throat. All I can think about is how Rowan will react to me being a dad and the fact that my son lives hundreds of miles away from me. I took off work, needing some emergency vacation days, but couldn't bring myself to tell Rowan I was going out of town. How do I even explain this to her when I barely understand it myself?

Regardless, as soon as I have all the details, she'll be the first to know. While Dawson bears an uncanny resemblance to me, it's important to have proof that he's mine. Once I have that, I'll figure out my next steps.

Chelsea has no idea I'm here, and my nerves get the best of me as I'm handed the keys to a rental car. Showing up unexpectedly is not what I wanted to do, but after I spoke to Laurel two days ago, she suggested it'd be better to blindside Chelsea because she'd never agree to meet me otherwise. I'm not the type of man who gets a woman pregnant and walks out on my kid, and even though I didn't know, I can't help feeling guilty for missing Dawson's first two years of life. After seeing how much Riley's in love with his kid and how much pride he takes in being a dad, it's a dagger straight to the heart.

Considering my life was finally going in the right direction with Rowan, I feel like the universe is laughing at me. Riley always said I'd hurt his sister, and though I'd never do it intentionally, this could be what it takes to screw things up. I hope she still gives me a chance after all this.

I feel uneasy as I drive to Chelsea's apartment. I've never felt this level of anxiety before, but it's like my mind can't stop racing, and my heart is pumping in overdrive. I've been living in the twilight zone ever since Laurel showed up, but when I pull into the complex with brick buildings and neat hedges, I know I have to do this.

I park, wondering if this is the right decision, but my mama raised me better than to be a coward. My conscience couldn't handle not stepping up, and running away from my problems isn't a way to solve them. Not to mention, if she does need help supporting my son, I want to contribute any way I can.

After a deep breath, I get out of the car and walk down the sidewalk until I see her duplex. I take the stairs two at a time, and when I get to her door, I hesitate for a moment. I can hear cartoons playing and child's laughter on the other side. Sucking in another breath, I tap on the door.

The handle jiggles, and the hard wood swings open. Our eyes meet for the first time in three years.

"Diesel," she gasps, then swallows hard. "W-what are you doing here?" she stutters, looking around until she realizes I'm alone.

"I'm askin' myself the same question," I say honestly.

Her brows furrow, but she keeps her voice in a hushed tone. "How'd you get my address?"

"Laurel found me."

"Fuck," she whisper-hisses. "I told her to stay out of this." Chelsea looks over her shoulder. "I'll be right back, sweetie," she says before stepping outside, but leaving the door cracked open.

"Look." I keep my voice as calm as I can. "She told me about Dawson. I felt it was my duty to come here and see for myself. If he's my kid, it's my right to know."

Her face softens, and she looks up at the sky, releasing a slow breath. Tears well on the rims of her eyes, and she tries to play it off, but I notice her wiping her cheeks.

"I'm sorry for showing up unannounced. Laurel has Dawson's and your best interest in mind. She cares about you, but I gotta admit, you've got a lot of explainin' to do." I pause briefly until our eyes meet. "Like why it wasn't you tellin' me."

Chelsea looks around as if she doesn't want any of her neighbors to hear us. "Would you like to come in?"

Shaking my head, I rub my palms down my jeans. This whole situation is making me sweat.

Chelsea gives me a small smile and tilts her head toward the inside of her apartment. "I think it's time you met your son, Diesel."

My mouth falls open, and I lick my dry lips. "Okay," I muster, but my emotions are going haywire, a convoluted internal mess.

She opens the door, stepping aside for me to enter. I see my son sitting on the couch with a toy tractor in his hand, watching TV. He smiles at me but has no idea who I am.

"Hi," he says in a small voice. When he grins, an overwhelming amount of joy and fear rushes through me. I'm his dad. *Holy fuck*.

"Hey," I say, then look back at Chelsea who's standing with her hands in her pocket, but she seems happy. She nods for me to move closer to him, so I do. "What kinda toy do you have there?"

"This is my favorite tractor," he says, raising it up high where I can see it better. Then he waves it proudly, giggling as he hands it to me.

I sit down next to him on the couch, angling my body toward his. "You know, I have one like this at my house. A real one. A big green John Deere."

"You do?" he asks with wide eyes.

"Yep. I have lots of tractors actually." I pause briefly, then continue, "Maybe I can show you someday?"

He smiles when I hand it back.

"Yeah!" he shouts loudly, causing Chelsea and me to laugh. "I'm thirsty."

I swallow hard, not sure how to interact with a two-and-a-half-year-old. This feels like some weird reality show, and I'm waiting for Ashton Kutcher to come out and say "You just got punk'd!" But now that I see Dawson, as scary as it sounds, a part of me wants it to be true.

Chelsea walks into the kitchen, then returns with a sippy cup of water and hands it to Dawson.

"What do you say?" She gives him a pointed look.

"Thank you, Mommy."

"You're welcome, baby." She glances at me, then lowers herself to Dawson's eye level. "My friend and I are going to talk in the other room. Can you be a good boy for me and stay here for a bit?"

"Okay, Mommy," he says, then sits back with his cup.

I stand and follow her to a small breakfast nook. It's hard not to look around her quaint home where she's raising our son. While it's small, it's clean and perfect for them.

"You want some coffee?" she asks as she pours water into the top of the maker.

"Sure, that'd be great."

Chelsea's stalling, that's more than obvious, but I'm happy for it. Once the drip is finished, she grabs two mugs from the cabinet and fills them.

"Cream?" she asks.

"Nah, I'm good."

She hands it over, then sits in front of me once she's added milk and sugar to hers.

We sigh in unison, which causes us both to let out our nervous laughter.

"I don't really know what to say." Her words break through the silence. "Except that I'm pissed off at my sister."

"Why?" I ask.

"Because it wasn't my plan to ever find you. I didn't know anything about you except that you lived in Texas. You were a complete stranger to me, and it made the most sense to keep it that way given we only hooked up once. Guys like you have handfuls of one-night stands, and it's not like it meant anything to either of us. It was purely physical, and I was being realistic with my expectations of a twenty-one-year-old."

"Realistic?" My nostrils flare at her assumptions. "You were being *selfish*, Chelsea. I have a son—who's had birthdays and celebrated holidays—and I didn't get to take part in that. I don't care what your preconceived notions about me were, didn't you think it was my right to know? What about his right to know his father?" I lean over the table, keeping my voice low so I don't alarm Dawson.

She stares down at her coffee, not making eye contact with me. I can tell she's trying to find her words, and I understand me barging into her life isn't the easiest thing to deal with. Not to mention, I'm pretty fired up now that I'm here and see he's real.

"I don't know what my reaction would've been three years ago, but I deserved a choice at least," I add. "Instead, you made it for me."

"Diesel, I'm sorry." Chelsea's eyes finally meet mine, and I see a tinge of regret. "You have to put yourself in my shoes for a minute. I'm not the type of girl who meets a guy on vacation and hooks up with him. When I got home, I went on about my life and realized I missed my period. My sister forced me to take a pregnancy test; though after being sick for a week, I had a feeling I was. When it was positive, I had an ultrasound to confirm it. I saw the little flutter on the screen, and my entire life changed." She chews her bottom lip and shrugs. "I was scared."

"And you're sure I'm the father?" I ask gently.

"I hadn't been with anyone else but you at that time. The last guy I was with was over six months before we met in Vegas. I knew for a fact it was your baby, but all I had was a stupid nickname because we didn't share personal details about ourselves. I thought about asking Zoey since I knew she ended up with Riley, but then I started second-guessing myself. I didn't know how you'd react or if you'd care, and my heart wouldn't be able to handle it if you wanted me to abort or give up the baby. I also didn't want to be forced to co-parent with a complete stranger who I knew nothing about. So instead of risking it, I didn't say anything at all. I guess at the time, being a single mom was easier than the what-ifs of telling you. You living in Texas meant sharing him would be super complicated, not to mention confusing since you'd be in and out of his life, assuming you'd even want to be in it. I know I'm rambling, but I did what I thought was best for Dawson and being shipped between states wasn't the right thing for a little kid."

I put myself in her situation and think about how we'd only hooked up that one time and didn't know each other. I really do get why she'd have concerns about telling me.

"I can understand your situation, Chelsea. It must've been hard for you to make that decision, and while I wish you'd told me sooner, I can't fault you for putting his needs first"

"I'm not saying what I did is inexcusable, but I'm relieved you know now and can accept *why* I didn't reach out. I love Dawson more than anything—more than life itself—and the thought of a stranger taking him from me was terrifying. I didn't want to be something you *had* to deal with."

Nodding, I take a sip of my coffee, happy it's cooled some. "I'd never think that, but there was no way of you knowing that. It takes two to tango, but I'd never *take* him from you. If anything, at least, Dawson deserves financial support. Laurel said you're strugglin' to make ends meet."

She groans and shakes her head. "And I hate that she told you that too. The last thing that I'd ever do is come to you for money."

"I know, but if he's mine—"

"You doubt he is?" She pops a brow. "He's your mini twin, down to your cocky attitude too." She chuckles, and I laugh with her, remembering I was quite arrogant the night we met.

"I'd still like to get a paternity test done so there's no doubt in either of our minds. That way it's a fact, and he can legally get my support and benefits.."

"Alright, then what?" she asks calmly.

"Then I'll help support Dawson and find a way to see him more. If he's my son, I'd love to form a relationship with him. It won't be easy being in two different states, but we'll come up with some sort of arrangement, even if we have to wing it. I can fly here, and you can fly there. We'll take turns."

She immediately starts shaking her head. "I can't afford that, Diesel."

"I'll take care of it." I smile genuinely. "Seems like we're both in a predicament. You don't want to leave here, and I can't leave my home either. So we'll have to make do the best we can."

A long breath escapes her. "Okay."

"My return flight is in two days. If we can get the test done before I leave, then we can move forward together and figure out the details of what to do next."

She nods, and I feel good we've found common ground, regardless if it's still shaky. We don't make small talk, but instead, I finish my coffee and then stand to leave. I thank her for the hospitality, and we exchange contact information. After her number is saved in my phone, I tell her I'll look into a testing facility and send all the details as soon as I have them.

"I'm staying in a hotel down the road, so I'm not far if you need anything…" I say when she walks me to the door.

"Thanks."

Turning, I smile at Dawson who's happily bouncing around the living room to the music playing on the TV. "Bye, Dawson. See you soon!" I wave, and my heart melts a little when he waves in return.

The next two days fly by. We go to the lab for the blood tests, have lunch and dinner, and try to get to know each other between all the craziness. My thoughts are all over the place, and I can't seem to focus past the fact that in a week I'll find out for sure if Dawson's my kid or not. Though a part of me is hoping he is because after spending time with him, I'm already wondering when I'll get to see him again.

I'm grateful for the five a.m. flight because I need to get back to work and more importantly, back to Rowan. She's texted and called, but I haven't figured out a way to tell her this yet. I'm nervous about what she'll say, but mostly what this'll mean for our relationship. No doubt she's asked Riley and he told her I had an emergency. I just hope he didn't tell her everything.

As the plane takes off, my nerves get the best of me as reality sets in that I will have a lot of explaining to do. Telling her I got a random woman I met in Vegas pregnant three years ago and it's quite possible I'm his dad. It'll take a week for the results to come in, however, after seeing Dawson in the flesh, and hearing Chelsea wasn't with anyone else, there's really no doubt. Hopefully, Rowan will understand, and she doesn't think less of me for something I did years ago. I told her that wasn't my lifestyle anymore, and I'm ready to prove that, but now I'm worried she'll think the worst.

I can't even be that surprised this happened. Riley always warned me that my party life would catch up with me someday.

I haven't been that reckless since I was twenty-one, but it doesn't change anything now. Once I was promoted to oversee the cattle operation, I realized there was no room for that type of lifestyle anymore. Kicking women out of my bed at four a.m. was no fun when I had to be at work at the butt crack of dawn.

All I've wanted since discovering my feelings for Rowan weren't one-sided and that she had them too was to settle down with one woman and build a family with her someday. I just never imagined it'd be like this. It's as if the universe gave me an Uno reverse card as soon as things got serious.

Rowan deserves to be more than my best-kept secret, and I want the whole world to know we're together and that she's mine. But after she finds out the news of my new reality, she may write me off completely. I'm not sure my heart would ever be able to recover from losing Rowan Bishop, especially when there's no doubt she's my past, present, and future.

CHAPTER FOURTEEN

ROWAN

I LOOK DOWN at my phone, turn it off, then turn it back on to make sure it's still working. After I go into my messages, I see the last one Diesel sent, which was yesterday morning. Since then, he's been eerily quiet and not responded to anything I've texted. They've all gone unanswered. Every. Single. One.

Alarm bells go off in my head, and I can't help but feel doubt creep in. My heart tells me something's wrong, but I tell myself he's probably just busy on a job. There are times when he doesn't have his cell phone on him, so I try not to overreact, especially after the amazing weekend we just had, but my thirteen-year-old insecurities are resurfacing after not hearing from him. He already thinks I'm a crazy ex-girlfriend, considering what I did to Nick's Corvette, which has proven to be a big mistake. No taking it back now, though. What's done is done.

The next morning, I still have zero text messages from Diesel. While I'm concerned something happened to him, all I can think is if I said or did something wrong. We shared an amazing night away, and now he's basically ghosted me. It's exactly what Diesel promised never to do and everything my brother said he does. Unable to lie in bed any longer, I sit up and pull my hair into a high bun. I can hear Mom chatting with someone in the kitchen. *Riley.*

I jump out of bed and rush through the hallway because if anyone knows where Diesel is, it's him. Once they're done with their conversation, and Mom briefly walks away, I glance at my brother who's looking more grown up with every passing day. Dad life is being good to him, which is nice to see.

"Hey," I say, casually. I don't know how to even start the conversation without him getting suspicious, but I go for it anyway. "I haven't seen your stupid best friend around lately. Where's he been?"

He looks at me incredulously. "Why do you care?"

I clear my throat, finding my courage. "Well, Maize needed him to help her yesterday and couldn't get in touch with him, so I texted him this morning and got no reply too. Just wondering if he's being his typical asshole self when a lady needs a hand. It wouldn't be the first time." A part of me feels guilty as hell for making up another story, but it's the most believable thing I could come up with on the spot. Also, I can't blow my cover.

Riley picks up his coffee cup and takes a sip. "He's in Arizona seeing his kid, apparently."

I glare at Riley, who laughs, but I'm almost certain I heard him wrong. "What'd you say?"

He shakes his head, grinning as if he's about to tell me a hilarious story. "It's a crazy story. Remember when I brought him to Vegas for his birthday?"

I nod, trying to keep a straight face, not wanting to react, but my temperature feels as if it's rising. "What about it?"

"He hooked up with a chick while we were there, and her sister came to the ranch the other day and told him he had a kid. Showed proof or whatever. So yesterday he went to Phoenix to figure it all out. What a total fucking shitshow!" He continues laughing. "I've been joking with him about having baby fever since Zoey got pregnant. Who would've ever thought he'd actually have his own?"

I feel sick to my goddamn stomach, and I'm actually happy I haven't had the chance to eat anything yet. Undoubtedly, it would've come up. My world feels like it's spinning out of control.

Why the fuck wouldn't Diesel tell me this? Why wouldn't he share something so personal and intimate, something that will most definitely affect our current relationship? I spilled my heart to him, and this is what he does to me?

"You okay?" Riley looks at me, and I know I've gone pale.

"Yeah, I'm perfectly fine. Also, your friend's a dumbass, so it doesn't surprise me one bit he knocked someone up. That's what he gets for sticking his dick in random pussy. Probably has a handful of other children out there too."

Riley shrugs. "That's what I said. He said he'd be back in two days. Wouldn't shock me if he marries the girl and returns with a wife and a kid. He'd consider it doing the right thing, then they'll probably have another right away."

I really wish Riley would shut the hell up. "Gross."

Mom walks back in the kitchen and looks back and forth between us. My emotions are unstable, so I take the opportunity to leave the room. "Gonna go shower," I say, not giving them a second glance.

Scalding hot water actually sounds great right about now and will give me the privacy I need. I go to the bathroom, turn on the shower, and step inside after I undress. The streams pound against my skin as the tears roll down my cheeks. I lean against the wall, pissed at myself for falling so quick and hard.

Is that why Diesel didn't tell me? Does he plan to come back with a wife, but more importantly, what does this mean for us? Our future? I let out a ragged sob, realizing that maybe we never had one to begin with. My broken heart almost felt whole, but now it's shattering all over again.

I knew something wasn't right when he didn't answer my texts yesterday or send me one before he went to work this morning. In the end, I guess he got what he wanted, another mark on his bedpost with my name all over it. He's officially at the top of my shit list, right above Nick.

Two days have passed since my world turned upside down, and I know Diesel's supposed to return today. He still hasn't responded to me, and I refuse to be the fool who reaches out again. I'm hurt that he didn't feel like he could tell me what was going on in his life and left me hanging. Diesel's lost my trust, and I'm not sure he'll ever be able to get it back.

I go to work, and Kenzie immediately notices I'm in a bad mood.

"Oh shit," she mumbles when I knock over a full bottle of beer, and it spills everywhere. George isn't upset and laughs it off, but I soaked him.

"I'm so sorry," I tell him. "I'm not myself today."

"It's okay, honey. Just get me another one quick." He throws me a wink, and I do and don't even charge him for the next one either. It's the least I can do, considering his crotch will be wet for the next few hours.

"You okay?" Kenzie asks me when I walk into the office. "You've been acting weird for the past few days." She looks at me concerned.

"Yeah, just a lot going through my head right now. Nick

wants his money for the damage I did to his car. Like now. And I'm just not feeling like myself today."

"I've heard Mercury's in retrograde." She laughs and glances down at the mood ring I've kept on my finger since Diesel gave it back to me.

I take it off and tuck it in my pocket. I'm pretty sure it's broken anyway, considering it's been stuck on the "in love" color for weeks. Or maybe I'm broken.

For the rest of my shift, I try to keep myself busy and clean every single nook and cranny I can while Kenzie works the bar top. Wednesdays are typically a slow night, but thankfully, the time passes by quickly.

After all the customers pay their tabs, Kenzie mops and wipes everything down as I finish counting the money and closing the drawers. "How'd you do tonight?" I ask her.

"Okay. Fifty bucks is better than zero because that's what I walked in with." She gives me a smile. "Becoming a stripper seems like a better gig every single day."

"Your parents would murder you, and Grandma Bishop would turn your body into a rug."

She chuckles, then shrugs. "Oh well. I'd be walking out with thousands right now."

Now I'm laughing. "No, you wouldn't. The guys around here are cheap. But becoming a nun seems like a real possibility these days, plus no bills. So there's that."

"Do you think nuns masturbate?" She's grinning so wide, I can't help the burst of laughter that escapes from me. She's definitely put me in a better mood without even trying.

"Oh my God. I have no idea. Probably not. But then again, maybe?"

I grab the deposit bag, lock up, and we walk outside together. She follows me to the bank drop, and then we go our separate ways. On the whole drive home, all I can think about is Diesel and how it's been radio silence between us. He has to know I'm concerned by my messages, and still, he doesn't respond or give me reassurance on anything.

Bastard.

I pull into the driveway, then get out of my car. As I'm walking to the front door, a dark shadow comes toward me, and I immediately open my mouth to scream, but he comes into view as I retreat a step.

"I'm sorry, Rowan. I didn't mean to scare you," Diesel says softly, coming closer.

With all the pent-up frustration and anger from the past seventy-two hours, I close the gap between us and push him. He's a marble statue compared to me and barely budges.

"I'm sorry," he whispers, defeated.

"You're sorry for a lot of fucking things, aren't you?" I glare at him, and he tilts his head, almost as if he's confused. "Riley told me, dumbass."

I'm brought back to eighth grade again when he denied me, but this is that on crack. Right now, I just want to go inside, shower off the night, and go to bed. I need to forget about him, about us, though I have a feeling it won't be so easy.

"Can we talk at least?" he asks.

"Oh…" I sarcastically laugh. "Now you want to talk after blowing me off for two days? Wow, how convenient for you. Hmm, let me think about it. No." I walk around him, but he grabs my hand, pulling me back toward him. His warmth sends swarms of butterflies through my body. My head's saying no, but my body's saying yes. I have to be strong, though. There's no excuse for him ignoring me, regardless of the situation. I'd never do that to him, especially after the intimate moments and open conversations we've shared.

"Please, Row…" He drops down on his knees and begs.

I frown at his pitiful expression. "You do realize that if my dad comes out here, you're gonna be a dead man, right?"

"It's worth the risk to explain myself to you."

I let out a sigh. "You've got ten minutes of my time, then that's it. I'm leaving."

He looks around, the porch light casting a warm glow on his face. Diesel stands, and I take a step back before he grabs my hand and leads me down one of the trails behind my parents' house.

In the distance, there's a clearing where a four-wheeler is parked. No wonder I didn't see his truck. The moonlight splashes shadows on the ground, and the warm summer breeze brushes against my cheeks. I try to keep my attention from him and look up at the moon.

"Rowan," he whispers. "I have a lot to tell you."

"You better get to talkin' because your time is running out," I snap, finally gazing into his eyes, seeing the hurt and frustration in them. "Riley told me you got one of your random Vegas hookups pregnant. So how about we start from there?"

He nods. "Her name is Chelsea. Her sister, Laurel, wrote me a letter saying I had a son, but I ignored it and brushed it off as a joke."

My eyes widen with shock.

"I know, I know. I should've reached out to her, but I didn't. Not much I can do about that now. Anyway, Laurel showed up at the ranch a few days ago and explained her sister had a baby, and is certain it's mine. She's struggling financially to raise him, but thought I deserved to know I have a son."

I watch him fidget with the hem of his shirt. "Okay, then what?"

"I got her address and flew to Phoenix to figure it all out. It didn't seem like a conversation to have over the phone, especially if she didn't want me knowing in the first place."

"And? How'd that go?" My heart hammers in my chest.

"She wasn't happy to see me at first and was annoyed that Laurel reached out to me, but she came around to the idea of knowing. I told her I wanted to take responsibility if he was mine, so I took a paternity test while I was there. The results won't be back for a week, so I won't know for sure, but he's the spitting image of me."

Diesel's words gut me. As crazy as it sounds, a part of me wanted to be the only woman who gave him a child. I've thought about what it would be like to start a family with him. How many kids we'd have. How me and Riley's children would grow up together. It's almost as if I'm mourning my fantasy, something I thought about once I realized my feelings for him. Those dreams feel demolished now.

I nod, trying to keep my emotions from spilling out. If it's his son, I don't want to be negative about it and make him choose between a new relationship and being a dad. "Maybe it's better that it happened this way, you know? Maybe we were never meant to last, and it was another shitty way for me to learn that I shouldn't trust men and the empty promises they give me. Or maybe it's the whole better to have loved and lost than to have never loved at all kind of situation. Either way, you have a child and a family to take care of now, Diesel. I think it's best if you focus on that right now instead of us."

Diesel grimaces and shakes his head, actually looking hurt and surprised by my words. "Are you serious, Rowan? You're just gonna walk away?"

"Why wouldn't I be?" I glare at him. "You have a family to focus on now. There's no point in starting something new when you have unfinished business to take care of." I'm so hurt that nothing he could say right now could mend my heart.

"A *family*? I have a kid, not a wife. I don't want Chelsea. You know who I want? Who I've always fucking wanted? You, Rowan. *You*. You're the woman I dream about every single night and have since I was a teenager. I just finally got you, and there's no way I'm going to allow this to wreck what we have. I'm not giving up on you or us. I won't."

I cross my arms over my chest, retreating a step. While I

appreciate his effort, it's not enough right now. "I'm not getting in the middle of this, Diesel. You need to be there for your son. You need to build a bond with him because you haven't been in his life. And who knows, maybe once you and Chelsea are around each other, sparks will fly again. There must've been an attraction between you, or you would've never fucked her in Vegas. I'm not stupid, okay? Y'all connected enough to make a baby, so you need to focus on getting to know the mother of your child and co-parenting. Trust me when I say I'll only get in the way, and I don't want to live with that." The tears build, but I push them away. I will not allow him to see how much this actually pains me. I can't.

"I can do both, Row. I can be a father, and I can be with you." He inches closer. "Please, let me prove it to you."

I tighten my jaw, wishing he would allow me to just walk away. I knew it wouldn't be easy, but he's making this much harder than it should be. I know I'm doing the right thing, even if it's breaking me in the process, and he doesn't agree.

"I'm not sure about that. You never replied back to my messages, Diesel. You ignored me for nearly three days after the most amazing night we had together. That meant something to me, and then you basically ghosted me. If it hadn't been for my brother telling me, I would've thought something horrible happened to you. It made me feel like I was just another hookup, and it meant nothing to you. For hours, I racked my brain on what went wrong, but all along, it was you being selfish. I poured my heart out to you, which you know wasn't easy for me, yet you still didn't feel the need to tell me what was going on. The moment I found out the truth, from someone who wasn't you, is the moment *you* walked away. And that's okay. I'll be just fine, and so will you."

"I should've told you," he says. "For that, I'm so goddamn sorry. I was so scared this would ruin us, and it looks like I fucked it up anyway." He lifts his hat, runs his fingers through his hair, then sets it back on. "I'll spend the rest of my life making it up to you. What can I do to fix this?"

Blinking, I stare at his lips, then back to his green eyes. "At this point? Nothing." My mind's made up. "If he's your son, you'll be talking to her all the time, and what if you start seeing her differently or she starts having feelings for you? I'd constantly feel like I'm getting in the way of you being with your son and you two being a family. Then we all risk getting hurt, and I won't be the other woman in this scenario. I'm sorry, Adam." I turn and begin walking down the trail.

"Row," I hear him say, but I don't stop. "Rowan, please give me another chance." I keep moving forward, knowing I can't turn around because I may not be strong enough to deny his pleas. This is the right thing to do with what's going on in his life. Leaving him before he can leave me is what has to happen because deep down, it feels inevitable.

As I continue putting one foot in front of the other, tears begin to fall in streams. A week ago, I would've never imagined I'd be breaking it off with him, but here we are. From now on, I'll guard my heart with everything I am and not trust men so easily. Not even those who I've known nearly all my life.

CHAPTER FIFTEEN

DIESEL

It's been one week since the paternity test, and the results come right on time. I call Chelsea when I receive them to let her know. Dawson's mine, but after seeing him in the flesh, there were no doubts. He's a mini version of me, down to his eye color. When she gets off work later in the day, she calls me back.

"I was thinking that maybe you and Dawson could come out and visit the ranch soon," I suggest.

There's silence on the other line.

"Ya there?" I ask.

There's hesitation in her voice. "Yeah, I just don't know if that's a good idea."

"Chelsea, it's really important to me. I want him to know my roots, where I grew up, what I do for a living. Who knows, he might enjoy the ranch life much better than the city life anyway."

"No," she snaps. "See, this is what I was afraid of, that you'd expect me to uproot my entire life and move away from my family to Texas. Maybe this—"

"Hey. I'm not asking you to move here. I just want you to

visit for the weekend. I have a spare bedroom you two can stay in. I'll show you around the ranch and introduce you to my family and friends. I haven't told my parents yet, but I know they're gonna be super excited to know they're grandparents. They'll want to spoil him rotten."

She lets out a ragged breath. "Okay, but we can really only come for a weekend. I'll have to fly out late Friday afternoon after I get off work and leave Sunday. I don't have many vacation days left."

"I understand. Let me know the details, and I'll be happy to book it for you. And Chelsea?"

"Yeah?"

"Thanks for giving me a chance to be his father," I tell her.

"You're welcome. Thank you for wanting to be. He deserves a good man in his life."

"I know you're concerned about it and probably think me finding out is a mistake, but I'm gonna do the best I can. I really don't know how to be a parent, but I want my son to know me, and my life, and where he comes from. The last thing I want is for Dawson to grow up thinking he has a deadbeat dad who didn't want him." Because I most definitely do.

"I don't think it was a mistake. But it's still new for all of us, and I was blindsided by you just showing up. While I want Dawson to get to know you, I need to as well. There's so much that's in the dark right now. You're a stranger to me, Diesel. We had sex three years ago and haven't spoken or seen each other since. I don't even remember what we talked about beforehand."

I laugh. "So you're saying it wasn't monumental?"

She snorts. "Oh my God. Men. I'll look up the flights and let you know."

"Sounds good," I tell her. We say our goodbyes, and I end the call, then stare up at the ceiling of the kitchen. My life is a goddamn mess.

Instead of staying home, I decide to go to the B&B and see what Maize cooked for dinner. I'm starving, and her food is the best in all of Eldorado. Well, after Grandma Bishop's.

When I walk in, I spot Rowan who looks at me and immediately turns. She's still being distant and pretending I don't exist. If it weren't such a serious matter, I'd say it's cute, but I know better. I hurt her, and just as I promised, I'll spend the rest of my life trying to make it up to her, as long as she doesn't move on before I can.

The night we had together in San Angelo was unforgettable. Being with her in such an intimate way was everything I ever dreamed it would be and more, then in a snap, it was ruined. I should've told her what was going on as soon as I found out, but I didn't know where to begin. Would it have changed anything? I'm not so sure. Rowan acted like she was a homewrecker or something, which is insane because I don't even know Chelsea or want her. Rowan's the only woman I've ever wanted, and now she's slipped through my fingers.

"Hey," I say, looking at Maize, then glancing at Rowan.

"What're you doing here?" Maize asks with judgment in her eyes.

"Thought I'd stop and grab some dinner," I say truthfully.

Rowan continues on as if I'm invisible and speaks directly to Maize. "Well, I gotta go to work. I'll see you tomorrow." She walks away, and I can smell the hint of her shampoo as she leaves.

I try to act as if I'm not gutted, but it's hard as hell. I don't know what to say or do. No one besides Wyatt knew we were together, and if I acted any other way, they'd all become overly suspicious.

Maize glares at me as she tucks loose strands of hair behind her ear. Flour is on the sleeves of her shirt, and she looks like she's had a rough day. "Don't you know how to cook?"

"Grandma B told me I could help myself anytime I wanted.

Should I call her and ask?" I taunt. Maize knows her grandma gave an open invitation to all of the workers on the ranch.

She groans and walks away, mumbling something under her breath. I grab a plate, fill it full of beef tips, rice, and brown gravy, then I stack a roll on top of my delicious pile and find a seat. Riley walks in and looks at me. I tell him hey, but my mouth is full, and it comes out garbled.

He sits and glares at me. "You know why my sister's pissed all the time?"

I nod and swallow. "Maybe she's on her period?"

"Dude." He groans, but his eyes don't leave mine. It's more than obvious he's suspicious. "You sure you don't know?"

"Yeah, I'm sure. Why?" I press, taking a huge bite of meat.

"Last week, I told her where you were, that you had a kid and all of that, and she's been moody and strange ever since. I started piecing some things together." He leans forward. "Diesel, I swear to fucking God if you messed with my sister, I will chop off your dick and shove it down your throat."

"Jesus…" I say, not having the words to be able to deny it. "Why the hell are you threatenin' my junk?"

He narrows his gaze at me, looking as though he's ready to murder me and hide my body. "I'm serious. She was upset and distant. She's been so freaking odd since you got back, and I have a feeling the common denominator here is you. If I find out you touched her, I will kick your ass to San Antonio and back. I'm not even kidding."

"Riley. You need to chill out. Geez. First of all, Rowan is a grown ass woman who doesn't need you making rules for her. Second, I don't know what's going through her head right now. I try to talk to her, and she ignores me, but then again, what else is new?" I leave out the part where I've texted her every single day since our chat on the trail, and she's ignored all of them. Nothing can shake her stance on this, but I'm determined to break her down. I've done it once, and I know I can do it again.

Rowan's gonna have to try a lot harder to keep me away because I'm not giving up on her or *us*, ever. What we have is real, and we both know it.

He glares at me just as his uncle Jackson walks through the back door, causing a much-needed distraction from this conversation. "What're you boys doin'?"

"Eatin'," I say, but that much is obvious as I stuff another spoonful into my mouth.

"Don't tell Maize, but I came to get a few slices of apple pie. Mama told me she baked a few for the guests tonight, and I haven't been able to stop thinkin' about it." He grins, walks over to the buffet, and grabs an *entire* pan, not just a few pieces like he said. When he turns around, Maize is standing there with her hands on her hips and nostrils flared. She's actually pretty damn scary when she's in a mood.

"What do you think you're doing, Uncle Jackson?"

I snort, but she's seriously pissed.

"That's no way to speak to your most favorite uncle now, is it?" He gives her a wink, then walks past her and leaves.

Maize's mouth falls open, then she turns and looks at us. "This—all of this—is for the guests. I don't need y'all eatin' everything when we have a full house. I'm gonna have to start making double."

Riley snickers. "I don't know why you haven't done that already. Nothing's changed, Maze."

"Shut. Up," she barks, then storms into the kitchen.

"I'm telling you, they're all experiencing the time of month at the same time," I quip, and Riley shakes his head before standing.

"Guess I should get going. Honestly, I came to get one of those apple pies too." He walks over and grabs one, leaving only one for the guests. Maize comes around the corner, and Riley takes off running with her right behind him. I can hear commotion through the living room, and eventually, she comes back huffing and puffing.

"At least I'm not *that* bad," I tell her as she walks by.

"I'd murder you if you were. I deal with them because I have to," she says matter-of-factly before disappearing out of sight.

I chuckle, finish eating, and set my perfectly cleaned plate in the dish tub before leaving. On my way out to the truck, I decide to go home, take a shower, and go to bed early. I have a ton of shit to do at work tomorrow, and though it's hard, I'm trying to give Rowan some space.

The next day, I'm in the saddle all day long rounding up cattle and moving them to another pasture. It might be late August, but it's still hot as hell outside. The temperature isn't expected to drop for a few more months, but we're prepping for winter already. Barns are full of hay, and I've made sure to get extra grain for the cows for when the grass completely dies. Today, Riley didn't ride my ass or even mention his sister, so I'm hoping the conversation we had yesterday eased his mind. Though I didn't completely lie to him, it wasn't the whole truth, which I hate, but he can't find out yet.

While I don't want Rowan and me to stay a secret, if she refuses to give me another chance, that might be how it goes. Though it'll be extremely hard for me to accept.

After work, I go home to clean up, then head up to the bar. Rowan may not want to see me, but it's killing me not to see her. Even if she gives me shit or ignores me, it's better than nothing at all. I put on the baseball cap I know she loves, spray some cologne I also know she loves, and dress in a T-shirt, jeans, and boots.

As I pull into the parking lot, the thought of seeing her has my heart hammering in my chest. I wish things weren't like this, and we could go back to the way we were, but it feels impossible now. My life has changed indefinitely, and all I can do is take it one day at a time.

When I walk in, she's smiling and talking to George, and that pretty grin immediately fades when she sees me.

"Well, hello to you too, beautiful," I say, sitting at the end of the bar.

Kenzie walks up, wearing a cheesy grin. "Hey, stranger. Where ya been?"

I lift an eyebrow at her. "What's up with the act?"

She leans closer. "Rowan said she doesn't want to talk to you, so I'll be helping you tonight."

"Seriously?" I can tell Kenzie has this all figured out, but she doesn't say anything. Damn, maybe we're more transparent than either one of us thought. "Rowan!" I yell across the bar. "Hey!" I wave, making a scene.

"Go away, Diesel," she says before turning around and going to the office. I let out a huff.

"Told ya," Kenzie gloats. "Want your usual?"

"I guess." Within a few seconds, she pops the cap off a Bud and sets it in front of me. I try to pay attention to the preseason football game on the TV screen, but it's so hard to focus when the woman I'm in love with is dead set on erasing our existence together. I order another beer and wait around until closing time. Rowan peeks around to see if I'm still at the end of the bar and rolls her eyes when I smile at her. I feel as if we're back to square one, right where we were when she moved home in May.

There's no way she could so easily forget everything we shared together. I refuse to accept that one bit.

Kenzie finishes cleaning, and I close out my tab, tipping her nicely for putting up with me all night. She tells Rowan she's leaving and smiles before walking out. Rowan comes from the office and looks at me.

"You need to leave," she says, and I can tell she's not playing around.

"No can do. You'll be here alone." I just look at her, taking the final sip of my beer. "Are you gonna ignore me for the rest of my life?"

"That's the plan," she snaps.

"Row," I whisper.

"*Don't* call me that."

I stand and walk around the bar until I'm mere inches from her. Resting my hands on her shoulders, I stare into her beautiful brown eyes. She tucks her bottom lip into her mouth, and I want nothing more than to pluck it from her teeth.

"I've missed you so fucking much," I tell her, gently lifting her chin. "I can't stop thinking about you."

She lets out a ragged breath, and it causes my heart to race. Without hesitation, I lean forward and gently slide my lips against hers. Instead of fighting it like I thought she would, or pulling away, she sinks into me. Our tongues twist as the kiss deepens, and I feel as if the world has tilted on its axis.

Rowan grabs the hem of my T-shirt, and we're so goddamn ravenous for one another, by the time she pulls away, we're breathless. She places her fingers on her swollen lips, and I swallow as I move loose strands of hair from her face. "I know you're scared, and you think walkin' away from me is the right thing to do, but it feels so fucking wrong."

"Diesel…"

"I'm not letting you go without a fight, Row. Never."

It's been a few days since I kissed Rowan at the bar, but it was all the encouragement I needed to know that not all is lost. She kissed me back without a fight, which means I still have a chance with her.

After work, I send her a text, telling her I'm coming to the bar, and she sends me a thumbs-up emoji in response. Not quite the attention I was aiming for, but it's better than her ignoring me completely.

She's started responding and has been supportive for the most part, though she's still guarded. I have hope that once she realizes Chelsea and I have nothing between us other than my son, we can move forward. At least that's what I keep telling myself while taking it one day at a time.

I walk in, and she tries to hold back a smile. There's hardly anyone at the bar tonight because it's been raining all day. Honestly, I'd swim here if it meant getting to see Rowan. Kenzie's no longer in town because she went back to college to finish her last year, but things typically slow down when school starts anyway. I'm actually happy she's not around because it means I don't have to be as careful. It's obvious she knew something was going on, but Kenzie didn't say a peep if she did for certain.

Rowan sets a beer down in front of me, then looks past me out the large front windows where the rain is pounding against the glass.

"It's still raining?"

"Yep, not supposed to stop until the morning," I tell her, taking a swig. I place my hand on top of hers and gently brush my thumb against the softness of her skin.

"I was thinking maybe we should tell everyone we're together." I'm being dead serious, and she knows it.

Rowan hesitates. "It's a bad idea."

"It's the *best* idea," I quickly say.

She nervously shifts on her feet because I've put her on the spot. "Diesel. I need more time. I'm sorry. I can't just jump into bed with you again because you kissed me."

"You mean, just because I took your breath away?" I smirk.

She rolls her eyes. "I can't. Not right now. You need to get adjusted to everything that's going on in your life. Learn to be a dad. Then if there's still room in your heart for me, we can talk about it."

I tilt my head, grab her hand, and press it against my chest. "My whole heart is yours, Rowan Bishop. It always has been and always will be. I want the whole fucking world to know you're mine and only mine, regardless of everything else going on in my life."

A blush hits her cheeks before she moves away from me. I am relentless and will always be when it comes to her. I stay the entire shift and help her clean up before we walk out. On the way out, I tell her about Chelsea and Dawson coming to visit, and she gives me a small smile. I want to kiss her goodbye, but I'm hesitant to cross that line again. I'd wait an eternity for her if that's what she wanted.

That night, I go to sleep with a smile on my face, hoping she truly understands what she means to me.

The next morning, I get to work early. Riley calls me out on the way I'm acting, and he thinks it's because I'm picking up Chelsea and Dawson from the airport this afternoon. Little does he know it's because his sister makes me the happiest fucking man on the planet. But I am also very excited about showing off my son.

I asked Chelsea what kind of car seat I needed to buy because I'm seriously bad at this parenting thing. There are too many choices, and I had no clue where to start, but she happily guided me. Knowing they were coming, I tried to do as many of the repairs to the house as I could to childproof the place better. The spare room is ready for them with clean sheets and freshly painted walls. I've worked hard to get it all together, and I hope she appreciates it. I want her to trust me so she thinks I'm suitable enough to be Dawson's dad. Even though I have proof he's mine, I'd never fight her for custody, knowing what she's done to support him on her own. I can only hope one day we'll be able to co-parent properly and both have time with him.

On the way to the airport, my nerves get the best of me. Chelsea's right; we're practically strangers, so introducing her and Dawson to my parents will undoubtedly be awkward. Last night, I told them about how I met Chelsea and her getting pregnant. I gave them all the details, and at first, they were upset she didn't tell me, but I explained why Chelsea felt that way. I do wish she would've told me as soon as she knew, but there's no point in being mad about the past. What's done is done, so all I can do is try to make up for the lost time.

When I arrive, I wait for ten minutes before I see her and my son. As soon as Dawson sees me, he smiles, which makes me do the same as I grab all of their bags. He's such a cute kid and well mannered, even for a two-and-a-half-year-old. I just hope he's nothing like I was as a teenager, or we'll both have our hands full. I gave my parents a run for their money, and they always said I'd have a payback kid who did the same to me. Hopefully, Dawson isn't it, but he does have his dad's good looks, so I'm not holding my breath.

Once we get to my truck, Chelsea shows me how to buckle him into the car seat.

"Dawson?" She looks at him. "Do you know who this man is?"

"Mommy's friend, Diesel." He grins proudly.

"Yes, baby, but remember when I said he was someone very special? He's your daddy," she explains.

Dawson blinks up at me, then giggles. "Nuh-uh." I chuckle at his expression.

The amount of happiness I feel is unfathomable. I didn't expect for her to tell him right then, but I'm glad she did so I could be here for it. "Yep, it's true. What do you think about that?"

All he does is laugh about it, which makes us both chuckle too.

After he's buckled in with his toy tractor in his hand, Chelsea and I climb in the truck. We head back to the ranch, and I explain some of the details of the area to her. The sun is barely setting over the horizon, and the sky has long whips of purple and pink. It doesn't take long before Dawson is happily asleep. I can't stop glancing at him in the rearview mirror, feeling overwhelmingly protective of him. I'm still in shock he's really mine.

When we make it to my cabin, Chelsea gets out and gently carries Dawson as I grab their luggage. I unlock the door and usher her inside. Chelsea looks around with a smile on her face. "Wow. This is not what I expected at all."

"You like it?" I ask. "It's not completely finished. I still have a lot to do, but I've been remodeling here and there on my days off."

There's a sparkle in her eye as she follows me to the spare bedroom. "It's really homey. I like the colors."

"Thanks." I set their bags down. "If you need anything, please let me know. The bed and breakfast is just down the road if you want a home-cooked meal, and I can borrow extra blankets if needed."

She sets Dawson on the bed, and he doesn't even stir. "I think everything is perfect. Really."

"Great. You hungry?" I ask.

"Nah, I ate before the flight. Just want a shower and to probably go to bed. I think the time change is going to catch up with me."

I nod and show her where the bathroom is and give her a mini tour of the place. When she goes to take a shower, I sit in the rocking chair I put in the corner of the spare bedroom and watch Dawson sleeping peacefully. My heart swells watching him, and I already don't know how I'm going to continue without getting to see him. I just hope everyone falls in love with him as quickly as I have, especially Rowan, because I know she's gonna be in both of our lives forever. Even if she's not convinced at the moment, she will be.

CHAPTER SIXTEEN

ROWAN

It's insane to think that Diesel has a son. He asked everyone to meet at the B&B so he could introduce the group of us to Chelsea and Dawson. I'm nothing but a ball of nerves, and I thought about not going. Seeing the woman he had a one-night stand with isn't really on my to-do list, but it's important to him, so I suck it up and push my feelings to the side.

"You coming?" my mother asks as she peeks into my room.

I shrug. "Do I really have to?" I'm only half-joking.

"Rowan, you better get in that car. You know Adam is a part of the family, and we have to be supportive of him."

"Fine," I say between gritted teeth. "But I don't wanna go."

She gives me a stern look, and I know better than to cross her, so I get up and follow her to the car. I hate the unknown of what it's going to be like, seeing him with his son and Chelsea or how seeing them around each other will feel like. What if they're flirty? Or worse, what if they look really good together? I don't want my jealousy to get in the way, though it undoubtedly will. The five-minute drive to the B&B has my stomach in knots, but I play it off as if I'm bored as hell instead.

I get out of the car, make my way up the steps, and walk inside to see Diesel holding a toddler who looks just like him. My mouth falls open, and my heart instantly swells when I see him. He hasn't noticed me yet because my uncles and aunts have his full attention.

Riley walks in behind me as Mom rushes forward.

"Isn't this some crazy shit?" He nudges me.

"Uh, yeah. Can't believe he reproduced."

"Reproduced or that someone actually slept with him?" Riley jokes, but I'm not laughing because at that moment I see her. *Chelsea.* And she's pretty. Blond with a perfect smile and bright blue eyes. There's a softness to her, and I see what Diesel saw, even if it was a random hookup. Immediately, a pang of envy and guilt rushes through me.

I watch the way they interact, and it's friendly, not crossing any lines beyond friendship. She says something, and he laughs as his little boy shows everyone his toy tractor. Grandma Bishop's tickled to death over him, and it's only going to get her started on wanting more great-grandkids. *Great.*

Mom waves Riley and me forward, and for the first time all day, Diesel sees me. He swallows, and it feels as if all the air in the room escapes, and I can't breathe.

"Rowan," he says, knowing my entire family is around and watching. So is his baby mama. "Come and meet Mr. Dawson."

I follow and tilt my head at one of the cutest little boys I've ever seen. "Hi, Dawson," I say, and he hides his face in Diesel's shoulder.

"Pretty ladies make him shy."

I shake my head and roll my eyes at him even though my heart's actually bursting. Seeing him being all fatherly is actually pretty sexy, but then I turn my head and notice Chelsea staring at our interaction.

"Oh hi," I say. "I'm Rowan." I hold out my hand and shake hers.

"Nice to meet you." She's polite and grins. I can only imagine how awkward this is for her to be around so many strangers, and I really try to imagine myself in her place.

I get out of the way and let my mom and dad visit. The living room is full of Bishops. Not wanting to draw any attention to myself, I sit on the couch on the other side of the room and listen to everyone talk.

"Was your mama excited to meet him?" Grandma asks Diesel.

He laughs. "Oh, of course. She's been on me like white on rice to give her some grandchildren. Little did any of us know, I already had." He's making jokes, and I hear my parents' laughter because it's actually not too different from their story. My mouth goes dry because my parents are still insanely in love with each other.

I try to zone out and ignore everything around me and dig deep. Is it possible for Diesel and me to actually make this work?

It literally feels like it's one hundred degrees in here, so I get up and step outside, needing the fresh air before I suffocate. Right now, I feel like the other woman, the mistress who has to hide her relationship.

My mom told us she and Dad had to really get to know each other after finding out she was pregnant with Riley even though they knew immediately when they met in Key West that they had an undeniable connection. Is this the same? Is it only a matter of time before Diesel and Chelsea's spark re-ignites and those old feelings are brought back to the surface? It's not out of the realm of possibilities regardless of what Diesel says. He hasn't spent enough time with her to know and surely hasn't given it a chance.

I lean against the railing of the front porch and look out at the bright blue sky and fluffy cotton-looking clouds.

My phone vibrates in my pocket, and I see it's a text from

Trace. We had planned a few months ago to get together and our schedules never really synced. I appreciate how he's not so pushy and gives me my space. Then again, I do like a pushy man. Diesel's a prime example of that.

Trace: Hey you! You got plans this weekend?

I laugh and shake my head. Is this the way it's supposed to be? I look up at the sky again, waiting for some sort of sign, but I'm given nothing. Maybe I'm supposed to be with Trace, and Diesel's supposed to be with Chelsea, or maybe I've quite possibly completely lost my mind over all of this.

Maize comes outside, looking at me incredulously. "You good?"

She's suspected something has been going on between Diesel and me for a while but hasn't asked about it. I'm praying she doesn't, either, because I'm not emotionally stable to have that conversation right now.

"Why wouldn't I be?"

She shrugs and doesn't push the conversation, thankfully.

"I need to get ready for work tonight, so Mom needs to stop gabbing and take me home."

"Good luck with that," Maize says, and before walking back inside, she stops. "You know you can tell me anything. I won't judge you or say a peep."

I search her face, and my expression softens. "I know. Thanks."

"I've noticed how different you've been. I saw you leaving the barn with Diesel, and I can't deny how things changed between you two. You're one of my very best friends, Rowan. I know you inside and out."

I let out a ragged breath, not wanting to completely crumple, but I don't feel like I can hold it in anymore. "I'm in love with him. Stupidly in love with him. And now he has a kid and might as well have a wife. They already look like the perfect little family."

She searches my face but doesn't seem shocked. "Does he know this? Have you told him?"

"I mean, sorta. Not in those exact words, but he knows I have feelings for him. We were sneaking around before the news broke about Dawson and Chelsea," I admit.

Maize sighs and frowns. "He's been in love with you since the beginning of time, Rowan. Everyone knows this. Even Riley as much as he wants to deny it. I'm actually relieved you have finally pulled the blinders back and see what's been right in front of you for so damn long." She smiles.

I'm shocked. Speechless, actually. I open my mouth and close it, which causes Maize to laugh.

"All those years, he threatened every guy to stay away from you, and you never noticed he wasn't interested in anyone else. He's been waiting for *you* for years," Maize tells me.

I adjust my ponytail. "I don't know what to do, Maze. I have no idea. I feel completely lost even though he's spilled his heart to me and told me how he feels. He wants us to be together forever and already talks about what our future will be. "

She places her hand on my back. "Then what the hell are you waiting for? Sounds like everything you've ever wanted."

I shrug and laugh as a tear falls down my cheek. "A sign?"

"If you're looking for a sign, you found it. Here it is." She places her palm over my racing heart. "You need to go for it so you don't look back years from now and regret not being with a man who will treat you like the queen you are and worship the ground you walk on. Hell, he already does that," Maize says matter-of-factly. "I'm actually quite jealous." She smirks.

Before I can respond, my mother opens the door and steps outside. "Ready?"

"Yep, sure am." I wipe my face and tuck my emotions back inside.

Maize gives me a big hug and whispers in my ear, "Follow your instincts. They'll always lead you to where you're supposed to go."

I pull away from her and smile appreciatively. "I love you."

"I am your favorite cousin for a reason, you know." She snickers, then walks inside.

Mom and I get into the car, then she drives us home. "Apparently, Maize is making homemade blueberry pies tonight. You should ask her to make an extra one for you and bring it home for me and your dad," Mom suggests with a wink.

"Nope. I'm not gonna make her head explode. You'll have to ask her yourself," I tell her as we park in the driveway. I get out and walk to my room, then send Diesel a text.

Rowan: Your kid is the cutest. He must take after his dad.

I don't expect him to reply immediately because he's currently being Bishop bombarded, but I know he will later. I change into something more comfortable and get ready for my shift tonight with a totally different outlook on this situation. Maybe I should've opened up to Maize much sooner instead of keeping it a secret. Or maybe I had to realize how much Diesel really meant to me before I could accept that we really have a future together. Either way, I'm looking forward to telling him exactly how I feel and apologizing for ever doubting him. Then again, that's what a broken heart will do to a woman.

The next morning when I wake up, I smile at the text Diesel sent me late last night.

Diesel: I knew you thought I was cute. Just imagine what our kids will look like :)

With a smile on my face, I climb out of bed and get dressed. I know Chelsea's leaving today because yesterday before I walked out, I overheard someone ask her when she was headed back to Phoenix.

After speaking with Maize yesterday, the conversation has been on my mind. For most of my life, one of my hobbies was ignoring Diesel and all his glory, regardless of how much he encouraged me to give him attention. I realize now what I've been missing. I have to give it to him for never giving up on me.

Excitement and nerves fill me as I pull my hair into a high ponytail. I need to talk to him right now and let him know how I feel. If he wants to be with me, and I want to be with him, then I don't give two shits what anyone thinks or says about it. If Riley knows what's good for him, he'll keep his opinions to himself. I'm a grown ass woman who's more than capable of choosing who I want to date, even if it is his best friend. If what Diesel says is true, then he deserves a second chance to prove he won't break my heart.

The smile that's planted on my face nearly hurts as I drive

over to Diesel's house. All the memories from the last time I was here begin to surface. The way he roughly said my name as he kissed me causes goose bumps to trail up my arm. Damn. How could I be so blind?

I park behind his truck and walk up the steps to his house. He's done an amazing job with the place, and I think about all the future plans we made together. I lightly tap on the door, not wanting to disturb his guests because it's still early in the morning. I wait, but he doesn't answer.

My heart is like a ticking time bomb in my chest as I knock again, but still nothing. I go to the front window and peek inside and that's when the blood rushes from my face.

Diesel's sitting at a barstool in the kitchen, and Chelsea is between his legs, nearly ready to climb on his lap. He's saying something to her with his hands firmly wrapped around her waist. I nearly choke on my thoughts, on my words, and feel like the biggest idiot in the entire world for believing that nothing was between them. Not able to keep watching, I turn and rush to my car, then back out of the driveway. I know I can't go home like this. Tears stream like a river down my face, and I'm so damn mad at myself for believing him.

I drive around for twenty minutes in an effort to calm down, needing to push the thoughts of him and her together out of my head. Their faces were inches apart, and Chelsea was leaning forward as if they were going to kiss. Maybe they already have? Maybe the two of them just had a morning quickie as their kid slept in the next room. The thoughts gut me and cut me straight to the bone.

I pull over at one of the lookouts and stare at the rolling hills until my vision blurs. Sucking in a deep breath, I wipe the tears away and text Maize.

Rowan: I was wrong about everything. Seeing Chelsea all over Diesel was the biggest sign of all.

Text bubbles immediately pop up, but I set my phone down and decide to finally go home. Thankfully, I'll have the house to myself because right now, I need to be alone.

CHAPTER SEVENTEEN

DIESEL

HAVING my son on the ranch with me has been everything I've ever dreamed of. Chelsea has been kind enough to let me have some time with him while she supervised from a distance. I showed him the big John Deere tractor, which he got a complete kick out of because it looked just like his favorite toy. I sat him on the seat, and he screamed with excitement. I made sure to snap a picture with plans to frame it. When I looked over my shoulder at Chelsea, she was smiling wide.

Even if he's a little shy, he has the same little quirks I did when I was a kid, but I think over time, he'll get to know me better and will open up more. Maybe even call me dad one day. So far, he hasn't, but that's okay. I'm sure he's just as confused as to what's going on as I am. Everyone knows where he came from, and that's enough right now.

I'm stuck between a rock and a hard place because I want to be involved in his life as much as I can, but Phoenix is too far to drive every weekend. Chelsea agreed to FaceTime me after work throughout the week so Dawson and I can talk regularly. I've also decided to try to visit him at least once a month if I can get off one weekend a month for the twelve-hour drive.

The second night Chelsea was here, I finally got her to open up about what she needed so I can help support Dawson. I'll do whatever she needs to make sure Dawson doesn't go without.

My parents were over the moon excited about having a grandkid, and I saw the instant love in my mother's eyes. She called me later that day with all sorts of stories about how I acted when I was Dawson's age.

Chelsea and I have found common ground and get along quite well, so I'm hopeful it'll be easy to work together. I've gotten to know her a little better and found out she works as a teller at a bank and hopes to one day become a loan officer. Most of the time, she's living paycheck to paycheck but has somehow made it work. I guaranteed her she'd no longer have to worry about buying whatever he needs.

The next morning, I wake up and go to the kitchen to make coffee. I have the day off and want to spend as much time with Dawson as possible before I have to take them to the airport this afternoon. As the maker stops dripping, Chelsea comes into the kitchen and pours herself a mug and leans against the counter.

"Mornin'. You sleep okay?" I ask.

She nods, then saunters closer.

She parts my legs and stands between them, leaning forward with lust in her eyes. There's nowhere for me to go, so instead, I firmly place my hands on her hips to stop this from going anywhere.

"Chelsea…" I quietly say, not wanting to disturb Dawson sleeping.

She gives me a side grin and bats her long lashes at me. "What?" she purrs. "We're both single."

"No." I shake my head. "I'm dating someone, and even if I weren't, I don't think it'd be a good idea. The last thing I want to do is confuse our son while trying to build a solid relationship with him. It's important to me. Plus, you and I hardly know each other and look at what happened the last time we jumped into bed together."

Defeat washes over her face. "Ouch. That hurts."

"I'm sorry," I tell her, hoping she understands. "I think you're nice and very pretty, but even if I were available, I wouldn't want to cross that line."

Chelsea backs away, creating the much-needed space between us. "Who is she? Why isn't she around then?" I try to keep my voice calm as I explain. "It's a new relationship, and we're keeping it under wraps at the moment. We haven't told anyone yet."

She rolls her eyes. "You don't have to lie."

"I'm *not* lying, but it doesn't matter anyway. I've grown up, Chelsea. I don't sleep with women just to do it. There has to be some sort of spark there. Any man would be lucky to have you, but it can't be me because I don't have feelings for you that way. I'm madly in love with someone else."

She releases a long, deep breath. "I can respect that, Diesel. Most guys would just use me. Sorry. I must look so desperate. I just thought things were going well, and there was a connection between us, but I shouldn't have assumed."

"There *was* a connection three years ago, and we made a beautiful kid, but being friends and raising our son is all that can be between us now."

She walks to the fridge, grabs some milk, and pours it into her coffee. "Do you have sugar?"

I know she's trying to change the subject, so I give her the escape. The last thing I wanted to do was embarrass her, but I can't cross that line, not when Rowan means so much to me. What I said to Chelsea is true—I'm in love with another woman. I'll be damned if I let my dick fuck that up any more than it already has.

Chelsea excuses herself and takes a shower. Once she's out and dressed, she brings Dawson into the living room. I make him scrambled eggs and add some fruit to his plate. Chelsea puts milk in a small cup, and he sits at the table in a booster chair like a big boy. He's talkative this morning, which I find adorable.

After he's done and Chelsea has changed his clothes, I ask if I can take him to the horse barn, just me and him.

She looks at me as if she's contemplating it but is still hesitant.

"Pretty please?" I beg with a grin. "I swear on my life that I won't let anything happen to him. It's safe as can be, and we're not going too far. Just to the horse barn at the B&B, right up the road."

She forces a smile and nods. "Okay, but only for a couple of hours. He'll need a nap before we travel. Otherwise, he'll be cranky on the flight, and I don't want anyone throwing me dirty looks."

I can't stop grinning. "Yes, of course. Thank you!"

Chelsea gives me a list of things to do. "Make sure he's buckled in the car seat really well. Don't let him out of your sight because he will take off running. If he—"

"Hey," I say, calmly. "He's gonna be fine. I won't let him run wild. I promise. Trust me, okay?"

"I have issues with trust. I'm sorry," she admits, and I feel for her in the same way that I feel for Rowan.

"I understand, completely."

She picks up Dawson and explains to him what's happening, and for the first time, he reaches for me. I hold him into my arms, and we go outside. Chelsea decides to help me buckle him in and continues with instructions. I squeeze her shoulder and grin. "He's in great hands."

"Not the first time I've heard that from you." She laughs, our eyes meet, and then she takes a step back, allowing me to shut the door.

I climb inside the truck and wave bye before backing out of

the driveway. During the ten-minute drive to the B&B, I chat with Dawson about ranch life. I tell him about the horses and then find myself talking about Rowan. He listens carefully, though I know he has no idea what I'm saying, but that's okay. One day, he will.

I park in front of the B&B, and I take him straight to the barn where the lessons for the guests are held. There are several horses saddled, which means Colton, one of the instructors, probably has some scheduled for the ten o'clock hour.

Carefully, I set Dawson on one of the ponies and support him so he won't fall. These horses are for beginners, so they're very gentle. He giggles and keeps leaning forward to pet the horse. It's the cutest thing ever. This is a part of his heritage, and I'm determined for him to know that. It hurts my heart that he won't get to grow up on the ranch, something I always wished I had. Seems he might get the city life too, unless I can somehow convince Chelsea to give Texas a chance, but as of now, she's not on board. I'll have to do what I can with what she's willing to give.

After we've been outside for an hour, I notice Dawson is sweating, so I bring him inside the B&B to cool off. I place him in one of the high chairs, grab some water, and then snag one of Maize's incredible chocolate chip cookies. I hold the cup for him so he can drink, then he gobbles the cookie with a smile on his face.

Feeling parched as well, I pour some water for myself but don't take my eyes off Dawson. An older lady chats with him, and he brags about the pony he rode, pointing outside. My heart's overflowing, that is, until someone smacks me in the back of her head with their hand. When I turn and see Maize, she gives me a scowl.

"What the fuck is wrong with you?" she whisper-hisses, trying not to draw attention to herself.

CATCHING THE COWBOY

"What?" I lift my ball cap and rub over the spot she smacked. "Why'd you hit me?"

"You're an idiot, Diesel," she says between gritted teeth.

"What else is new?" I ask with a shrug, but I have no idea what she's referring to this time. Then again, it's not uncommon for her to call me names.

"Rowan told me everything. *Everything*. And then you went and messed things up. She told me what she saw this morning." She cocks her hip, placing her hands on them.

I search her face, confused. Rowan told her about us? "What are you talkin' about? Saw what?"

"Rowan went to your house this morning to talk to you. You didn't answer the door so she looked through the window and saw Chelsea wrapped up in your arms." Maize shakes her head, grimacing. "I was rooting for you, too." She sarcastically laughs. "Riley's gonna lose his shit. I ought to kick your ass myself for leading her on."

My eyes go wide, and I start to panic at what Rowan must've seen before I pushed Chelsea away. "It wasn't like that. I *swear*."

"And to think Rowan wanted to come clean to everyone about your relationship, too. But you fucked it up," Maize grits. "You ruined *everything*."

"Come clean about what relationship?" Riley asks from behind, and I close my eyes, wishing this wasn't happening right now. I turn around and see him and John staring like they're ready to murder me.

"Please let me explain…" I hold up my hands, hoping he'll take mercy on me since I'm here with my son and there are guests around.

Riley's tight jaw and daggers tell me he doesn't give any fucks about that. "I warned you, Diesel." He fists his hands in my shirt and pushes me against the wall. Maize squeals, telling Riley to take it outside, but he's too pissed to listen. "I warned you to stay the fuck away from my sister. And now I'm gonna punch your pretty face in for hurting her. I knew you'd do this. You just couldn't stay away, could you? Just wouldn't feel content until you hurt my sister, the way I always knew you would." Before I can get a word in, Riley rears back and punches me in the face. I try to block it, but he's too fast. If it were any other person in the world, I would've laid them out flat, but I don't fight him back. I can't.

"Hey!" I hear a woman's voice shout.

"Mama," Dawson says, holding his arms out. She takes him from the high chair and kisses his cheek.

"What's going on here?" Chelsea asks, walking toward the group of us, and Riley retreats, putting space between us.

"What are you doin' here?" I ask, holding a hand to my face. I'm gonna have a black eye now. "And *how* did you get here?" I'm actually shocked to see her. I hope she didn't walk because that's miles down a dirt road, and it's hot outside.

"I might be from the city, but I know how to drive a four-wheeler, Diesel." She laughs. "Truthfully, I got nervous. This is new territory for me, and I just wanted to check on Dawson for my own sanity."

She notices my face fall, but I don't blame her. This is new territory for us all.

"It's nothing against you. He's around strangers and an unknown environment, and I started to worry. I just needed to see him and make sure he was safe."

I nod. "I understand, it's okay. He was having a good time. He saw the horses, and then we stopped in here for a snack and water."

Dawson begins to tell her about the pony. "Hold on, baby, one second."

Chelsea looks at all of us.

Maize is annoyed and crosses her arms over her chest. "Glad your girlfriend could show up and save your ass."

Riley is ready to beat me to a pulp, and John is overly annoyed because we caused a scene…*again*.

I look at Chelsea. "Rowan saw us together this morning."

Her face drops. "Oh no. I'm so sorry," she says to me, then looks at everyone. "Whatever you think happened between Diesel and me this morning didn't and was one hundred percent my fault," she explains. "I made a move, but he stopped me, then admitted he was dating someone. It's all a really big misunderstanding, honestly. There's nothing between us," she says, and I'm so damn thankful she's here because they wouldn't have believed me, thanks to my past. Riley's still tense and so is John. Maize's eyes soften, though.

Silence cuts through the room as my heart erratically beats. I never thought Rowan's and my relationship would be announced like this, especially since she's not even here, but I'm glad the news is out there finally. Assuming she'll give us another chance, I'll fight to prove how much she means to me.

"Is that the truth?" Riley asks me.

"I swear. I would never do anything to hurt Rowan, man. I'm in love with her and have been for years. She's the only woman I've ever felt that way for. I love her," I confess, then wait for Riley to say something. But the only sound heard is a loud gasp behind us.

We turn around, and that's when I see Rowan standing at the top of the staircase, looking as beautiful as ever with her hair down and pushed to the side. Her eyes are bloodshot, like she's been crying. I fucking hate knowing I upset her. She stares at us, and I know she heard what I said by the shocked expression on her face. I'm not sure if it's because of what I just said or the fact Riley knows about us now. Either way, I'm in love with her, and I want the whole goddamn world to know.

CHAPTER EIGHTEEN

ROWAN

Maize refused to let me go home to an empty house for the rest of the morning, though I had every intention of doing so. She threatened to come over, but she had work to do. So instead, she suggested I hang out at the B&B and even bribed me with my own personal breakfast full of strawberry pancakes, bacon, eggs, and homemade hashbrowns.

One thing's for certain—if Maize Bishop ever volunteers to cook something special for you, you do not deny her. It'll be one of the best meals of your life. She should open her own restaurant but enjoys working for the family too much. Maize acts modest, but she one hundred percent knows she could win contests with her food, and people drive over an hour away to eat it.

When I arrive, she's wearing an apron with her name embroidered across the chest. Her dark hair's in a high bun, and though she's smiling, there's also a sad look in her eyes. She pulls a tall barstool up to the prep table and pats it for me to sit as she prepares my breakfast. She listens to me spill my truths as she shreds a potato, mushes fresh strawberries into the batter, and warms the skillet. It doesn't take long before I have a beautiful picture-worthy plate of yummy food to eat. I didn't realize how hungry I was until she put it in front of me. I'm happy we're alone, and I can speak so candidly about what's happened over the past few months. It feels good to tell someone because I've kept this tucked deep inside for way too long.

"I'm so upset, Maze. Diesel hurt me more than Nick ever could, and I think it's because I didn't actually love Nick. I was just infatuated with the thought of us being together, though he never treated me right. I was always too much for him to handle, and he tried to mold me into something I wasn't—a housewife. I've never felt so defeated in my life. Diesel likes me for who I authentically am. I didn't have to pretend to be anyone other than myself around him. Do you have any idea how that feels? To be yourself in front of a man because that's what he loves about you? I actually feel sick talking about it," I explain. She pushes my plate closer and hands me some syrup she hand mixed.

I force a smile and take a bite. It's comfort food at its finest.

"I'm gonna chop off his balls and make a gumbo out of them, then I'm gonna make him eat the whole damn pot."

I snort. "You wouldn't."

"I would, and I am. He better not show his stupid face in the B&B for the rest of his life, or we're gonna have words," she threatens, snagging a piece of my bacon, but I can't even be mad about it. She made way too much anyway, but that's just how it is here. Full plates are an everyday occurrence.

"First, he strings you along and gets you to have sex with him. Then his baby mama just shows up with his kid in tow, and he screws her too? This is such bullshit. I'm livid right now." She grabs a butter knife and holds it in her fist. I take it from her hand and set it down on the table.

"Has anyone ever told you how scary you are?" I giggle-snort, and I'm so happy to be spending time with her. She's right, going home would've done me no good. I would've just sulked and felt like total shit the rest of the day. Maize makes me feel a little better about the whole situation.

She shrugs. "A few times. Just don't mess with my feelings, food, or my family, and everything will be just fine."

"Noted, but you not wanting us to eat the food at the B&B really isn't fair. You know it's addicting, but then you don't want us to eat it. Pretty mean if you ask me," I say, stuffing my mouth full.

"Says the person who got their own personal breakfast buffet this morning." She snickers.

"Also, you make it sound like Diesel made me sleep with him. It takes two to tango, and trust me when I say I'll be thinking about the times I had with him for the rest of my life—even if I hate him. No man has ever…" I whisper, keeping my voice low. "Pleasured me the way he did."

She blushes. "It was that good?"

"Better than good. Mind-blowing. So I can see why Chelsea came back." I frown, swallowing down my food. "I really thought what we had was more than that. I believed we had something special. Maybe I was nothing more than a forbidden fuck," I tell her.

"You're much more than that, Rowan. I honestly can't believe any of this because of the way he's always acted when it comes to you. Something isn't right, but if you saw them together, I will believe you any day of the week."

"I know. It doesn't add up, especially when he was dead set on announcing to everyone we're together just a few days ago. Maybe it's my fault? Maybe I pushed him away?"

Maize shakes her head. "No, he's just a man slut. That's all."

I yawn and realize I'm still tired from last night, plus I'm emotionally drained from what I witnessed today. I need a nap.

"Why don't you go upstairs and rest? Our favorite room has no guests in it right now," she suggests.

"The purple room?" I laugh.

"Mm-hmm. Bed's made and waitin' for ya. I'm gonna have to start preparing lunch soon."

"Whatcha making?" I ask as I finish picking at my plate until it's nearly empty, but I literally can't take another bite, or she'll have to roll me up the stairs.

"Grandma's Southern chicken salad sandwiches."

My eyes go wide. "With homemade sourdough bread?"

"Yep." She nods and laughs. "I'll make extra for you."

"You love me so much," I tell her, standing.

We exchange a hug. "I do, and it's not just because we're gonna become nuns together."

I roll my eyes, thank her for listening to me, then head upstairs. When we were kids, we'd get lost playing in the B&B. It holds so much history and happy memories. We'd use to take our Barbies in here and pretend it was our house. It's almost fitting that it's the only room available at the moment.

I walk inside and lie on the tall four-poster bed. My heart hurts, and I'm not sure anything could heal it at this point. After rolling over onto my side and staring out at the blue sky for nearly an hour, tears well and then fall in streams. I really thought we had a future together, but I was so wrong. My eyes feel heavy from crying, and somehow, I eventually fall asleep. When I wake up, I smell the bread Maize's baking, and though I'm still full from earlier, I could eat her cooking again.

I step into the hallway and immediately hear commotion at the bottom of the stairs. My pulse races when I see Riley reach back and sock Diesel right in the jaw. Surprisingly, Diesel doesn't try to retaliate against him. Though if I were willing to bet, I think he could take Riley. He's nearly double his size, but then again, Riley does have some strength behind him.

Before I can break it up, Chelsea walks in and admits what happened this morning. She made a move on him, and he denied her. I must've walked away before that happened, too upset to continue spying.

"Is that the truth?" Riley asks.

"I swear. I would never do anything to hurt Rowan, man. I'm in love with her and have been for years. She's the only woman I've ever felt that way for. I love her," Diesel admits.

All I can do is gasp, then cover my mouth. They turn and look at me before I can disappear. My timing is terrible today. My words and thoughts, everything has completely escaped me.

"Rowan?" Diesel says, walking toward me and searching my face. He feels the same way I feel about him, and I'm so fucking happy that I could cry *again*.

He stalks toward me, climbing the stairs two at a time until he's a step below me. "Hey." He grabs my hand. "I'm so sorry you saw that. It's not what—"

"Did you mean it?" I whisper, interrupting.

That boyish grin that I love so much sweeps across his perfect lips. "I've been in love with you for quite some time now, baby."

I wrap my arms around his neck, and our lips crash together. At this moment, I want to devour him as we lose ourselves in each other's touch, taste, and kiss. The only thing that stops us from a full-blown make-out session is a deep clearing of a throat. I pull away to see my uncle John standing there with his arms crossed over his chest, but he's smiling.

"Do you mind? Some of us are about to lose our stomachs here," he says from across the room, and I see everyone staring at us.

I laugh as happy tears spill from my eyes. Diesel wipes them away with his thumbs and holds my cheeks with his warm hands. "I love you so much, Rowan Bishop."

"I love you too," I confess, and I feel those words in every fiber of my being. Finally, our relationship is out in the open. It's not how I expected any of this to happen, but it feels like a giant weight has been lifted off my shoulders. No more hiding and no more sneaking. Now we can just be together and openly love each other. It doesn't mean I won't get shit from my family—nothing would allow me to escape that—but it's okay. I just hope Grandma doesn't start talking about me giving her a handful of great-grandkids anytime soon. I don't want to rush this and want to savor every second with him.

Diesel laughs, grabs my hand, then leads me down the stairs. Riley scowls, and I lift my eyebrows at him, daring him to say a word. The boys in school weren't scared of me for no reason. I pack a punch hard enough to knock a man down.

Chelsea walks up to me with Dawson in her arms, and I can see the embarrassment written all over her face. Diesel takes Dawson from her arms for just a moment so the two of us can have some alone time.

"Rowan...I owe you an apology," she says.

I give her a smile. "Really, don't worry about it. You didn't know."

"I know, but I just don't want you to think I was trying to steal him. I would've never crossed that line if I'd known. Neither of us talked about our relationship status, but I also didn't ask. If I could take it all back, I would."

I try to imagine being a single mom for the past two and a half years without a partner. She went through the delivery and raised a newborn all on her own. This woman is strong as hell, and I have so much respect for her, and even more now because she can admit her mistakes. "Listen. I'm not upset with you, Chelsea. Not at all. I should've asked Diesel what was going on. I shouldn't have just assumed."

"I know what it looked like and what you saw, and that's not your fault," she insists.

I search her face and notice how sincere her words are. "Diesel really loves his son, and I really love him, so that means we're gonna be in each other's lives for a long time.

Maybe it started off on the wrong foot, but that's okay. We understand each other more and the whole situation. It seems just like a big misunderstanding." I laugh. "And I have really bad timing."

She grins. "I'd like that...being friends, at least. I know this probably hasn't been easy for you. Diesel told me your relationship was new, and no one really knew about it, and then I roll up here with a kid. Trust me when I say it wasn't my idea, but it's for the best for Dawson."

"I agree one hundred percent. They both deserve the opportunity to form a relationship, and I have so much respect for you for allowing that."

I can see she's getting emotional, and we both laugh as I pull her in for a hug. "Hormones are such a bitch," I say.

Diesel walks up, breaking up the moment because Dawson starts getting fussy. She turns and takes him from Diesel. "Told you he needed a nap or he'd be cranky."

"Mama knows best," Diesel says. "If you wanna wait in the truck, I can bring you home in just a few minutes."

Chelsea nods. "Actually, would you mind if I grabbed some lunch? It smells delicious."

Diesel chuckles. "Help yourself. Might have a wheelbarrow in the back after you're done because Maize's cookin' is the best in the area."

Chelsea laughs and walks to the dining area as Riley moves toward us.

"This is really gonna be a thing? You two all lovey-dovey, smoochin' in front of everyone, and causin' a show?"

"Riley," I warn. "Mind your own damn business. You don't get to tell me what to do, who to date, or any of those things. And if you do have a problem with it..." I take a step forward, ready to knock him down, but he takes a step back.

"Hey..." He lifts his hands. "I know I can't control you. I just don't want you gettin' hurt, Rowan. I've only wanted the best for you, my only little sister, even if it means you choosing this dickhead."

"I'm your best friend in the entire world!" Diesel argues. "Don't you trust me?" He places a hand to his chest, pretending to be insulted.

Riley gives him a pointed look and tilts his head.

"If anyone's gonna treat your sister right…" Diesel thrusts his hips, and Riley groans, grinding his teeth. I can't help but laugh because through all of this, the man still has jokes.

"If you hurt her, I won't think twice about punching you again," Riley warns.

"And when he's done with you, I'll chop off your dick," Maize adds, walking up to us.

I glance at Diesel, and he winks at me, and I know this is what true happiness feels like. Maize tells Riley to stop causing a scene and pulls him away. I wrap my arms around Diesel's neck, finally getting a tad bit of privacy.

"It's gonna take him some time to get used to this, Cowboy," I say. His strong hands rest on my hips, and he pulls me even closer to him. "I'm sorry for assuming the worst. I should've known better, but my emotions had me thinking back on my past when I caught Nick cheating."

"No, I get it. This is new for all of us, and I probably would've thought the same thing had I seen another man's hands on you. Except I would've barged in and flattened him out."

I chuckle, knowing he definitely would have. I nearly get lost in his eyes before mine flutter closed, and I'm ready to taste him. Before our lips can touch, the door slams, and I pull away. My eyes go wide, and I can't believe who's standing in the living room of the B&B.

Trace, and my ex, Nick.

My mouth falls open, and the only thought that runs through my mind is *what the actual fuck?*

CHAPTER NINETEEN

DIESEL

I SEE red the minute my eyes land on the two guys standing in front of me.

Rowan's tool bag ex-boyfriend and Trace.

Why the fuck are they here?

Better yet, why are they here together?

Rowan pulls away and steps toward them before they can come any farther into the B&B. "What's going on?"

"You know why I'm here—" Nick stands taller. The cocky son of a bitch is about to meet my fist, more personally this time.

"I just came to check on you," Trace interrupts. "You seemed upset this morning and stopped responding to my messages."

My jaw clenches. I glance at Rowan who's fidgeting with the hem of her shirt.

"You texted him?" I ask.

"I was upset…it was after I saw you and Chelsea and wanted someone to talk to."

"I thought you talked with Maize?"

She turns toward me, her eyes wandering before they land on mine. "I did, but I needed a guy's perspective too. I was only reaching out for a friend..." she reassures, but it doesn't make me any less annoyed.

Rowan faces Trace, who looks confused as hell. "I'm so sorry, Trace. I didn't mean to leave you hanging or have you worry about me. I really appreciate that you care, but it was all a misunderstanding and things are fine now."

"That's good to hear," he says. "Sorry I just showed up unannounced."

"Nah, man, it's fine," I chime in, wrapping my arm around her waist so both of them know she's mine. "I appreciate you coming to check on her."

"Of course."

"Lovely..." Nick interjects. "If this cheesy Hallmark moment is over, can we get back to the money you owe me?"

I swallow hard, trying like hell to contain myself in a room filled with Bishops and guests.

Snapping my eyes to Trace, I smile. "Why don't you go into the dining area and help yourself? My son's mother is in there and a few of Rowan's family members."

"Alright, sure. Thanks." Trace walks around me, and then I turn to Rowan. "I'm going to take Nick outside for a little chat."

Her eyes widen in fear, but I flash her a wink. Then I stalk toward Nick and nod toward the back door. He follows, and once we're off the porch, I turn around and cross my arms. Nick matches my stance, and his smug frat boy look has me wanting to punch him in the face.

"You're brave comin' here like this, especially after the last time."

"She owes me money," he counters.

I bring a finger to my lips and tap twice. "You broke her heart, and she broke your car in return. Sounds even to me, so ya need to go back to where you came from and never step your preppy ass on this property again."

"This doesn't involve you." He scowls.

I squint and tilt my head at the dumb motherfucker. "See, that's where you're wrong." Stepping forward, I push his chest, and he stumbles back, losing his balance. "Anything involving my girl involves *me*."

He pushes back. "She owes me money, and I'm not leaving till she pays."

This little cocky fucker. "Perhaps you didn't hear me the first time?" I crack my knuckles. "No one's paying you a dime."

"Then I'll report that whore for vandalizing my property. I have the video and will hand it over to the cops." He flashes an arrogant grin and spins around.

I quickly grab his collar before he can walk away. Fisting his shirt in my fingers, I rear back and deck him in the face. His hands cover his nose as he hunches over.

"I warned you," I remind him. "You threaten her with that video or the money, I'll fuckin' hit you. Your stupid ass didn't believe me."

"You broke my nose!" he whines, moving his hands away to reveal blood.

"It won't be the only thing I break if you don't stop harassing Rowan. But if you be a good little boy and stay the fuck away, I won't break any more of your bones. Deal?"

"Fuck you," he spits, blood dripping from his chin.

I pat his shoulder with a smirk. "Good. Glad we had this nice chat. Should I walk you to your car?"

He shoves me away, then makes his way around the B&B to the parking lot. Looking at my knuckles, I see they're already red and starting to swell.

The asshole better stay away this time.

I walk back into the B&B and smile when I see Rowan sitting with Dawson on her lap. My whole world in one beautiful view.

Chelsea and Trace are in the middle of a conversation, so I sit on the other side and grab Rowan's hand.

"He likes you," I tell her.

"He's a toddler. He'll like anyone who plays with him," she retorts.

"I doubt that." I laugh. "It means a lot that you still want to be in my life after everything I've put you through. I didn't exactly handle it in the best way and—"

"Adam," she says my name, stopping me. "Yes, you should've told me what was going on sooner, and I should've confronted you about Chelsea. We're gonna need to work on communicating if we want this to work long-term."

I nod in agreement. Rowan's my everything and future. The last thing I want is to fuck it all up. "Definitely. Complete transparency from now on, Scout's honor."

She snorts. "You weren't a Boy Scout."

"I totally could've been!"

Dawson starts giggling at our laughter. "You think I'm funny, right?" I smirk.

He nods and starts talking. I love hearing him ask questions and point at things.

"He's precious," Rowan swoons. "Definitely your mini."

I hate that they have to leave today. "I'm gonna miss him."

Chelsea stands and frowns. "He's gonna miss you, too."

Holding back my emotions, my throat goes dry, but I nod. This is all so new, yet it feels natural. I was meant to be Dawson's dad.

Diesel: Hey, I'm back. Wanna sneak over here? ;)

After everything that went down at the B&B, it was time to take Chelsea and Dawson to the airport. I hated saying goodbye, but I made plans to visit in a few weeks. Until then, we'll FaceTime, and she promised to send me daily pictures of him.

Rowan: You know we don't have to hide anymore, though it was kinda fun…maybe you should leave your window open for me, and I'll crawl in.

Diesel: You know the entire town knows by now anyway.

Rowan: Yep. My parents already had "the talk" with me after you left. Then my grandma. It was embarrassing…I had to keep reminding them I was twenty-three years old and not a child anymore.

Diesel: They think I corrupted you now, don't they?

Rowan: Ooooh yeah. Riley's still walking around with a pissed-off expression. I hope I didn't ruin your friendship.

Diesel: Nah, he'll get over it. We'll be laughing over beers in no time.

Rowan: I hope so. Zoey already texted me and said he was grunting around the house.

I shake my head as I envision my best friend having a fit. He should know by now that I'd never intentionally hurt Rowan, but I can't fault him for being protective. I am too.

Diesel: I'll see him tomorrow and clear the air. He already got one hit in, so we should be even.

Rowan: Okay, good. Then I don't feel so bad coming over.

Diesel: Well, I did punch your ex for you. Again. You kinda owe me…

She sends me an eye-roll emoji, and I laugh.

Rowan: Be right there.

We haven't been alone since our date two weekends ago, and I'm dying to have her all to myself again.

When I hear her car pull up, I rush to the door and whip it open. I don't bother waiting for her to get to the house before I walk toward her. As soon as she parks and gets out, I pin her to the side and claim her mouth.

Rowan wraps her arms and legs around me as I press my body into hers. She groans against my mouth as I slide my tongue between her soft lips.

"I missed you so fuckin' much," I tell her. We hardly talked or saw each other for a week, and it was miserable. "I was devastated when you wouldn't answer my calls or messages."

"I missed you too," she admits. "I needed time to process it all."

Setting her back on her feet, I tilt her chin, and she meets my eyes. "I know. We both did. But I want you in my life and hopefully Dawson's too."

"I'm not goin' anywhere, Cowboy." She smiles wide.

I blow out a relieved breath. "Thank fuck."

"When will you see him again?" she asks as I take her hand and guide her into the house.

"Hopefully in three or four weeks. I'd like to go visit for a few days. After that, I'm not sure. We're playing it by ear."

"Maybe she'll decide to move here."

We walk to the kitchen so I can get her something to drink. "Doubtful. She sounded pretty hell-bent on staying in Phoenix."

"I don't know…" Rowan sing-songs when I hand her a bottle of Bud. "She and Trace were hitting it off at the B&B."

"Trace?" I muse.

"Yep," she says with a smile, popping the p. "Trace was smooth-talking her, and she was eating it up like candy."

"I better not have to punch his face in," I growl.

"Trust me, Chelsea was *all* over it. You wouldn't have to worry about Trace. He's really one of the good ones around." I give her a pointed look. "We're only friends!" she reiterates, chuckling. "The most we ever did was kiss, but there was no real spark between us."

"He does seem nice, so I'll give him the benefit of the doubt. However, it's unlikely she'd move here just for a guy. She won't for her son's father."

"Maybe she'll surprise you and do it for all three of you."

"I'd love having Dawson around all the time. Show him the real ranch lifestyle and watch him grow up here. Then we can give him a few siblings along the way."

Rowan chokes as she takes a sip and starts coughing.

"Too soon?" I tease.

"Not according to Grandma Bishop."

I waggle my brows, getting a giggle out of her. "Back up, Cowboy. You're a few years too soon."

"*Years*?" I frown.

"Just because Riley jumped into marriage and having a kid

doesn't mean you should," she scolds. "Well, besides the kid you already have, but you know what I mean."

I cup her face and smirk. "Alright, got it. Make you my wife before knocking you up, just like Grandma B said."

"Precisely." The blush on her cheeks is adorable, though I know she tries to hide it. Talking about our future doesn't scare me in the least. I've been ready for Rowan for as long as I can remember.

"Then right now, I'll make sure to enjoy having you all to myself." I grab her hips and lift her body until she wraps her legs around me.

"Yes, please." She laughs when I trip over the stool as I rush out of the kitchen and into my bedroom. "If you don't kill us in the process."

Once I successfully set her down on the bed, I tower over her and crash my lips to hers. Settling between her legs, she arches her back. Rowan rubs against me, and while my cock's already hard, she's making it harder.

"Shit…that already feels amazing." I chuckle.

Her hands slide beneath my shirt, and she scratches her nails down my chest. I want to take things slow and really show her how much I love her, but she's just as ravenous as I am.

Groaning, I try to hold on to my willpower, but it's a losing battle with her. Rowan's skin is so soft, and all I want to do is touch and kiss her all night long.

"Fuck it." I lean back and grip my shirt behind my neck, then pull it off.

Rowan giggles and openly gawks at me. "I could stare at that eight-pack all damn day." She licks her lips and waggles her brows.

"You're gonna be doing a lot more than just starin'."

"Arrogant," she mocks. "But yes, take off those jeans."

I hurriedly undress, then help her out of her shorts and top.

Staring down at her, I'm still so amazed she's mine. Shocked, really.

"Why are you looking at me like that?" The corner of her lips tilts up.

"Feels surreal."

"What does?"

"You being mine, and the world finally knowing." I rub my thumb along her cheek. "Being able to tell you how much I love you."

She leans up on her elbows, then cups the back of my neck until my face is close to hers. Rowan's lips crash into mine, and she releases a low hum when our tongues dance together.

"I love you, too," she whispers as we rest our foreheads together. "I'm gonna try really hard not to let my issues with my past relationships mess this up. It almost did already."

"Between me having no relationship experience and the douchebags you've dated, we're a match made in heaven," I tease, tipping her chin up. "Don't worry. We've got this, baby."

I pull her in for a deep kiss, and when she moans, I shift our bodies until she's on top of me.

"I wanna watch you ride me." I fist my dick and pump it a couple of times.

Rowan pops a brow. "Ride your cock or your face?"

"Shit. *Both*."

She laughs, placing her palms on my chest to lift herself. Slowly, she slides down my length, and with every inch, I smile wider at the vision in front of me. Rowan's a gorgeous woman, but she's also stunning inside. Once you get through her hard exterior, she really shows who she is. Funny, hard-working, loyal as hell. Sometimes a little crazy, but those are all the qualities I love about her.

Even at thirteen, she was beating all the guys at barrel racing.

"Jesus," I hiss between gritted teeth, grabbing one of her breasts. "Your tits bouncing in my face is hot as fuck."

Rowan rotates her hips, taking me even deeper as she increases her pace. She leans back, and I nearly come at the sight of her body on display for me. Her adorable braids, her smooth, soft skin, the cute freckles on her shoulders—I can't fucking get enough.

I bring the pad of my thumb between us and rub her clit in quick circles until her back straightens, and she moans out my name.

"That was sexy as hell," I tell her, wrapping an arm around her waist to flip us over.

She squeals, hanging on before I drop her underneath me.

"Bend over. You and those braids are driving me insane."

Rowan turns, and I immediately grip her hips, positioning her into place. I line us up and slowly re-enter her, feeling her tight walls around me. She feels so damn good, and my heart nearly bursts at the emotions bubbling inside me. I've never made love to a woman before Rowan.

Once I'm deeper inside her, I thrust my hips and move us into a steady rhythm. I watch as she fists the sheets, moaning and moving her body with mine. I reach up and grab the ends of her braids, then tug until her head falls back toward me.

"You feel this, baby?" I growl against her ear. "You and me."

"Yes," she whispers. "*So* good."

Squeezing her hip with my other hand, I pick up my speed, knowing she's close. Soon she's whimpering, begging me to let her come.

Releasing her hair, I slide my hand down her stomach and rub between her legs. "Enjoy it, baby."

She grips my wrist and squeezes as I bring her over the edge, thrusting deeper as she throws her head back and moans out my name.

"Fuck, Row..." I grit between my teeth as her pussy tightens around my dick.

Her chest rises and falls as she pants, and when I release her, she lays flat with her ass up. I smack a cheek, and I smirk when she lets out a little squeal.

"Hang on, sweet Rowan," I warn, gripping her hips and driving into her hard and fast. The sounds of our skin slapping together and heavy breathing echo throughout the room as I come undone and release inside her.

My arms are jelly, and I quickly roll over so I don't crush her. Rowan's legs fall with a grunt.

"See whatcha been missin' out on?" I smirk at her.

"I don't even have the energy to scold you for being a smug asshole."

Chuckling, I turn on my side and wrap my arm around her, moving her closer to me. "Thanks for giving us a chance. I promise I won't let you down."

Rowan blinks and looks at me. "Stop acting like you don't deserve to be happy. I'm the lucky one."

With a grin, I shrug. "Agree to disagree."

Last night and a quickie this morning with Rowan were pure perfection, and I can't remember a time I was ever this damn happy. Between having Dawson here over the weekend and working things out with Rowan, I'm on cloud nine. Though

I'm exhausted as hell working on only an hour of sleep, every second with her was worth it.

"Hey, dipshit. Quit smilin' like a moron," Riley harasses when we meet in the shop for our daily list.

I can't help it. It's just too easy to piss him off. "Can't help it when I'm thinkin' about your sister."

"I swear to God, Diesel…" He grits his teeth.

"Oh, c'mon. You can't be *that* mad. I've been telling you I liked Rowan for years. You just didn't listen."

"And I told you to stay away. *You* didn't listen."

"What's more important? Her happiness or being pissed at your best friend?" I challenge, knowing he'll cave. "You know I'm not gonna hurt her. I love her."

"You've never had a relationship."

"You didn't either until Zoey!" I remind him. "And you went and married her on a dare."

"He's gotcha there," Alex walks in and adds. "You two seriously having a pissing contest about this right now?"

I open my arms. "I'm ready to kiss and make up."

Riley rolls his eyes at my laughter.

"Well, you better soon because I have a new guy I wanna introduce you to. So hug it out or whatever you kids do."

"I promised Rowan I'd clear the air with you today, so whaddya say?" I arch a brow, waiting. "Gonna make me a liar already, or realize I'm the only one who can make her happy?"

"Some big words there, Diesel," Alex says. "I see Riley already gave you a shiner."

"Yes, sir. Only because I let him."

"God, you're such a fuckin' smartass," Riley hisses.

"And you owe me, so just quit being bitter so we can move on."

"Owe you for what exactly?"

"I could think about a hundred things, but specifically, the night of Rowan's formal dance in eighth grade. Remember?"

"What about that night?" Alex asks, looking back and forth between us.

It takes Riley a minute to realize what I'm talking about. The night he got so shit-faced, I had to drive his truck at only fourteen years old to pick up Rowan from school. "I hate you."

I snicker, shaking my head. "So, we good now or what?" I prompt, holding out my hand and knowing he'll take it.

After a moment, Riley grabs it, and I pull him in for a hug. "You should be excited to have me as a brother-in-law someday."

He laughs, adjusting his hat. "I wouldn't go *that* far."

"Our kids will be cousins."

"Alright, if you ladies are done, Gavin's here," Alex says, interrupting us.

We both turn to a hulk of a man, tall and chiseled. He's stacked like me but bulkier. I have no idea who he is, but he looks like he's ready for a fight. He's at least ten years older than me.

"Gavin, this is my son, Riley," he introduces them, and they shake hands. "This is Diesel, he runs the cattle operation."

"Nice to meet you," I tell him, taking his hand.

"He's new to Eldorado and will be staying in one of the ranch hand cabins. He'll be working with Jackson on breaking in the wild horses. He has bull riding experience and trains riders too."

"Bull riding?" My brows shoot up. "Impressive."

"Thanks. It was dangerous work, won some competitions, got some trophies, but I'm retired now."

"I bet you have some insane stories about traveling to rodeos and competing, huh?" Riley asks.

"Or how much ass you got?" I taunt.

The corner of Gavin's lips tilts up as if he could tell us crazy shit for days. "You could say that." He strokes his fingers over his scruffy jawline, smirking. "On both accounts."

"Maybe over a round of beers," I suggest. "My girlfriend works at the Circle B Saloon in town and will hook us up. We could meet up after work."

Riley groans at the mention of me calling his sister my girlfriend, but I hid it for too long to keep on for his sake. I'm gonna tell everyone and anyone I want now.

"Uh, sure. I've been there a couple of times." He pinches the back of his neck. "How about nine?"

"Sounds good."

"Alright, now that our *team meeting* is over…" Alex snickers. "I'm gonna give Gavin a tour of the property and get him settled in with Jackson and Kiera."

"Your cousins are gonna lose their shit over him…" I say once Alex and Gavin leave.

"Great, another guy I have to threaten to stay away from my family."

I pat him on his shoulder. "Good luck, bro. You'll be fighting *them* off him."

CHAPTER TWENTY

ROWAN

Diesel: I'm meeting your brother and a new worker at the bar at 9 tonight.

Rowan: Does this mean Riley doesn't want to kill you anymore?

Diesel: Told you he'd get over it…I'm very convincing ;)

Rowan: Yeah, I'm sure…

Diesel: Can't wait to see you. Wear those cowboy boots I like. And pigtails.

Rowan: With the jean skirt?

Diesel: HELL YES!

Rowan: You know every guy will see me wearing it in the bar, not just you…

Diesel: I've been scaring men away from you since we were in middle school. I'm a pro at this.

Rowan: Oh my God, you're so possessive.

Diesel: Damn right. And it worked :)

Rowan: …ten years later.

Diesel: Love's a marathon, not a sprint.

Rowan: Ha! Says the guy who was talking about marriage and babies last night.

Diesel: Shh…don't say that in front of your brother. He really will kill me.

Rowan: It'll be our little secret.

MY CHEEKS HURT from smiling so much. Ever since leaving his house this morning, I just can't stop. I'm so happy I don't have to hide my feelings anymore. Especially when my cousins are making faces at me.

"Bite me," I say at their expressions.

Kenzie and I met at the B&B to hang out with Maize while she cooks. I don't work till later, so hanging out with them means we can officially catch up since Kenzie decided to come home from the weekend, considering her university is only a few hours away.

"So how's the sex?" Kenzie blurts out.

"Kenzie!" Maize scolds.

"What?" She takes a bite of her omelet. "You were thinking it too. I just care enough to ask."

"When it's with the right person…" I let out a dreamy sigh. "It's perfect."

Maize makes a gagging noise, and we all laugh.

"Don't be a love hater. Someday, Maze…you're gonna find the one."

She rolls her eyes as she beats her fist into a ball of bread dough.

"Speaking of which, Diesel and Riley are coming to the bar tonight with the new guy who just got hired. You should come. Kenzie and I are working."

"Hells yes, you should!" Kenzie's face lights up. "Stay until after my shift so I can use my newfound drinking freedom to do it legally." She turned twenty-one a month ago and has been using any opportunity to remind us all.

"I'm busy tonight," Maize says.

"Doing what?" I ask doubtfully. "Bingeing *Love is Blind* and shoving dark chocolate into your mouth doesn't qualify as busy."

Maize glares at me, knowing I'm right.

"But you gotta admit, it's a train wreck you can't look away from…" Kenzie says about Netflix's new reality show. "Cameron's my favorite. I'd marry him in a heartbeat."

"See?" Maize holds a hand out toward Kenzie. "I need to catch up." I've always admired Maize and Mackenzie's sisterly relationship. Though I'm close with both of them, I've always wondered what it'd be like to have a sister.

"You can do it tomorrow. Tonight, you're coming to the bar! No arguing!"

"Damn, I thought getting laid would make you nicer," Maize mutters with a smirk.

"Maybe you're the one who needs to get laid, meanie," I retort.

"I *definitely* need to get laid," Kenzie adds, and the three of us burst out laughing.

"What's all the noise I'm hearing in here?" Uncle John enters the kitchen, and I hope he didn't just hear his daughters talking about needing to get some.

"None of your business," Maize smarts off. "Girl talk. No boys allowed."

"Pretty sassy for someone who still lives under my roof," he teases.

"Kenzie and I are gonna get an apartment in the city," she says casually, knowing damn well her father will blow a gasket at the idea.

"Not a chance in hell," he states firmly. "Nice try, though." Uncle John reaches over and steals one of the apple turnovers that Kat delivered this morning.

"Dad…" Maize begins. "I'm almost twenty-five and live at home. Do you know how pathetic I sound? I need my own place."

"You can move out when you get married."

Maize snorts loudly. "And did you and Mom wait till marriage to move in with each other?"

We all know the answer to that one. No.

"Do as I say…"

"Not as I do," Kenzie finishes for him.

"That's right." He kisses Kenzie on the head. "Your mom isn't ready to be an empty nester yet, and frankly, I think she'll go crazy without you two there, so until you're in a serious relationship, no talk of moving out."

"My parents are halfway there. I wonder if they'll get all sappy on me when I move out?" I question.

"Knowing your mom and dad, they're ready to relive their youth days and have their privacy back." Uncle John chuckles. "They didn't exactly take the slow and steady route."

"Thanks for that visual…" I groan. "Now I need to throw up my breakfast."

After another couple of hours of hanging out at the B&B, I

head home and do some house chores with Mom. She talks my ear off about Diesel and how she just knew we'd eventually get together.

"Adam's so sweet," she gushes. "Reminds me a lot of your father."

"Ugh, Mom. Don't say that." I shiver, trying to push the comparison out of my head. "That's really the last thing you wanna hear about your boyfriend."

Boyfriend.

It's still weird to call Diesel that. But also amazing.

"I just meant how attentive and loyal he is. Your dad was ready to fight anyone who came near me or threatened our relationship. As soon as I moved here, he jumped in with two feet, eager to make us work no matter what. I was expecting the worst when I told him I was pregnant, but he fell to his knees and almost cried. He was so happy."

"Do you ever think back and wish you'd gone a little slower? Like enjoyed the honeymoon phase a bit longer? Or are you glad you guys had a baby and got married right away?" I ask as we fold a basket of towels.

"I've thought a lot about that over the years, and I can honestly say it all worked out the way it was supposed to. It's never ideal to get pregnant that soon, especially when we weren't technically even dating, but it brought two people from different parts of the country together, and we formed an undeniable connection. I fell in love with him within a matter of weeks. He's always been my rock."

I nearly swoon at the way my mom talks about my dad. Though they're my parents and thinking about them romantically is still gross no matter how old I am, I can't deny how sweet it is when she talks about how far they've come.

"Why do you ask, sweetie?" she asks.

I shrug, not making eye contact. "You said Diesel reminds you of Dad, and it just had me thinking about these early dating years and how we should enjoy them before all the marriage and baby stuff happens."

"Are you pregnant?" she rushes out.

"Ma! No!" I burst out laughing when she tilts her head, doubtfully. "I swear!"

"Well, I can't say I'd be mad about the idea. Even though you two have known each other for most of your lives, not rushing is smart. Get to know each other on a more personal and deeper level before you bring in more responsibility. I love your brother, but he was a helluva lotta work."

I chuckle. "He still is."

I'm ecstatic when Diesel shows up at the bar earlier than he said. He's not with Riley or the new guy, so I get to steal a few private moments with him.

"Hey, Cowboy," I say, wrapping my arms around his neck. He's wearing his black hat, which I love.

"Howdy, cowgirl." He pulls on one of my french braids. "You fulfilled my requests." He eyes my outfit with an arrogant smirk.

"Of course…" I squeeze him tighter. "Only because I'm hoping you'll take it all off later."

"Goddammit, woman." He brings a hand down to his groin. "Don't talk like that here or I'm gonna have to excuse myself."

"You asked for it," I remind him of his earlier text messages.

"Listen, lovebirds…" Maize groans from one of the stools. "I agreed to come hang out, not watch you two make out."

"Stop being a grump." Kenzie sets a shot glass in front of her. "Blow jobs on me!"

"What?" Riley enters the bar at that precise moment with another guy behind him. "That's the very last thing I *ever* wanna hear from my cousin."

"Shots, perv!" Kenzie pours the liquor and then tops it with whipped cream. "Now, Maze. Take it without using your hands."

"Seriously? This is dumb."

I stand behind the bar next to Kenzie and laugh at her sour mood. "Be glad she didn't top it with a cherry. I nearly choked on the stem the last time she made me do one!"

Maize furrows her brows, then sighs. "Fine." With a groan, she leans down, wraps her mouth around the shot, then tilts her head all the way back. Once the liquid slides down her throat, she drops the glass down.

There's whipped cream all over her face, which has us laughing.

"You. All. Suck." She points at us as I hand her a napkin.

"But it's good, right?" Kenzie teases.

"Uh…anyway." Riley clears his throat, directing our attention to him. "This is Gavin. He'll be working with Jackson training horses."

Kenzie's eyes widen as her face lights up. Gavin looks like sex on a stick, so it's no surprise she's seconds away from jumping his bones.

"You already met Diesel," Riley says, waving his hand toward him. "That one behind the bar is my pain in the ass little sister, Rowan…"

"Just call me Rowan. Hold the 'pain in the ass' part," I mock.

Gavin flashes the smallest of smiles. "Nice to meet you."

"Then my cousin, Kenzie, who works here sometimes. Also a pain in the ass."

"Excuse you?" Kenzie places her hands on her hips. "If anyone's a ginormous ass, it's Riley."

"Noted," Gavin says.

Riley chuckles, moving on. "This is my other cousin, Maize. She's the cook at the B&B."

"Ooh, the one who makes amazing pancakes," Gavin states. They must've gone there this morning when we were busy talking in the kitchen.

Maize turns slightly to shake his hand and then quickly retreats. She blinks hard as if she's trying to clear the fog from her eyes because she just noticed how good-looking he is. Her not knowing how to act is almost comical, but I don't want to embarrass her so I don't say anything.

"So Gavin…" I say, bringing the attention to me instead of Maize's sudden inability to speak. "Where're you from?"

"Houston," he says in a thick drawl. "But I've traveled a lot in the past twelve years or so. I've been all over the state."

"Gavin's a retired bull rider," Riley explains. "Trains riders now on the side."

"Oh my God," Kenzie gushes. "That is so cool. I would love to see you ride."

I'm five seconds away from pouring a glass of cold water over her because she's about to internally combust.

"Told ya…" Diesel says to Riley. I'm not sure what he's referring to, but they both start cracking up.

"Told him what?" I ask, stepping closer.

Diesel leans into my ear, and whispers, "That your cousins would act like cats in heat around him."

I snort, shaking my head.

Maize looks pale as hell. "You okay, Maze?"

She blinks, then licks her lips. "Um, yeah. I'm just gonna

run to the bathroom real quick." Then she shifts her eyes and moves them to the side, motioning for me to follow her.

After she hops off the stool and walks toward the back, I wait a few seconds before excusing myself from the conversation and then meet Maize in the single-stall bathroom.

"Hey, what's goin' on?" I ask, shutting the door behind me. "You look like you've seen a ghost."

"That guy…"

"Gavin? What about him?"

"That's *Gavin*."

I blink. "Right, I just said that."

"No, I mean, yes. That's the Gavin I slept with a few weeks ago."

"Wait…" I rack my brain. "The guy you bailed on the next morning?"

"Yes!"

I quickly cover my mouth with my hands, trying to hold back my laughter. "Oh my God, Maze!"

"Shut up!" She smacks my arm. "This is humiliating!"

"This is freaking awesome." I chuckle. "Did he recognize you?"

"I don't know. I recognized him right away. That's why I quickly turned away."

"Well, go out there and say hi!" I push her toward the door, and she digs her heels in, not budging.

"Hell. No!" She frantically shakes her head.

"Weren't you just tellin' your daddy you were almost twenty-five years old and old enough to move out?" I cock my hip and place my hand on it. "This isn't very mature." I snicker, knowing she's growing more agitated by me.

"I didn't realize how much older than me he was. He looks older, right?"

I nod, agreeing. "He definitely does. Probably ten years older?"

"Oh my God." She drops her face into her hands. "I'm leaving through the back."

"I don't think so."

"Fine, then I'm staying in here."

"The bathroom?"

She drops her arms. "Rowan, please! Help me."

I sigh. "Alright, fine. I'll make sure the coast is clear."

Slowly, I open the door and peek around. I step out and see the guys laughing and chatting with Kenzie, who's the star of the show right now.

"Okay, you're good," I say. Turning to face her, I wave her on, and she rushes for the employees' only exit.

"Thank you!" she whispers.

As soon as she's gone, I quickly wash my hands, then return to the bar.

Kenzie furrows her brows as she looks at me. "Where's Maze?"

"She left. Wasn't feeling well." I shrug.

"What a lightweight." Kenzie laughs. "She had one beer and a shot."

"She throwing up after only that?" Riley cackles.

"Right?" Kenzie adds as I turn around and wipe down the counters. "Maybe she's pregnant."

My eyes widen at the thought. She did look awfully pale tonight. Could she be?

She said they hooked up a few weeks ago.

I grab my phone from my pocket and text her.

Rowan: Totally random question for no reason, but when was your last period?

She doesn't respond until she's back home twenty minutes later.

Maize: Uh...I don't know? Why?

Rowan: Well, any chance you could be pregnant?

Maize: WHAT? No!

Rowan: Are you sure? Like 100%?

Maize: I'm on the pill, and we used a condom.

Rowan: Did you remember to take your pill?

Maize: I think so...I mean, sometimes I forget, but typically I do!

Rowan: Oh my God...

Maize: Shut up. I swear. I'm not pregnant.

Rowan: Then take a test.

Maize: We hooked up like three weeks ago. It'd be too soon to know anyway.

Rowan: Maybe. I'm buying you a test, though, just to be sure.

Maize: And when I prove to you I'm NOT, you owe me $100!

Rowan: Ha! You better cross your fingers and toes you aren't. Unless you want Mr. Brooding Cowboy as your baby daddy ;)

Maize: I hate you so much.

"What are you laughin' about?" Diesel grabs my attention and asks. I slide my phone back into my pocket so he doesn't see the conversation.

"Just checking on Maize."

"She okay?"

"Yeah, I think so."

"You gonna come over tonight?" he asks, bringing the conversation back to him.

"Hmm...that depends. You gonna make it worth my while?" I taunt, willingly giving him all my attention.

"Oh hell yes, you know I will."

Once my shift is over, I follow Diesel back to his place, and though it's almost three a.m., neither of us is tired enough to go to bed.

"I think I'm gonna take a shower and wash the bar smell off me." I kick off my boots. "You wanna join me?"

"You even gotta ask?"

We race to the bathroom, and Diesel wraps me in his arms. Our lips fuse as we frantically undress each other. Diesel turns on the water, and once it's hot, we both step in and mold our bodies together.

"So there's a fundraiser hoedown in San Angelo next month."

"Really?" I slide my palms over his hard chest, then down his rock-hard abs.

"I was thinking of taking my best girl and dancing with her all night long. Whaddya think?"

I pinch my lips together, teasingly. "Hmm...I bet she'd like that."

"Maybe relive our first kiss."

I smile, raising my brows. "Hopefully not the 'getting interrupted by my brother' part."

He shakes his head, groaning. "That asshole. I was just about to stick my tongue in your mouth too."

Bursting into laughter, I wrap my palm around his cock. "I'm sure you were."

"Mm-hmm. Then I was gonna slide into second base."

"Right there on the dance floor, huh?"

"Yep. Make sure everyone there knew you were mine and only mine. Forever."

"Fourteen-year-old boys must have wild imaginations," I taunt, stroking him faster.

He releases a moan. "You have no idea, baby."

Diesel cups my breasts and squeezes before leaning down to take a nipple into his mouth. His rough hands rub over my skin, grabbing my ass and pulling me closer to his chest. "I loved you then, and I love you now. Even if you hated me." He winks, then brushes his lips over mine.

"It took me a while to see who was right in front of me, but I'm glad I caught you when I did." I have no doubt Chelsea would've climbed in his lap had he let her and he'd been single. I'm still getting used to the idea that he has a son and will have contact with Dawson's mom on a regular basis. I don't want to be the jealous girlfriend, but I see what a catch Diesel is, and I'm not about to let him go.

"I see the wheels spinning in your head," he says. "Stop overthinking."

"I'm not," I lie.

He chuckles, then slides his hand between my legs. "I'm about to make sure of that."

CHAPTER TWENTY-ONE

DIESEL

Rowan and I stand at the gate hand in hand as we wait for Chelsea's and Dawson's arrival. It's been four long weeks since I've seen him, and I can't believe how much I missed the little guy. Chelsea has sent me pictures nearly every day, and we see each other on FaceTime a few times a week.

The moment Chelsea spots me, she sets Dawson down, and he comes running toward me. Kneeling, I open my arms and wait for him. He tackles me, and we both go down laughing.

"Hey, buddy." I hug him, then bring him back to his feet. "I missed you."

I stand, then pick him up.

"Hey." Rowan waves.

"Hi, guys," Chelsea says as she catches up to him.

"How was the flight?"

"He talked everyone's ear off." She chuckles. "And besides trying to potty-train a toddler during a flight, it was fine."

"Oh no," Rowan says. "Did he have an accident?"

"No, he's wearing a pull-up, but he likes to sit on the potty forever, and those plane bathrooms are so tiny, and some people aren't very patient."

"I'll teach him how to stand and pee," I say proudly.

Chelsea gives me a look.

"What? It'll be my contribution. I have some makin' up to do."

"Throw Cheerios or Froot Loops in the toilet and tell him to aim for them," Rowan says with a laugh. "That's how my mom said they trained Riley." She shrugs.

"I'll keep that in mind," Chelsea responds, chuckling.

We all walk together to the baggage claim, and once we have their luggage, we take my truck back to the ranch. It's an hour drive, so we use that time to catch up.

"So, there's something I wanted to talk to you about…" Chelsea says when we get into the house.

"Spill it."

I look over at Dawson, who's playing with Rowan on the couch. Hearing their laughter is music to my ears.

"Well, okay, don't freak out." She bites her bottom lip.

"Oh hell, Chelsea. Don't say that." I remove my cowboy hat, brush a hand through my hair, then put it back. I'm already starting to sweat.

"Sorry, it's not bad. I swear."

I release a breath. "Alright, good. Then tell me."

"I had a phone interview at a bank in San Angelo last week, and I'm going in for a second one while I'm here."

"Wait. What?" I tilt my head, confused. "You're movin' here?"

"Well, we'd move to San Angelo so the commute wouldn't be too long, but—"

"You'd be close!" I exclaim before she can finish.

She laughs, nodding. "Yes, we'd be really close."

I lean down so I'm eye to eye with Dawson. "You hear that? We'll get to see each other more than once a month!" I pick him up and pull him to my chest, then I turn to Chelsea and smile. "Thank you."

"Dawson deserves to have a dad," she simply says with a shrug. I would've never asked her to move here for me, but the fact that she made this decision on her own has me so damn excited.

"Can I ask you something?" I say to Chelsea, and she nods. Swallowing hard, I look at Dawson and then back at her. "I'd really like him to have my last name."

She nods again. "I'm already working on it. I planned on changing it before we move here."

"Dawson Hayes..." I say aloud with pride.

"He's gonna be a heartbreaker," Rowan chimes in. "Especially with his father's genes."

"Hey!"

Chelsea and Rowan both laugh.

"Daddy!"

The three of us go quiet and look at Dawson.

"Did he...?" I point at him.

Rowan's eyes light up. "He did!"

"You just called me daddy?" My heart is about to burst, and tears well in my eyes. I can't help it; this is one of the happiest moments of my life.

Dawson giggles when I tickle him. "I love being your dad, kid."

"This is the right decision," Chelsea says. "Plus, it'll give Trace and me a chance to get to know each other."

Rowan's jaw drops. "I knew it!" She points at me. "I told you!"

I snort at her dramatics. "You did."

"Told you what?" Chelsea asks.

Dawson gets restless on my hip, so I set him down and watch him carefully as he wanders around the room. If he's going to be here more often, I'll have to toddler-proof the house a lot better. There are too many things he could get into.

"That you two were totally flirting at the B&B that one day," Rowan explains.

Chelsea blushes, and I couldn't be happier that she's interested in someone. "We exchanged numbers and have been *casually* talking. I knew there was no point if we were in different states, but then a bank job opened, and Dawson's been asking to visit you more, and it just felt like all the pieces were coming together for us to move here."

"So…it wasn't just for me?" I tease, popping a brow.

"Oh, shut up." Chelsea throws a pillow at me.

I'm so relieved that things aren't awkward between us, especially with Rowan and her, and that the three of us get along. We're going to be co-parenting, and though I'm still new to it, I'm excited to spend time with him and teach him everything I know about country living. Rowan's been patient and understanding, and we've grown even closer.

"When's the interview?" I ask.

"It's tomorrow, so I was hoping you'd be able to watch him."

"What time? I have to work in the morning, but I can in the afternoon," I tell her.

"Otherwise, I can help," Rowan adds. "I have off tomorrow. I'll take him to Grandma Bishop's, and she'll just die over him while spoiling him properly."

I laugh, knowing she's right. "If that's okay with Chelsea? I'll come over as soon as I'm done."

"I mean, yeah, that's fine as long as Rowan doesn't mind. Dawson can be a handful."

"Absolutely! My cousins are looking forward to playing with him too," Rowan reassures her.

"Okay, thank you. I appreciate it. I'm not used to getting much help and always feel like a burden when someone offers. When I'm at work, he goes to daycare, and my sister's shifts are the same as mine so I didn't have extra hands." She blows out a breath as if the whole world isn't all on her shoulders now.

"I'm here, Chelsea. You don't have to do this alone anymore. When you move here, we'll come up with a schedule so you have some nights to yourself. You deserve it."

"I can't remember the last time I had an entire night to myself," she says with a laugh. "Or an uninterrupted bath."

Dawson grabs my cowboy hat off the coffee table and puts it on his head, covering his eyes and nose. He starts giggling, which makes the three of us burst out laughing too.

"How ya doing over there?" Rowan asks from the doorway, leaning against it with her arms crossed. The smartass look on her face tells me she knows damn well how things are going.

"Half his dinner is on the floor, so…not great."

She walks toward me with a smile, then she looks at the table. "Did you try to feed him spinach?" She wrinkles her nose.

"It's healthy for him," I retort.

"Only if it makes it into his mouth," she teases.

"Daddy, no!" He swipes my hand again when I hand him a fork. "I want candy!"

"You can't have candy, buddy. How about some fruit?"

He nods and shoves a piece of hot dog in his mouth. Of course he'll eat that, but nothing with actual nutrients.

"Don't get discouraged," Rowan tells me as I cut up an apple and banana. "Toddlers are picky shits."

"How did Chelsea do this by herself for so long?" I ask,

setting the slices in a bowl. "He's been here for three hours, and I'm exhausted. I chased him all over the house, put him on the potty ten billion times, and then he screamed for food but won't eat."

"Is that why he's not wearing any pants?" Rowan chuckles, and the sound causes me to smile. I lower my gaze down her body and appreciate her curves.

"Yep," I say. "He's wearing his big boy underwear because it's faster to get him on the toilet without removing the extra layers."

"Did you try the cereal trick?"

"Also, yep. He grabbed the Cheerio out of the water and then popped it into his mouth before I could stop him."

Rowan covers her mouth to hold back her laughter, but I see the corner of her lips tilts up.

"Oh my God…" She pats my arm. "He's as much work as you were, I'm sure."

"My mother's already confirmed that as true when I called and asked for advice." I grunt.

It's been a few weeks since Chelsea and Dawson moved to Texas for good. It's the first night he's sleeping over, and while I'm happy to have him here and give his mother a break, I'm nervous as hell. I've been getting the spare room ready for him, but I have a feeling he's not going to stay in his toddler bed without a fight. Chelsea's already warned me he likes to get out.

"Well, maybe once he's asleep, I can help ease some of your tension," Rowan says seductively.

I pop a brow. "I might be down for that…" Grinning, I take the bowl of sliced fruit and set it down in front of Dawson. I don't even bother with the fork this time. He's flung it four times already.

After dinner, we give Dawson a bath, get him into his pajamas, and then read him two bedtime stories. Just as Chelsea warned, he snuck out of his bed, and I repeatedly tucked him back in. After the seventh time, he wore himself out and finally fell asleep.

"I am *so* tired…" I groan as I collapse on the bed next to Rowan. She's been watching TV while she waits for me. "Any chance I can just lie here while you pleasure me? I don't think I can move."

Rowan grabs the remote and turns it off. Then she straddles my lap and wraps her arms around my neck. "You did good," she praises. "And I gotta admit, watching you be a dad is sexy as hell."

I arch a brow. "Oh, really? How sexy are we talkin'?"

"Mmm…like blow job sexy. Slide your cock between my breasts and let you come all over my chest sexy."

"Don't fuck with me, woman," I warn. "My dick is already hard."

She rocks her hips and grins when she feels me between her legs. "Or you can just lie there while I ride you. Your pick."

"Pick?" I huff. "I choose all three. Blow job. Ride me. Fuck your tits. In that order."

Her head falls back as she releases a deep laugh, and I lean forward, kissing her neck and sucking hard. She rocks her hips against me, and I groan at the friction.

"Christ…" I hiss. "Take off your clothes right now."

Within seconds, we're undressed, tripping over ourselves before falling back on the bed. Rowan pushes me down and eagerly slides over my length, and I grip her thighs, moving her against me faster.

I fucking love the way she looks on top of me. It's not just sex, it never has been, but making love to my dream girl and knowing someday I'm going to marry her have me craving more of her every day.

"Should we make him a little sister?" she taunts as she leans closer.

"Don't even joke," I say seriously. "I'll knock you up right now."

She grins wide. "Not yet, Cowboy. Dawson gets you to himself for a while."

"Okay, that's fair." I smirk.

Rowan brings her mouth to mine, and I cup the back of her head, deepening our kiss. "I love you," I whisper against her lips.

"I love you, too," she whispers back as I slide my other hand down her body, then smack her ass.

She squeals, and we pull apart. Quickly, I flip us over and lift her leg until her calf rests on my shoulder. Rocking harder, she arches her back, then covers both of her hands over her mouth as she screams out her orgasm. I follow behind her moments later, burying my face in her neck as we fall over the edge.

We lie in bed with my arms wrapped around her. My body feels like jelly, but I want to absorb every tender moment with Rowan.

"So how are things going with the new guy around the ranch?" she asks after we catch our breaths.

"Gavin?" I furrow my brows, and she nods. He's been working with Jackson for almost a month now. "I guess fine. I don't see him much. Why do you ask?"

"Just wondered if he's said anything about Maize."

"No, not to me. What would he say about her?" I'm confused as hell as to where this conversation is going. "Rowan..."

"What?"

"What aren't you telling me?"

"Um...it's just girl stuff. Nothing. Forget I said anything." She waves me off, and it's cute she thinks I'm just going to so easily *forget*.

I tilt her chin up and arch a brow. "It's nothing like actually *nothing* or nothing like I need to punch him in the face?"

She squints her eyes and twists her lips. "Neither?"

"So it's something…"

She sighs, rolling her eyes. "They might've hooked up when he first arrived."

"No fucking way."

"It was the night you and I went to San Angelo actually. They met at the bar, and of course it was a night I wasn't working."

"Holy shit."

"I know…" She inhales. "She took a pregnancy test."

"Jesus, Row." I blink hard. "Please tell me she's not—"

"It was negative," she interjects. "Then I had to pay her a hundred bucks for losing the bet."

I breathe out a sigh of relief, my brain still spinning from this news. "So they hooked up, and then what?"

"Then nothing. She avoids him at all costs, which is why I asked if he's ever brought her up. 'Cause if he did, I thought maybe he was thinking about her."

"I don't see him that much. When I'm not working, I'm with you and Dawson. But I have a feeling even if I did, he wouldn't say a damn thing. In fact, he doesn't talk that much. He looks pissed off most of the time."

Rowan snorts, giggling. "Yeah, it's always the quiet ones you have to worry about. He does have that whole sexy, brooding thing goin' on, too."

My brows shoot up. "'Scuse me?"

"Not to mention, he's way older. Probably more experienced."

"I'm older," I remind her.

"By one year!" She chuckles, climbing on top of me. "Aww…is someone jealous?"

"Is someone tryin' to *make* me jealous?" I brush loose strands of hair behind her ear and smile at her.

"I didn't even have to try in school. You scared every guy away who breathed in my direction."

I puff out my chest. "Damn straight."

"We better get to sleep. Dawson will probably be up in four hours," she tells me. "And he'll want your full attention."

"I plan to take him out to see the cows after breakfast anyway. They'll burn him out, or he'll burn them out. Win-win either way."

Rowan leans down and softly kisses my lips. "You're a great dad."

"I'm trying to be." I wrap my arms around her. "Hopefully, a great husband one day, too." When I waggle my brows, she rolls her eyes at me, but she knows I'll put a ring on her finger one day.

"Gonna finish fixing up this place this winter, and then you won't be able to resist movin' in with me."

"Alright, Cowboy. Challenge accepted."

CHAPTER TWENTY-TWO

ROWAN

FOUR MONTHS LATER

Diesel: You wearing that sexy red thong I like?

Rowan: I was thinking commando might be more your style?

Diesel: Screw dinner. Gonna fuck you against the table instead.

Rowan: That is not the romance package I signed up for on our first Valentine's Day.

Diesel: Okay, fair point. I'll wine and dine you, then fuck you senseless.

Rowan: Deal.

"You sure you're okay babysitting?" I ask Elle who's

sitting on my bed, waiting for me to finish getting ready for my hot date tonight.

"I think I can handle a three-year-old," she states. "Plus, Kenzie and I are having a singles-only party after Dawson goes to bed, so she'll be there to help me."

It's been a crazy five months since Chelsea and Dawson moved to Texas. In fact, it's been quite the adventure since the night Diesel kissed me in the bar office.

But I wouldn't change it for the world. I've never been happier and love seeing this side of Diesel.

"Alright, I'm ready," I tell Elle, staring into the mirror and inhaling a deep breath. I'm dressed up more than usual, and I hope I knock Diesel on his ass when he sees me. "How do I look?" I spin around for her to get a good look.

She examines me from head to toe with a cheeky grin. "Like you're about to get laid six ways to Sunday."

"Well, then I guess that's perfect!" I chuckle, brushing my hands down my skintight dress. "Though I'm like ninety-percent positive I won't be able to sit in this thing without it splitting at the ass."

"I'm wondering how you're going to even walk in those shoes…" She raises her brows at my five-inch platforms. I've worn heels less than five times in my whole life, and it's possible I might trip and break my neck.

I walk around my bed, and my ankle jerks, making me stumble. "Dammit. How do women wear these things?"

"You should've practiced," she scolds.

"No, no. I think I have this…" I straighten my back and walk around my room. "I'll be fine."

"You're walking in slow motion," Elle deadpans.

"It's the only way."

She snickers, shaking her head at me.

"You're basically a doctor, so if I twist something, you can fix me up!" I grin.

"A *vet*," she emphasizes. "An animal doctor."

"Potato, *potahto*."

"No, ma'am. Now, if you're birthing a calf or a foal, then I'm your girl. Otherwise, you'd be going to see my parents at the ER." Both my uncle Evan and aunt Emily would no doubt give me a hard time for wearing these, especially if they saw me at the hospital banged up.

"Yeah, I don't want that. Would kinda ruin my whole rough sex plans for tonight."

Elle gags, making me laugh.

"Please, let's go before you hurt something." She stands, and we head for the door.

We drive to Diesel's house where Dawson's staying tonight. He wanted to give Chelsea and Trace a chance to have a romantic night without worrying about getting up with a toddler in the morning. They've been seriously dating for the past few months, and they're great together. Trace adores Dawson and is great with him. He's surrounded by so much love and is the luckiest little kid to have four adults who get along and can co-parent together.

Elle parks her truck, and I slowly get out, adjusting my dress before making my way to the door. As soon as it opens and he sees me walking up his steps, his jaw drops.

"Hooooly fuck."

Seeing Diesel's face was totally worth it.

"You like?" I ask, swallowing hard.

Elle comes to my side. "He better, considering what it took to get you in that thing."

"I definitely do, but now I don't want anyone else to see you…" He pulls me into his arms and slides one hand down my back. "Especially with your legs and ass on display. Hell, you're tryin' to kill me, aren't you?"

"She's gonna kill herself in those heels," Elle says, snickering as she walks into the house, and Dawson comes running toward her.

"I don't think I've ever seen you wear those before." His gaze lowers, admiring every inch of me.

"Nope, but I wanted to wear them for a special occasion."

"Then we better get going because my mind is running wild with ideas..." He closes the gap between us and kisses me. "Like right now, I'm envisioning you bent over wearing *only* those heels."

"Mmm...now that I can probably arrange," I whisper, brushing my lips against his again.

"Daddy!" Dawson interrupts, tugging on his jeans.

We quickly pull apart. I forgot we had an audience.

"What is it, bud?" Diesel kneels, removing his cowboy hat.

"Aunt Ellie said I could have cereal for supper!" His smile's so wide and genuine, it's impossible to tell him no.

"Is that so?"

I crack up laughing because Dawson's obsessed with cereal. Ever since we tried that potty training trick, it's all he wants to eat.

"Would you rather I feed him something I make? Because trust me, it won't be good. That's Maize's area."

Elizabeth Bishop is smart as a whip, but her cooking skills are null.

Diesel picks him up and stands. "Alright, buddy. You have fun with Aunt Ellie." He kisses his head, then hands him off to Elle. "In bed by eight," he reminds her.

"This isn't my first babysitting rodeo," she mocks. "I have this. We're gonna get high on sugar, run a mile, then crash out. Easy peasy."

Diesel groans.

"ABye, lovebirds!" Elle all but pushes us out the door, and Diesel takes my hand, threading our fingers together as we walk to his truck.

"Can you actually walk in those things?" he asks, opening the passenger side for me.

"Where's your confidence in me?"

He lifts me, and I settle into the seat.

"About three inches lower." He snickers.

I glare at him, buckling in. "We're on a date, mister. You're supposed to be charming and romantic, remember?"

Diesel clears his throat and slides his hands down his dressy button-up shirt. "Startin' now." He throws me a wink, then shuts the door and runs to his side.

As soon as we're on the road, he grabs my hand and presses his lips to my knuckles, planting a sweet kiss there.

"In case I wasn't clear, you look gorgeous."

"You look quite handsome yourself. That shirt is making me want to rip off the buttons and slide my tongue up your abs."

"You better watch that naughty mouth."

"My mouth most definitely wants to be on you."

"Rowan…" he warns in a deep drawl. "Getting my dick hard in these jeans is uncomfortable, so start talkin' about something else."

I grin, tightening my grip on his hand. "So I shouldn't tell you I'm wearing a new black thong and bra set tonight?"

"Goddammit, woman." His jaw tenses. "That black piece of fabric you call a dress is already drivin' me insane."

Although we spend as much time together as we can between our work schedules, we don't always get nights alone, so after fourteen days of no sex, I'm dying for him. He gets Dawson three to four times a week, and by the end of the night, Diesel's usually so exhausted he falls asleep the second his head hits the pillow. I'm still working late at the bar, so I need to make tonight count.

"Or that I haven't touched myself since you last did, and I'm so wet right now."

"Row…I won't hesitate to pull this truck over and put you

up on my lap, so unless you want us to miss our dinner reservations, you better stop."

I know he wants this to be super special, but all I want is him.

"I think you should do just that…"

Diesel jerks the steering wheel to the right until we're off the road. Gravel spits up under the tires as he takes a hidden path, and I squeal, hanging on tight as he laughs.

"What're you doing?" I shout. "You tryin' to kill us?"

"Hang on, sweetheart."

It's been raining for three days straight, which is more than we typically get in an entire month this time of year, but it means it's muddy as hell. The truck dips into a deep puddle and then water rises and splashes against the side.

"Adam!" I shriek through my laughter.

He quickly turns the wheel again, and we drive through another muddy puddle. Dirty water flies everywhere, covering my window.

Diesel looks over at me with a shit-eating grin on his adorable face before he does another donut, and the truck spins in circles.

I hang on for dear life, gripping the safety handle, and can't stop smiling and laughing. I've gone mudding on four-wheelers through the woods before, but nothing like this.

After ten minutes, Diesel finds a dry spot and parks the truck.

"What the hell was that?" I ask, still trying to catch my breath from the rush of adrenaline.

"That was the equivalent of me dumping a bucket of cold water over your head so you'd stop looking at me like I was your next meal."

"But that's all I want," I pout, sticking out my lower lip.

He adjusts his seat so it slides all the way back and then

grabs my hand and helps me climb over the middle console. My dress is too tight to straddle his lap, so I sit on his legs.

"Why do I even bother trying to plan a romantic night for you?" he asks, brushing a strand of hair behind my ear.

I shrug, grinning. "Good question. You know I'm not high maintenance."

"One of these days, I'm gonna try to propose, and you're gonna jump me before I even get the chance to ask."

Smiling wide at the thought of him putting a ring on my finger, I nod in agreement. "Probably. So you might wanna ask me when I'm least expecting it."

"Duly noted." He winks. "But I actually have something for you."

"A gift?" I prompt.

"Perhaps." He stretches back and reaches for a small box behind him. "This is one of them. The other is at the house."

"You really didn't have to get me anything," I tell him. "I just wanted to spend time with you."

He grabs my chin. "I know. But this gift is a little selfish."

I narrow my eyes as he sets it in my palm. "What do you mean?"

"It's for both of us," he clarifies.

"Oh God. Is it one of those remote vibrators?"

"Huh?"

"Like I put it inside me, and you have the remote to control the speed…"

Diesel furrows his brows, looking at me like I've lost my mind.

"Okay, so by your expression, I'm gonna say no."

He smirks. "Rowan, just open it."

My heart races as I lift the top and unwrap the tissue paper. Whatever it is feels light. My fingers rub against metal, and when I pull it out, I narrow my eyes in confusion. "A key?"

"Yep," he says.

I hesitate. "Because I have the key to your heart?"

He releases a laugh. "Well, yes. But this is the key to my cabin."

"You're giving me a key to your house?" I ask. Is this the next part of a relationship? Exchanging house keys?

"I am."

"Oh." I flip the key and study it. "Thank you."

"But I'm also giving you the key to *your* house."

My eyes meet his, and I frown. "Wait. What?"

Diesel grabs my hand and rubs the pad of his thumb over my knuckles. "I want you to move in with me."

With wide eyes I blink, and my throat goes dry.

"I want to wake up with you every morning and go to bed with you every night. I'm tired of cramming time with you between our work schedules and hectic lives. Now that the cabin is all fixed up, I want it to be *our* home. Decorate the walls. Fill it with pictures and candles. Pick out new pillows and blankets in your favorite color. Hell, new china and silverware. I've been ready for the next step with you for months but didn't want to rush you. However, I know I want you in my life forever."

Diesel's looking at me as though I'm his whole world with his cowboy hat sitting just right and his green eyes sparkling at me. The scruff on his chin is newly trimmed. He's my everything.

There's no doubt in my heart that I want him.

"Rowan, what do you say? Do you want to live together?"

My eyes swell with happy tears. I frantically nod and wrap my arms around his neck. "Yes, absolutely!"

I pull his lips to mine, and he tightens his hold on me. "I love you," I murmur.

"I love you more." His hands slide up my thighs, moving my dress up to my waist, and he shifts my body until I'm straddling him. Rocking my hips, I feel him harden between my thighs. Diesel groans as I rub his cock against me.

"You want to take another one of my firsts?" I whisper.

He pulls back slightly, furrowing his brows. "What's that?"

"Sex in a truck," I explain. "I've never."

The corner of his lips tilts up into a wide grin. "Good, neither have I."

Leaning back, I flash him a skeptical look. "Really?"

"Serious! I was saving all the fun places for you."

I snort, laughing. "I'm sure."

He manages to undo his buckle and jeans, sliding them down until I palm his cock and stroke him.

"Fuck…" he hisses. "Why does it feel like it's been too damn long?"

"Because it has!"

Sliding my panties to the side, he pushes a finger inside me. "Now you'll have me all the time."

"Finally," I say, gasping as he adds a second finger. When Dawson sleeps over, we have to be quiet since his room isn't far from the master, but now that we're in his truck, we can be as loud as we want. "I need you inside me."

He lifts me slightly to position himself against me, and I slowly slide down his length. I wrap my arms around his shoulders, and my head falls back as we rock in unison and come together.

It's the best Valentine's Day ever.

"You're what?" Riley shouts as I tape up the boxes in my room.

"You heard me." I smirk.

"You and Diesel are moving in together? Like…legit?"

I nod.

"No one asked me."

Snorting, I laugh. "Why does this surprise you so much? We've been dating for six months. You married Zoey after twelve hours," I remind him with a shit-eating grin.

"Am I ever gonna live that down?" he huffs.

"Nope," Diesel answers, rounding the door and walking in.

"That's different. You're moving in with my best friend," Riley retorts, then points at Diesel. "And you…"

Diesel holds up his hands in surrender. "What now?"

"You know the rules. You break her heart; I break your neck."

Diesel smirks. "Crystal clear, boss."

"Relax." I stand and pat Riley's shoulder. "We're living in sin, not getting hitched in Vegas."

Riley groans, and without another word, he turns around and leaves.

"You'd think he'd be used to us dating by now," I say, wrapping my arms around his waist.

Diesel leans down and gently presses his lips to mine.

"I could be the King of England, and I still wouldn't be good enough for his little sister." He shrugs, knowing there's no use in worrying about it.

"Would that make me your queen?"

"You are most definitely my queen. Royal title or not."

I smile. "Ready to be roomies with me?"

"Ready to have a three-year-old around half the time?"

"Well, I grew up with Riley so…" We both laugh, and we hear him shout from the room across the hall.

"I heard that!"

"Dawson's a good kid. I love watching you be a dad and getting to experience him learning something new. Do you think Chelsea will be okay with me being around more?"

"Of course. I told her so she's aware, but Trace is around him all the time too. As long as his parents are happy, he'll be happy."

"And that's all that matters, right?"

"All that matters to me is you, my son, and this ranch. I don't think I could be happier if I tried." He cups my face, and our lips merge.

A throat clearing from behind interrupts us, and we pull apart. "Y'all can't wait till you're under your own roof to make out?" my mother scolds. Then she looks at Diesel. "I hope you take good care of her. You hear me?" She steps in and hugs me. "This is my baby."

"Mom." I grin. "I'm not going very far," I remind her.

"But still. I wasn't ready for this. Seems too soon."

"If it helps, I'll still come over and raid the fridge while you do my laundry."

"Nice try." She pats my butt.

Like clockwork, my father enters. He's been working all morning and gives Diesel a curt nod. "You're really leavin'?" he asks, crossing his arms over his chest.

"Five minutes away," I say. "You won't even notice I'm gone."

He pulls me in for a long hug. "I'll always notice the absence of your bobby pins lying around the house and tripping over your boots you never put away."

"Geez, it's like you two want me to be here until I'm eighty."

He pulls back and kisses the top of my head. "We're gonna miss you. You know we will."

"I'll miss you guys too. As soon as I figure out how to cook, we'll have you over for dinner."

They both laugh and nod. I'll have Maize help me.

"Well, we're burning daylight. Let's get your stuff loaded up and outta here," my dad says and recruits Riley to help.

It only takes one trip to bring my essential boxes over. Since Dawson needs room for his things too, I left some of my stuff at my parents. Most of it I need to go through and toss or donate anyway. I don't want to crowd the house with all my useless crap.

After everything is unloaded, I say goodbye to my parents and Riley, and then it's just Diesel and me in a house surrounded by boxes.

"Well, this is it. No turning back now," I tease as he wraps me up in his arms, and we fall onto the couch.

"You wouldn't get very far. I'd chase you."

I sit on his lap. "Ahh, yes. The stalker is back."

"Always and forever, baby." He cups my ass. "You're mine."

Smiling, I bring our lips together. "And I couldn't be happier about it."

EPILOGUE

DIESEL

FIVE MONTHS LATER

I CAN'T BELIEVE Rowan and I have been together for almost a year. Knowing that she took a chance on me and loves my son as much as I do is everything I could've ever wished for. Today's the big Fourth of July party at the Bishop Ranch, but it's also going to be a day to remember for everyone, especially Rowan.

John and Jackson are busy grilling burgers and hot dogs while the other men are setting up the firework display. Alex takes me off to the side, and Riley follows suit. "You ready for this?"

Riley looks at me, smiling. He's finally somewhat used to me being with his sister, which is a relief.

I glance over my shoulder and see Chelsea sitting on a blanket next to Trace. Elle and Kenzie chat with Rowan as Dawson sits on her lap. I'm so goddamn lucky.

"Yeah, I'm ready," I tell him without hesitation. Riley calls one of his friends on the phone and makes sure all of my plans are in place. "You've got ten minutes."

Alex gives me a side hug and grins. "Mama B is gonna start asking about babies."

A chuckle escapes me. "She already has! What are you talkin' about?"

"Before marriage?" Alex asks with his eyebrows raised.

I shake my head. "She said ring first, five babies second. In that order."

"Of course she did." Alex snickers before we go our separate ways.

Five minutes later, Alex turns on the stereo and blasts it while everyone sits on blankets and picnic tables, waiting for the sun to set so we can start popping fireworks.

"Life of the Party" by Shawn Mendes blasts through the speakers, and I walk across the pasture and mouth the words to Rowan. Her eyes widen with recognition and shock.

"What're you doin'?" she mouths back.

Chelsea takes Dawson as I grab Rowan's hand and pull her to her feet. I start dancing with her in front of everyone, re-creating the night of her winter formal when we first danced to her favorite song. I spin her around and dip her a few times until the airplane flies overhead. It's low in the sky, and the engine's loud, grabbing the entire town's attention. Behind it flies a sign that reads: "Will You Marry Me, Rowan Bishop?"

Everyone in a fifty-mile radius can read it without a doubt. She looks up, then glances back at me, her lips parted.

"What does that say?" she asks just as I drop down on one knee.

I'm nervous as hell, knowing all eyes are watching us, but I try to focus on the beautiful woman in front of me who I'm going to make my wife. I fidget and pull the ring box from my pocket and flip it open. Rowan's eyes are full of tears, but the smile hasn't left her face.

"I knew when we were kids that you were the only woman for me. So many people have told me that when you know, you *know*, and I knew you were meant to be mine when we danced and shared our first kiss that night. Somehow, I've always known." She covers her mouth with her hands, tears sliding down her cheeks and fingers. "Rowan, you make me the happiest man alive. You've taught me so much in so little time, and I can't imagine a life without you. You love me wholeheartedly. You love and welcome my son in your life. I love you more than words can express. You're everything I've ever wanted." I reach up and grab her hand. "Sweetheart, will you marry me?"

Rowan nearly knocks me down as she wraps her arms around my neck. The ring goes flying as she kisses me in front of her whole family.

"Rowan Bishop," her grandma says. "You better give that man an answer and not keep him and the rest of us waitin'."

ROWAN

Everyone surrounding us laughs at Grandma Bishop's outburst. She has her hand on her hips, impatiently waiting.

"Yes, yes, yes! I will marry you." I scream out for the whole town to hear.

I'm nearly straddling him in front of God and country, but all I want to do is kiss his soft, perfect lips. Eventually, we break apart, and he helps me back to my feet.

"Oh, the ring," he says, seeing the box on the ground. Neither of us cared about it and were too caught up in the moment of being together for the rest of our lives. He pulls the sparkling diamond out and slips it on my finger. I can't help but gasp at how stunning it looks on me.

"This is too much," I whisper, looking down at the rock.

"You deserve it all, baby," he says, just loud enough for me to hear. "So let's get you knocked up."

I smack him across the chest, but the truth is, I have my own secret to tell. After everyone has given us a stupid amount of hugs and congratulations, Diesel takes me off to the side, away from everyone so we can have some privacy for the first time all day.

"Are you happy, Row?"

I look at him, feeling the tears creeping in my eyes. "You have no idea. I…I…didn't expect any of this. Not today. I don't know how you managed to buy a ring and plan all of this without me knowing."

A sneaky grin sweeps across his lips. "You think all we do all day is work on the ranch? You're sadly mistaken."

I shake my head. "You're so bad."

He leans over, and I press my lips against his and melt into him. By the time we pull apart, we're both breathless, and I'm more than ready to get out of here and consummate this proposal, but not before I say what I need to.

"Adam," I say seriously, looking up into his eyes.

He tilts his head, furrowing his brows. "Yes?"

"I don't know how to say this without just telling you…." I hesitate.

He searches my face and looks alarmed, so I give him a reassuring smile.

"I'm pregnant," I say, swallowing hard, watching him process what I just said.

He blinks hard. "Wait, what?"

"I found out a few days ago. I was feeling weird at the bar and picked up a handful of tests from the store after work. They were all positive." I shrug.

His mouth falls open before cups my face and smashes his lips against mine. "Really? We're having a baby?"

The excitement in his voice is so damn contagious that I can barely contain my happiness. "Yes, really. It's happening. I mean, I didn't expect it so soon, but Dawson is gonna have a brother or sister next year." Though we joked about having babies and making a big family, I was on the pill, and we weren't trying. However, it looks like the universe had other plans for us.

Tears well in his eyes, and seeing him overjoyed with emotion has me crying too. We kiss and laugh, and he holds me as though he's never letting me go. I know he won't. I'm his forever.

"You've truly made me the happiest man in the world," he says. "You have no idea. I didn't get to experience all the baby things with Dawson. I love my son more than life itself, but I missed out on a lot. I'm so damn excited right now. I just can't even explain myself. My words seem like pig mush."

I giggle at his analogy. "I can wait to grow our family, babe. This is everything I ever wanted."

"Me too, Row. A houseful of kids who get to grow up on the ranch while I grow old with you." Diesel leans over and nuzzles against my neck.

Butterflies stream through me as I lean into his touch. "Same, Cowboy. Also, can we wait a while before we tell everyone our news? Keep it our little secret for old times' sake?" Truthfully, I just want confirmation from my doctor first before we tell our parents. The moment they know, the entire town will know.

He chuckles. "I'm good with that. You know we're gonna get bombarded with questions and loads of baby stuff."

"I know." I sigh with an enthusiastic smile. "That's why I kinda just wanna enjoy the news with you for a while before we share it with our families."

"Our relationship started out a secret, so we might as well have another." He winks with a mischievous smirk.

I kiss him deeply, and we both smile before walking back to the group. They're happily eating and goofing off. The ring shines and sparkles, and I can't stop staring at it as I interlock my fingers with Diesel's. After we grab a burger and chips, we sit on a big blanket, and I lean against his chest, waiting for the firework show to begin. Fourth of July is my favorite holiday, and each year the show gets bigger and better because my uncles act like they're trying to set a Guinness Record or something.

Looking around, I'm so grateful to be able to raise a child on the ranch with my family close by. I know it's exactly what Diesel wants, and it's been my dream for as long as I can remember.

Before the first explosion goes off, I see Maize standing off to the side with her arms crossed, looking pissed as ever. I tell Diesel I'm gonna grab something to drink and go over to her. When I move closer, I notice how tense her jaw is and narrowed her eyes are. Holding her temper is not her strong suit.

"Everything okay?" I ask, grabbing her hand and pulling her away from Uncle Evan, who's too close for this conversation.

She lets out a huff. "No, it's not."

I search her face. "What's going on?"

"Did you see who Gavin brought with him to the party?" she asks, more irritated than when the ranch hands steal food off the buffet table.

"So? You haven't given him a lick of attention since he moved here," I tell her.

"That is Sarah Cooke, Rowan. She was such a bitch to me in high school. Made fun of me every single chance she got. Seeing her flirt with him makes me want to break her skull in," she says between gritted teeth.

"Whoa there, Maze. You gotta calm your tits, or you'll stroke out or something. Let's get something to drink. If I didn't know better, I'd say you were envious," I tell her with a wink, going to the lemonade and punch table. Before I can grab a cup for Maize and me, Gavin walks up. I pretend to contemplate what I want to drink as he leads Maize to the side. They're far enough away to have some privacy, but still close enough for me to eavesdrop.

"I've put the pieces together, Maize," he says in a hushed tone.

"What're you talkin' about exactly?" Maize asks, playing dumb. Even I know what he's referring to. They had a one-night stand, she spent the last year avoiding him like an STD, and now that he's brought another girl around, she's jealous as hell.

For a moment, silence draws on between them, and I can imagine Maize's staring him down like he's grown a third eye. I slowly put ice cubes in some cups, taking my sweet time. It's too easy to be nosy when they're right there.

He chuckles, unfazed by her antics. "I've tamed wild horses, Maize Bishop, and I'll tame your *attitude* too. I like a good challenge."

She scoffs. "Is that a threat or somethin'?" Maybe she doesn't notice, but I can hear the shakiness in her voice as I pour my punch.

"Not a threat, sweetheart. That's a damn promise," Gavin keeps his voice low, but the confidence oozes off his words before he walks away. Maize comes up to me completely infuriated.

My eyes are as wide as saucers as I glance at her, and she groans before pulling a flask from her back pocket and taking a long swig. "I hate him. I hate him *so* much! Egotistical, bigheaded, tight blue jean wearing bastard!"

"You forgot to say brooding and sexy as sin in there somewhere," I say, snorting at how annoyed she is.

"He just needs to go away. I don't shit where I eat for a damn reason, yet here I am," she says as Gavin walks back to Sarah with a cocky grin. Maize watches them for a minute, and

I swear laser beams are going to shoot from her eyes at any moment. It has me holding back laughter.

"Come on, ignore them," I say and grab our drinks and meet Diesel back on the blanket. Maize follows me, bitching under her breath as she plops down next to Kenzie with her arms crossed.

"I thought you got lost or something. What took so long?" he asks, kissing me right behind the ear, causing me to squirm.

I giggle and turn toward him, whispering. "Oh nothing other than Maize and Gavin exchanging words. He *totally* confronted her."

His stares at me, and his mouth falls open. "No way."

"Yep, and she's ready to murder him and his date," I explain.

He laughs. "Welp, my money's on her. She's scary as hell."

"I guess we'll see," I say, chuckling, then lean over and plant kisses on his mouth. "That was us at one point."

Diesel grins. "It was, and now look whatcha've gone and done."

"What's that?" I ask.

"You roped Big D," he gloats. "You actually caught the uncatchable cowboy."

I shake my head and slide my lips across his as our kiss deepens. "No, Cowboy, you're wrong. You caught me."

We hope you enjoyed Diesel & Rowan's story! There is a lot more to come in the Circle B Ranch series, featuring the Bishop's and finding their happily ever afters. Even though this can be read as a stand-alone, some of the characters will interconnect to the next one, so we hope you'll join us for Maize Bishop & Gavin's story next in *Wrangling the Cowboy!*

THE TWO OF US

A brand new series coming from Kennedy Fox
THE LOVE IN ISOLATION SERIES

What do you do when the entire nation is on lockdown?

If you're an heiress to a billion-dollar fashion company, then you quarantine in a glamorous cabin and finish your final semester of NYU online. The best way to focus on her upcoming valedictorian honor is away from her family, classmates, and the paparazzi. Cameron St. James is ready to get out of the big city and head Upstate for seclusion, despite her parents' pleas to stay home.

What do you do when a pandemic is sweeping the world?

If you're barely making ends meet, then you isolate yourself in your best friend's mountain cabin with breathtaking views and no neighbors for miles. It's the perfect safe place away from three roommates who don't take the life-threatening epidemic seriously. Elijah Ross is ready to work remotely and focus on his next big promotion, assuming he'll still have a job after this.

What happens when things don't go as planned, and you're stuck with the one person you dislike the most?

You improvise and do whatever it takes to avoid each other, though it proves to be impossible. The cold evenings alone turn into movie and popcorn nights together by the fireplace. Days turn into weeks, and eventually, more than just a friendship blossoms. As the unknown haunts them, they lean on one another for comfort—until someone pops their safety bubble and threatens everything.

***The Two of Us* is an enemies to lovers, brother's best friend standalone romance set in the current affairs of history in the making. Though the character's storyline is fiction, the virus is very real, and we've made sure to be sensitive on this topic.**

KEEPING YOU AWAY

TYLER & GEMMA, #1

A brand new series coming from Kennedy Fox
THE EX-CON DUET SERIES

I never planned on returning to Alabama, but circumstances brought me here after years of being gone. Though Lawton Ridge is my hometown, I was hesitant to go back because of *her*—my sister's best friend. The last time we were together, she was eighteen, and I was a broken soldier transitioning to civilian life.

Gemma wrote to me while I was overseas and we developed a bond I hadn't anticipated. I crushed her heart the day I left, and it's something I've never forgotten. But now that her dad is my new boss, life just got way more complicated.

Too sweet, too innocent, too good for a guy like me—I should walk away again.

After serving five years in prison for something I didn't do, I'm constantly on guard. Though I've taught people how to protect themselves in a boxing ring, no one can help prepare me for my next move. I'm about to enter the fight of my life and face the mafia princess who put me behind bars. She thinks I fear her and will stay away, but she has another thing coming. I plan to make her pay, but that means risking everything.

I trust no one, but Gemma gradually breaks down my walls and exposes the pain I've hidden underneath. For her own sake, I should keep my distance, but it's nearly impossible when I hear her sweet humming while I work and she slowly draws me back in. It's a battle I didn't train for, and one I'll lose if I don't keep my restraint—especially since she's engaged to another man.

KEEPING YOU AWAY is a slow-burn, angsty romance wrapped up in an intense love story. It's book 1 in the Tyler & Gemma duet and must be read first.

ABOUT THE AUTHOR

Brooke Cumberland and Lyra Parish are a duo of romance authors who teamed up under the USA *Today* pseudonym, Kennedy Fox. They share a love of Hallmark movies & overpriced coffee. When they aren't bonding over romantic comedies, they like to brainstorm new book ideas. One day, they decided to collaborate under a pseudonym and have some fun creating new characters that'll make you blush and your heart melt. If you enjoy romance stories with sexy, tattooed alpha males and smart, quirky, independent women, then a Kennedy Fox book is for you! They're looking forward to bringing you many more stories to fall in love with!

CONNECT WITH US

Find us on our website:
kennedyfoxbooks.com

- facebook.com/kennedyfoxbooks
- twitter.com/kennedyfoxbooks
- instagram.com/kennedyfoxbooks
- amazon.com/author/kennedyfoxbooks
- goodreads.com/kennedyfox
- bookbub.com/authors/kennedy-fox

BOOKS BY KENNEDY FOX

CHECKMATE DUET SERIES

BISHOP BROTHERS SERIES

BEDTIME READS SERIES

ROOMMATE DUET SERIES

CIRCLE B RANCH SERIES

EX-CON DUET SERIES

LOVE IN ISOLATION SERIES

Find the entire Kennedy Fox reading order at
Kennedyfoxbooks.com/reading-order

Find all of our current freebies at
Kennedyfoxbooks.com/freeromance